All That Sparkles

Glitter Bay Mysteries, Book 1

Diane Bator

Escape With a Writer Publishing

ISBN Print: 978-1-7383328-2-3

Published by Escape With a Writer Publishing

1312-400 Towerlane Drive, Airdrie, Alberta, T4B 2K7

Previously published in A Witch of a Scandal, Aconite Cafe, October 2023

Dedication

To my dear friends & family who encourage me and keep me accountable!

To my fans old and new, thank you for coming along for the ride!

To the Monday Muses, who kept me grounded and nudged me along my path,

Darryl & Kathy for road trips, long talks, and never-ending support and encouragement.

My mom, Trudy, for life and love.

Matt, Will, & Athena – You are my heart and soul! Love you forever and always!

I know I've forgotten some but please know you are loved and cherished for being a part of my life!

Contents

Chapter One

Curiosity was about to kill me no matter how hard I fought it. Someone had taken a great deal of care in packaging two gowns in separate black garment bags with peekaboo windows and heavy metal zippers. Clothes and me together in one room spelled trouble.

As I unzipped one bag to reveal an ornate gown with a sleeveless, crystal-coated bodice, dozens of feet of tulle skirt exploded out of the bag like spray foam. Within seconds, the skirt took over the entire changing room. I stared with my mouth hanging open.

It was the one dress I refused to try on.

A wedding gown was bad karma. I did not want to get married again. Ever.

I used my entire body to stuff the wedding gown into one changing room. My hands, feet, hips, and knees all went into action to shove the frisky fabric inside and pull the heavy tapestry curtain shut. The curtain billowed, but it managed to hold the demon dress at bay.

Stepping into the second changing room, I held the other bag out at arm's length. The second gown was a blush, two-piece with a layer of dark lace over both the halter-style top and the elegant A-line skirt. It was fabulous. No designer label, in fact, no label at all. Someone had sewn crystals around the straight choker collar and waistband of the skirt, as well as all over the halter. I barely had enough time to tug on the blush halter top before the front door opened.

I'd been literally caught with my pants—in this case, skirt—down. "I'll be right out."

The more I studied my reflection in the changing room mirror, however, the more I took a shine to the two-piece gown with the veil of sun-faded black lace over the skirt and dozens upon dozens of crystals sewn into the halter.

"Hey, Laken, where are you?" my sister called out.

"I'm in the changing room."

I made that old dress look good. Even if I never wore it again, I wanted it. More as a reminder about how far I'd come. Or fallen, depending on your point of view.

"Will you please not try on the merchandise before I get a chance to look them over?" Sage whipped open the curtain. Her face paled and a small gasp filled the air as she took a step back.

"What? Did I tear the lace?" I searched the fabric. "I'll pay for the repairs. I swear. Where's the hole?"

Sage shook her head and whispered, "You look amazing."

"Wow." Considering I used to be a model that came as no surprise, even though I no longer lived among the Hollywood Who's Who. "People paid me truckloads of money for years because I look amazing, and you just realized it now?"

I was the taller, thinner sister, who ran off to L.A. to make it big, and I did. Even married a movie star. Then I caught Mr. Not-so-Right in our bed with several other women. And two men. All at once. Not my cuppa tea. Our divorce was ugly, and I ended up an even wealthier woman thanks to the hush money from his publicity people.

I sucked up my sudden attack of self-pity and flicked my short red hair over my ear. "Pretty, isn't it? I want to buy this one. Not many people in Glitter Bay wear size two anyway. It would only hang around the shop gathering dust if I don't take it."

Sage huffed. "Where did it come from?"

I waved toward a large trunk near the counter. "Some kid with blue hair and a nose ring dropped that off. He said there were clothes and paperwork inside. Gill from Sweet Eden Tea House is supposed to call you later. He had to take his wife to the hospital."

"Gill San Vicente?" she asked. "Then the blue-haired guy was Abbie."

"Are there a lot of guys with blue hair are there around here?"

Sage seemed distracted. "Did Abbie say what was wrong with Tilly?"

"Nope. He just took off like the cops were after him." I began to unzip the skirt.

"Don't you have any shame?" Sage asked, closing the tapestry curtain. "Those of us who are not models close curtains, so no one else sees us naked."

I smiled, loving her modesty. "Sorry. In my industry, you get used to not caring."

"Well, not me. I like a little mystery." She huffed. "Actually, I'm surprised Tilly would send anything over to my boutique. We don't exactly see eye to eye, especially after I caught Abbie shoplifting and called the police. Tilly insisted the poor boy had been through enough humiliation and I shouldn't press charges."

"So did you?" I pulled on my von Furstenberg sleeveless scarf dress in aqua, Klein blue and fern. No knockoffs for me. My ex provided only the best. Whether he knew it or not.

"No. I let him work it off while carefully monitored. I made him clean every square inch of this place. Maybe giving me her things to sell is her way of saying thanks."

"Maybe. That or her grandson is looking to make some quick cash."

My sister gave a barking laugh. "Quick cash? Then he doesn't understand my business all that well. Quick cash isn't always guaranteed."

Speaking of the best, I fingered the delicate fabrics of the beautiful blush gown. The glitz and glamor brought back memories that seemed a lifetime away now. Red carpet events, galas and movie premieres with my now ex-husband who thought he was God's gift to the galaxy. The stones on the gown were definitely not rhinestones. More like Swarovski crystals, or even diamonds. Nah. Couldn't be.

"How much would you want for the gown?" I asked, packaging the dress before I carried it out to the front counter.

Sage had knelt next to the trunk and was poking around inside. "Did you take anything else out of here?"

"Just this gown and the wedding dress." I said, handing her the garment bag.

"A wedding dress. Where is it?"

Returning to the first changing room, I pulled aside the curtain and stood back. Once it settled, I removed the armfuls of white tulle before handing it to her.

Her green eyes grew round as a small rush of air escaped her. "Wow. That's beautiful."

"Too fluffy for my taste. The crystals on the bodice are nice, though. If no one wants to buy the dress, you could always recycle them. They'd be worth some money."

Sage let out a squawk. "It's perfect the way it is. If no one wants it..."

"Then you're stuck with it, just like a lot of the other perfect stuff in the store."

Her face reddened. My older sister was shorter, more athletic than I'd ever be. She wore her long, flaming red hair tied back into a perpetual ponytail and seemed to have an endless supply of smiles. I both loved and envied her to no end.

"I sell things," she said, throwing me a look that could've burned through the beige cement walls.

"Yeah, mostly to me when a good deal walks through the door." I chuckled as I slid on my jade, pointed toe. "Sage, I know you do well here, but you need a nicer showroom to draw customers in. A place with more light and space. The beige walls are kind of depressing."

"It's called Antique White, which seemed suitable at the time." She retorted, pulling a sparkling necklace out of the trunk. "Ooh, this is nice. I can't believe Tilly wants to sell this."

How had I missed seeing that? "May I?"

Sage hesitated long enough for me to scowl before she handed it over.

I squinted as I examined it. "These stones aren't as nice as the ones on the gowns. Cheap rhinestones. You might get fifteen or twenty dollars for it."

"That's why I keep you around," she said. "If nothing else, you have good taste."

"I'm not sure how to take that." I nudged her.

Digging through the rest of the trunk, we found lots of costume jewelry, some worth more than Sage would've charged before I moved to town. Also, a pair of red shoes that looked like Gilda the Good Fairy dumped glitter all over them. Cute and shiny, but not my style, which was good since they weren't my size.

By the time we locked up the store at six, we'd inventoried the entire contents of the trunk. My sister had a long list of items to research and price. Minus one fabulous sparkling gown that I brought home and tried on one more time. After I took several selfies—yes, I still loved cameras, some things would never change—then hung the gown in the back of my closet door before making dinner.

I'd met Gill and Tilly, the owners of the tea house, when I'd first moved to Glitter Bay. They seemed modest and down to earth. What kind of life had they led in the past to allow Tilly such extravagant belongings? It must've been a while since she'd fit into those tiny clothes.

Here I was doing the one thing I detested others doing. Judging a book by its proverbial cover. I might have to crack the spine on this one to find out more. Good thing my first stop in the morning was the Sweet Eden Tea House. I itched to ask Tilly if she had any more amazing gowns tucked away for safekeeping. A girl could never have too many fabulous gowns, could she?

Chapter Two

Before dawn broke the next day, I tiptoed down the creaky stairs of Sage's hundred-year-old fixer-upper and slipped on my sandals. I tugged my bike from the weeds at the side of the house and rode to where the majestic Sweet Eden Tea House overlooked the Pacific Ocean. I arrived at six a.m., before most of town crawled out of bed and right after Gill San Vicente put the first pot of water on to boil.

Since I moved to Glitter Bay four months ago, every morning I'd claimed the corner table on the front patio of the tea house, where the power of the ocean breathed life back into my chemotherapy-weakened body. Armed with a cup of tea and a buttered tea biscuit, the first hour of my day became pure bliss. I could forget about my ex, forget about cancer and daydream about what I wanted to do with my life.

"What'll it be today, Laken, my dear? Darjeeling? Earl Grey? Dragon Well?" Gill ran a hand over his silver hair and flashed a wide smile. Every morning, Gill brought my tea to my table while I watched the sun cast shadows across the grass before creating sparkles on the waves.

It was far too early to hide my curiosity, even with a well-timed yawn. "Dragon Well? What's that? I've never heard of it."

His wife, Tilly, who certainly couldn't wear those fabulous gowns now, waited behind the cash register taking orders and money without cracking a smile. She straightened her multicolored blouse, a throwback to the seventies, and snorted. "Some fancy tea from China that Gill found in Portland to sell to tourists."

Gill patted his wife's hand before turning his attention to me. "It's a Chinese green tea that tastes less grassy than the Japanese Green. It goes well with those lemon scones from the Sweets and Treats Bakery."

Good thing Gill was a far better salesman than his wife or I would have never returned to the tea house. I hoped my unease wasn't palpable. "I guess I'll try the Dragon Well tea. I'll take one of those yummy lemon scones too."

"Of course, Laken, my dear." He smiled. "Shall I bring everything to your usual table?"

"That would be great. Thanks." I paid Tilly for a small pot of tea and a scone, glad my hands no longer shook from chemo the way they did when I'd first arrived in town.

When I first met her, I thought she didn't like me, but, after overhearing arguments between her and several customers, I realized her attitude was nothing personal. Tilly didn't like anyone. I wanted to ask about the gowns and assorted pieces of jewelry but chickened out.

"Lake." Tilly snorted. "What sort of name is that for a girl? Were your parents hippies?"

"Lake with an 'n.'" Gill rolled his eyes as he enunciated my name for about the twentieth time. "Lay-ken. She works at Vintage Sage, that antique clothing place."

"Oh. You'd never catch me setting foot in that place." She huffed.

I headed for the wide front porch that hugged the tea house. In fact, my parents *were* hippies when I was born, but now that Sage and I were grown, they'd become absorbed in the pursuit of a golden retirement. My sister and I lived on granola and herbs. Nothing illegal, mind you. Just the kind both Gill and the health food store sold.

Behind me, Tilly snarled. "Gill, did you take money out of the till yesterday? We were short twenty dollars again. You know you need to give me your receipts."

"I uh..." He seemed to hesitate. When I glanced back, his cheek twitched as his gaze met mine. "I needed to get butter for today."

"Yeah?" she asked, "All I saw was the same half bar of butter in the fridge this morning that sat there all day yesterday."

He winked. "That's because I haven't gone to the store yet. The twenty is in my wallet."

Tilly reached for a stack of cloth napkins. "So go, then. It's not like you're doing anything else."

I turned away as she began to fold the napkins. None of my business. I had tea to drink, a view to take in and the rest of my life to plan. There was no way I'd impose on my sister forever.

As I stepped outside, the breeze off the ocean ruffled my chin-length red hair. Since no other customers had arrived at the tea house yet, I snagged my usual table in the corner. I wiggled out of my sandals and stretched my toes to where the morning sun would reach before long. The temperature rose nearly ten degrees by the time the sun peeked over Glitter Bay to make the entire body of water before me...well...glitter.

Gill emerged through the front door carrying an ornate wooden tray that held a small, flowered teapot, a matching teacup, milk and sugar. A small square of butter, already sweating in the heat, sat next to the lemon scone. He set my tray down then arched a kink out of his back as he took a deep breath. "Looks like another lovely day in paradise."

I chuckled. "You make it sound like we're in Tahiti or something."

"Tahiti's far too hot." He waved an arm. "Glitter Bay is just right. Rainy in the winter, sunny in the summer, plus all the amenities you could need. Far better than Tahiti or even L.A., for that matter."

His mention of Los Angeles sent a shudder through me. My smile froze on my face. As much as I'd loved the sunshine and the crazy, extravagant life of a movie star's wife, I treasured the peace and tranquility of Glitter Bay even more. "I wouldn't know."

"Oh, that's right." Gill winked as he poured my tea. "You're from Portland."

Since I hadn't talked about my past, I assumed Sage had filled him in on my behalf.

"You know." He set the teapot on the table. "We could use a hand around the tea house, especially with Tilly's heart condition. She needs time to rest. I should've retired long ago."

"Then what would you do?" I laughed. "You'd be bored silly."

"Me? I'd move to a retirement home so someone can take care of me for a change." He hesitated. "Are you sure you're not interested in a job? Maybe part-time?"

"I already work with Sage at her clothing store. Which reminds me, I wanted to ask you about that trunk the blue-haired kid..."

"Come on." He cut me off. "You're young. I'm sure you could juggle two jobs. Twenty hours a week at most."

I was flattered that he offered me a job every time I walked through the door. "I'm in Glitter Bay for my health, Gill, not my pocketbook."

"Right. Sage said you got some big inheritance." He sighed. "Lucky girl. I'd love for someone to leave me a ton of money."

Inheritance nothing. A chunk of my money came from my divorce settlement. A great deal of money sat in my bank account in Los Angeles until I figured out what to do with my life. After being married for five years to Emery Samson, movie star and flirt extraordinaire, I'd earned every dime.

"Hey, Sage and I went through that trunk you sent over to Vintage Sage." I picked at my scone. "Does Tilly have any other great pieces I could look at?"

"I'll have to get back to you on that." He hesitated and shifted his weight. "Let me talk to her before you say anything."

I winced. "Yeah, it's probably best if you talk to her. She doesn't seem to like me much."

"She doesn't seem to like anyone much." Gill gave a shrug then returned inside to another of Tilly's tirades. She constantly seemed angry about something. No wonder she had a heart condition. It didn't seem like anyone told her about yoga and a healthy diet.

"Don't get involved." I picked up my teacup to breath in the light scent of the green tea. I'd had enough drama in my life for another ten years.

I'd barely touched the cup to my lips when something soft and furry brushed against my bare foot. I shrieked, dropped the teacup onto the wooden porch and upended the table as I nearly leaped over the railing.

A small, grey and white dog cowered beneath the chair. It wobbled before tucking its snout beneath its paws.

"Sorry, buddy, I didn't even see you there." I crouched for a better look. "Oh my. You're just a baby, aren't you?"

Gill rushed outside wielding a broom. "What happened? Are you okay?"

The puppy shrank away and whimpered.

"I didn't notice I had a visitor until he touched me." I wiggled my fingers in a feeble attempt to coax the puppy into the open. "Is this your dog?"

He shook his head but lowered the broom. "Not a chance. Tilly breaks out in hives. I've always wanted one, but she's already mad enough to burst a blood vessel on the best of days. Adding a dog wouldn't be good for my health."

"I can imagine."

He leaned the broom against the wall then knelt for a closer look. "Cute little thing. Looks like one of them English Sheepdogs. I wonder where it came from."

"You've never seen him before?" I dusted off the scone and held out a piece. The puppy wiggled its nose but didn't move. "The poor thing seems hungry."

"I can sneak him a piece of ham or something from the kitchen," Gill said.

"Ham?" I reached farther until the bit of scone was almost within the puppy's reach. "I thought you just served tea and stuff from the bakery."

Gill groaned as he straightened up. "We do soups and high tea with sandwiches and those expensive little cakes. You'll have to come by for lunch one day. I'll be back in a minute."

Alone with the greyish lump of fur, I became braver. "Poor thing. I can see your ribs through your fur. Scones might not be your favorite, but it's something."

The puppy gave a low whine as it sniffed the morsel of lemon scone. A heartbeat later, it licked the crumbs off my fingers then shimmied closer.

I broke off another piece. "Okay. Just one more bite before Gill gets back."

The door creaked then he walked out. "I found a chunk of turkey in the fridge. Did he eat some of the scone?"

"The whole thing." I smiled. "I doubt he's eaten anything but garbage for a while."

Gill knelt to hand the puppy a chunk of turkey breast the size of my hand.

"Are you sure Tilly won't miss that?" I asked. "That's a pretty big piece."

"He needs it more than she does." He stroked the puppy's back. "It's got no collar and probably no home, either. You should take it to the shelter."

I gasped. "Why me?"

"I can't leave the shop. Besides, Tilly will have a reaction from the fur on my clothes then she won't speak to me. That's not such a bad thing for one day, but it's hell when she's ticked for a week. Do you know how hard it is to run a Mom and Pop store when Mom won't speak to Pop? It's best to keep Mom happy. Or else."

Not my drama. I blew out a breath and sat down on the porch as I reached out to the puppy. "How am I supposed to take him to the shelter? All I have is a bike."

"I'll think on that." He stood and dusted off his pants. "Why don't you two make friends while I fetch a fresh pot of tea and a new scone? Maybe we can get him into a box or something so you can figure out how to get him home."

"No way." I held up both hands in protest. "He's not coming home with me. I'll take him to the shelter, but that's where he stays."

Gill sighed. "For a while. If no one claims him, I hate to think what might happen."

A lump of guilt grew in my throat as Gill returned inside. I righted the table, set the remaining crumbs on the plate and picked up shards of the teacup, thankful the teapot only had a chipped handle. The puppy licked the tidbits of scone I'd missed.

I sat on the chair then picked him up. He hardly weighed anything. "Maybe I should take you home. Sage and I can put posters up once we get you cleaned up. Someone must miss you. You couldn't have appeared out of thin air."

The puppy, its fur matted by burrs and dirt, settled on my lap and then closed its eyes and sighed. I stroked its fur, pulling out each burr one at a time. I'd never looked after anyone but Emery who'd never had burrs.

Tears filled my eyes. When my treatments cramped his lifestyle, Emery took roles around the planet to escape. His public relations people insisted he appear with starlets while I hid from the paparazzi. Then I caught him "entertaining" his entourage. Once I was in remission, he moved in with an eighteen-year-old pop singer. I packed my bags and came home.

Home.

I'd never lived in Glitter Bay before, but Sage was the one person who kept me grounded. First, when I got my diagnosis, then again when my ex-husband had a long string of affairs. She'd chauffeured me to appointments right up until we popped a bottle of Prosecco to celebrate my remission.

"It looks like you two hit it off." Gill set a clean tray on the table.

I hadn't heard him return. "He's so tired."

"It's a boy?"

I shrugged. "I have no idea. How do I check that on a dog?"

"Same way as you'd check on any other male." Gill lifted the puppy off my lap and held it at arm's length while he examined it. "Congratulations, Laken, it's a boy. He needs a little food, a lot of love and a name."

"Not a chance!" I held up both hands. "I'll take him to the shelter, but that's as far as this romance goes. I'm staying with my sister. I don't even have a house of my own."

"Do we know the same Sage Miller?" Gill placed the puppy in my lap then chuckled as he poured my cup of tea. "She'll never let you take that dog to the shelter. She'll be head over heels in love as soon as she sees him."

"What if I just take him to the shelter and leave him there? She'll never need to know he exists." I managed to sip hot tea with the puppy on my lap.

"Hey, Laken!" Sage rode up to the tea house right on cue on her antique blue bike.

No time to hide. I was doomed.

"Good luck with that." He winked then turned to wave. "Sage, my dear, what can I get for you today?"

"Nothing right now. Thanks." She stopped at the bottom of the steps. "I'm off to yoga before work. Can you hang on to one of those yummy blueberry muffins for me? I'll stop by on my way to the store."

"Done." Gill took the broom into the tea house.

"Um, Laken? What's that in your lap?" Sage peered over the top of her sunglasses. "Why, Laken Miller, if I didn't know better, I'd say you were snuggling a small dog."

The puppy glanced up, yawned then dropped its head against my blue linen capris.

"I found him on the porch under my chair. He seems either neglected or homeless." When I realized I stroked his matted fur as I spoke, I lifted my hand away.

No, no, no! I do not want a dog, especially one that could fit in a shoebox.

Sage leaned her bike against the railing then came up to kneel beside me. "He's maybe three months old at the most. Definitely an English Sheepdog."

"Is that bad?" I reached for my scone.

She winced. "They grow to be pretty big. Look at the size of those paws."

I glanced down. His paws *were* large for a small dog. "Well, don't worry. I don't plan to keep him. In fact, I'll take him to the shelter after tea."

Sage's eyes widened. "Don't you dare. Take him to the vet clinic and make sure he's healthy. I'll stop by the house after yoga so we can figure out what to do about him."

"We'll what?" I stared, slack jawed.

She ran down the stairs and grabbed her bike, mounting it as she ran down the street. "Don't forget to give him a name."

The tea house door swung open again. "Give who a name?"

Both the puppy and I jumped when Tilly shuffled out. I'd never seen her off her stool before. My mouth went dry as I pointed. "Um. Him."

Her dark eyes narrowed to thin, black slits. "Get that mutt off my property."

My heart raced as I hugged the puppy to my chest. "I found him under the chair."

"Yeah?" She reached for the broom. "Well, get it out of here. I'm allergic."

"I'm sorry." I winced as the puppy whined in my arms. "I'll take him to the shelter as soon as I'm done with my tea."

"You're done." Tilly's face reddened. "Get him out of here. I'm getting in hives."

"What's going on?" Gill ran outside with a blue cloth in one hand and snatched the broom from his wife.

Tilly scowled. "She has a dog. Get them out of here. You know I'm allergic."

He placed his hands on her shoulders. "You go inside and take your medication before your blood pressure skyrockets. I'll take care of things. Why don't you start a pot of soup for lunch?"

"Fine." Tilly's nostrils flared. "My turkey soup takes time to simmer, anyway. Just get that mangy mutt out of here."

Since Gill gave a large chunk of turkey to the stray, he'd be in bigger trouble after I left. Once Tilly closed the door, he released a long sigh and lowered his voice. "I'm so sorry, Laken. She has this weird phobia about dogs."

"It's okay." I gulped some tea and tried to calm my shaking body. Tilly San Vicente was downright scary when she was upset. "I'll carry the dog and walk my bike home. He needs a bath before I take him anywhere. He smells funky."

"This might help." He handed me a scrap of blue fabric. "My daughter carried Abbie in it when he was a baby."

With Gill's help, I strapped the baby carrier to my chest, stuck in an old towel to line the bottom, then eased the puppy inside. Once Gill was satisfied it wouldn't fall out of the leg holes, he poured the rest of my tea in a to-go cup.

"This is a first." I kept one eye on the door in case Tilly reappeared. "I never thought I'd ever pack anything in a baby carrier."

Gill smiled. "Did you give him a name yet?"

A name? Not a chance. I didn't want to get attached.

"I'll think about it," I promised, crossing my fingers beneath the puppy's wiggly body. Why would I name a dog I didn't want?

As I left, a tall man with a black trench coat passed me on his way inside. The type of man who would've caught my eye at one time, handsome and dark-haired. He smelled faintly of some kind of spice. I cringed when he flashed an amused grin.

I struggled to get onto my bike, trying to convince myself I was taking the puppy home for my sister. The baby carrier straps dug into my back as the puppy slid one leg out the hole in the bottom.

"Let's get you out of there," I said, once we got to the house. "Come on, Sammy."

Sammy. The name rolled off my tongue without hesitation. It did seem like a suitable name. Emery Samson deserved a namesake that caused every bit as much trouble as he did. If this morning was any indication, the puppy was right on track. I hoped no one thought I still had feelings for my ex because if it. We were through. Done. Finite.

I set the puppy in the lush grass. Once he'd done his business under one of the rose bushes, he wagged his tail and trotted toward me. He smelled worse than before.

I held him at arm's length and carried him into the house. He needed a bath and a visit to the vet before I went to work.

"Okay, pal, we have a few rules around here," I announced, sitting in an armchair with Sammy in my lap. "Number one, there are two humans and a devious cat named Muumuu who also live here. You can't eat any of them. Number two, you need a bath. You're filthy and you smell awful. Three, you need a checkup before you can even think about living here."

Sammy stood on his hind legs, pressed his paws to my chest, and licked my face as if in acknowledgment.

So much for the stern lecture.

I hugged him, then carried him up to the bathtub. Fifteen minutes of scrubbing later, Sammy looked like a soaked ball of yarn, and I was drenched. He'd tried to eat a bar of soap before shaking water everywhere. The bathroom looked like a tornado hit.

Sage would not be amused. The new addition—if we kept him—would make life a lot more interesting.

Muumuu appeared in the doorway just as I wrapped Sammy in a towel. Sage's cat looked large and intimidating, but without her layer of two-inch long grey fur she probably weighed less than five pounds. The cat let out a squeak as ten pounds of wet dog launched out of the towel like a bottle rocket down the hallway. Both animals landed on Sage's bed with a thud and sent a pillow flying. It knocked the lamp off my sister's bedside table.

At this rate, Sammy and I would be homeless before Vintage Sage opened at ten.

Chapter Three

Sage took one look at me and Sammy before she huffed and left for the shop. So much for discussing options. Lucky me got the morning off to deal with the dog—and the destruction of the living room thanks to Muumuu and Sammy.

The vet turned out to be tall, blond, and handsome. He seemed like the sort who ran every morning, ate a vegan diet, and was nice to everyone. A male version of my sister.

By ten o'clock, Doctor Cameron Dale gave Sammy a clean bill of health, then suggested I tack up posters around town to find his owner. He ran a hand through his disheveled blond hair and flashed a smile before selling me a leash, a collar, and a huge, expensive bag of dog food that I couldn't possibly carry home. In return, Sammy left teeth marks on the vet's monogrammed stethoscope. Seemed like a fair trade to me.

Doctor Cameron, as he insisted I call him, offered to deliver my purchases to Sage's house personally. I got the impression he had a crush on my sister. The poor guy didn't stand a chance. She was dating a bodybuilder from Portland who could bench press both the lanky vet and his red sports car with the personalized license plate "ANMLDC."

Clipping Sammy's new blue leash onto his leather collar for the walk home, we made our way down the hill. He kept wanting to veer toward the beach, but I directed him to the Sweet Eden Tea House. Tilly sat behind the counter but there was no sign of her much better half. Didn't that woman ever leave her seat except to yell at people?

Sammy yanked at the leash and whined.

"Yeah, we're going," I told him, taking two steps before he squatted in the grass. "Great. You'd think the first thing that con-artist vet would've sold me were designer doggy doo bags."

While Sammy did his business, I gave him privacy and admired the tea house's weathered yellow exterior hugged by the wide, white wooden porch. The tea house had always struck me as a charming, romantic place, aside from Tilly's presence. What would it be like to live in the upstairs apartment. To be lulled to sleep by the ocean at night, then wake up and walk along the beach every morning.

The main level would be ideal for Vintage Sage. The light and space would give it more of a boutique vibe than the current thrift shop feel.

Since Sammy was still relatively clean, aside from rolling on the grass for a minute, we walked over to the store. My sister let out a groan when she saw us and asked, "Did you have to bring the dog with you?"

"What else should I do with him?"

Sage closed her eyes and took a deep breath. "Didn't you buy a crate he can stay in while we're at the shop?"

"Yeah, but I couldn't carry it home," I told her. "Do you want me to take him back to the house and leave him in the yard?"

"No, he's a puppy. Who knows what he'd get into? How do you plan to get the crate to the house?"

"The vet said he'd drop it off after he's done work."

"He's delivering it personally?" Sage asked, then thought for a moment. "Why don't you watch the shop so I can get lunch and do some errands? I'll come back by three so you can be home when the crate arrives."

"Are you avoiding Cameron?"

"No." Sage snatched Sammy then was out the front door before I could launch into teasing her.

The afternoon was so quiet I gave up checking the clock. None of the hands seemed to move anyway. At twenty to five, the door opened. I sighed in relieve until Tilly's nostrils flared as her gaze met mine.

"You," she said. "Where's that mangy dog?"

This was the second time I'd seen her off her stool in two days. Whatever was on her mind must be important.

"Sammy? He's with Sage." I placed my hands on the counter, so she didn't see me shake. "What can I do for you, Tilly?"

Tiny beads of sweat covered her brow. "My grandson delivered a trunk here the other day. I want it back, along with everything that was inside."

Sage hadn't only inventoried the contents, but we'd sold a couple items. One gown for sure. "I'll talk to my sister when she gets back."

Tilly's face paled. She clenched her jaw and tightened her grip on her purse straps. "Gill brought it here without my permission. I need my things back."

I glanced at the list Sage had left on the counter. Either Tilly was more sentimental than I thought, or we'd missed something. Nothing in that trunk had any real value.

"I want my belongings back today before you close today." Her face grew even whiter.

Considering the shop closed at five, and Sage should've been back two hours ago, that wasn't likely. I inched around the counter. "Are you okay? You look kind of pale. There's a chair near the changing rooms, why don't you sit down for a minute. I'll get you some water."

"I just need my things back," Tilly said. She took two shuffling steps toward the door, then fell to her knees. A blink later, she leaned to her right and struck the side of her head on a two-tiered table covered in hats before toppling to the wooden floor.

"Tilly!" I shrieked. My heart leaped into my throat.

She remained motionless.

I ran toward her. "Tilly? Are you okay?"

No answer.

"Do you need a doctor?"

Still no answer. Did she have a heart attack? I crouched to touch her neck. No pulse. "Oh crap!"

Right then, the front door opened. Gill came inside with two large paper shopping bags. "I'm done with the shopping. I got the milk, butter, and eggs, but they didn't have fresh raspberries. What's going on?"

My mouth opened and closed like a beached carp. No sound came out.

"What happened? Tilly? Are you okay?" He set the bags on the floor while he checked his wife's wrist.

"I think she's...," I whispered. The rest of the sentence stuck in my throat.

"Call an ambulance," Gill said, grasping her wrist. "Her pulse is faint."

He began CPR without hesitation. Tears zigzagged through the stubble in his chin, then soaked Tilly's blouse as he alternated chest compressions with puffs of breath.

I grabbed my phone. "I'll call an ambulance."

"You need to go to the tea house and put the groceries away before she wakes up," he told me. "They'll go bad if they sit out for too long. I don't want her even angrier at me."

In mid-dial, I stared at him and asked, "Are you serious? You want me to go to the tea house and put your groceries away?"

While it seemed like an odd reaction to finding his wife on the floor, shock did weird things to people. I called 9-1-1 while carrying the bags to the back room. Tilly already didn't like me. I didn't want to give her another reason. Just in case.

The tiny kitchen overflowed with excess merchandise, a small table, a lone chair, and an antique fridge Sage found in the junk shop next door. Inside the fridge, sat carefully labeled containers of leftovers and vegetables. I stuck both bags inside, then returned to the front. When Gill refused to let me help with CPR, I texted Sage to get to the store immediately. I desperately wanted to wake up. The whole situation seemed surreal.

Less than a minute later, an ambulance arrived. Two paramedics wheeled in a gurney. The shorter, blond man checked for Tilly's pulse before unwrapping a syringe. He tossed the wrapper in his kit, then gave her an injection. As both men worked feverishly to save her, I held a breath of hope.

Finally, the taller paramedic ran a hand through his light brown hair. He met my gaze as he helped Gill to his feet and said, "I'm sorry, Gill. We did everything we could. Do you need a ride to the hospital?"

Gill shook off his hand. "Thanks, Keyon, but we need to call the police."

Keyon frowned. "She probably had a heart attack."

"She didn't just drop dead," Gill insisted. "Somebody killed her."

My mouth fell open. Since the only other person in the shop when she collapsed was me, I didn't like his insinuation.

"Maybe we should let the doctor decide," the blond paramedic said as he and his partner loaded Tilly onto the gurney.

"Andy's right," Keyon said. "There's no reason to suspect anything. Unless they do and autopsy, we won't know if there's probable cause."

Gill shook his head and told them, "There's no way that woman would die on me. She promised to make my life miserable for another twenty years."

I smiled wishing my ex had felt the same way about me.

"This was only a matter of time, Gill," Andy said, placing a hand on the older man's arm. "Everyone in town knows Tilly had a heart condition."

Gill's chin quivered as they covered Tilly's ashen face and raised the gurney. "I just the truth."

Keyon averted his gaze as they wheeled Tilly to the door.

"I'm sorry for your loss, Gill," Andy said, flashing a sad glance at me. He looked like he wanted to say something, but his partner tugged the gurney out of the store. Within a minute, they were gone. Lights flashing, but no siren. No emergency.

Gill sat on the bench outside the shop. "I should go make sure they treat her right."

"Is there anyone I should call?" I asked, sitting next to him.

"No. You've done enough. Thank you." He placed a shaky hand on my arm as he stood and walked away.

His words pierced my skin, more hurtful than comforting. Did he blame me?

Sage ran toward the shop with Sammy in tow. Gill was half a block away before she dragged me into the shop away from onlookers. Barely winded, she said, "I got here as soon as fast I could. What happened?"

Blinking away tears, I told her, "Tilly wanted her stuff back. She said there were things in the trunk that she needed."

"What things?"

"She didn't get to tell me. She collapsed, hit her head on the table, and fell to the floor. That's when Gill came in. He thinks I killed her, Sage."

"I doubt that," my sister said, rubbing my arm. "She was probably dead by the time she hit the floor. Are you okay?"

I couldn't think straight anymore. "Rattled. Gill's groceries are in the fridge. He wanted me to take them back to Sweet Eden, but I—"

She gave me a long hug before handing me Sammy's leash. "Why don't you take Sammy home and relax? I'll close the store and hide that trunk for now. We won't sell anything else of hers until I talk to Gill."

As I walked Sammy home, the reality of Tilly's death set in. Shock chilled my body like a fine mist. Unlocking the door, I nearly tripped over both Sammy and Muumuu when they circled my feet.

I nudged both animals aside, collapsed onto the couch, and pulled a plush blanket around me. For a few brief seconds, I forgot about everything aside from the sight of Tilly falling to the floor.

Long enough for Sammy to sink his teeth into the remote control on the coffee table. The television turned on and flipped through several channels.

"Do you plan to eat everything you find lying around?" I asked, picking him up before I curled onto the couch and snuggled him against my chest.

Muumuu lowered her head as if glaring at us from the doorway. She probably wished I'd dropped Sammy off at the shelter instead of disrupting the entire household. Her domain. Heck, she probably would've been happy for Sage to drop me off at the shelter. Sammy's presence only made her dislike me more.

Seconds later, Muumuu leaped onto the back of the couch and nestled behind my head. I closed my eyes to brace for her usual attack.

For once, she didn't bite me. She purred and licked my hair. Rather than chase each other around the house while I blubbered, Sammy and Muumuu curled up next to me. Their warmth comforted me.

Tears rolled down my cheeks. Tilly terrified me after she'd yelled at me and Sammy. Now she was gone and there I was crying like we'd been best friends.

A few minutes later, I was jolted awake from a horrible dream where someone killed Tilly all over again. In my dream, her death had to do with the trunk that blue-haired boy brought to Vintage Sage.

As my heartrate slowed and the picture in my head abated, one thought haunted me. What if Gill was right?

Grateful I wasn't renowned for my psychic abilities, I snuggled into the warm spot between the two animals once more. My thoughts drifted to those beautiful gowns and the glittering stones. I couldn't picture Tilly wearing either, so why did she have them?

Realizing Gill might need some extra money to pay for her funeral. I decided to help by reappraising the contents of the trunk and eking the prices up a little. After all, shopping for a bargain was my specialty. Hopefully, there were other bargain hunters in Glitter Bay.

Chapter Four

By the time Doctor Cameron, the veterinarian, arrived at Sage's house around five fifteen, he'd changed into a pale purple shirt that brightened his eyes, put on cologne, and combed his hair. On the other hand, I must've looked like I'd wandered off the set of a zombie flick. Hair disheveled and stuck to my cheeks, red eyes, and a pillow-lined face.

While I'd napped, Sammy and Muumuu broke one vase and unstuffed a throw pillow. It wasn't safe to let anyone else inside until I'd cleaned up.

"Laken," the vet said, shuffling his feet as he peered past me. "I brought your things for the dog. Is Sage home?"

"Um. No. We had a... a little problem at the store. Hopefully, she'll be here soon."

As I struggled to keep Sammy and Muumuu from running out the open door, the side-to-side dance I did matched the bob of the vet's head. The man kept trying to peer around me while he looked for my sister. He moved like an awkward teenager struggling to catch up to his latest growth spurt.

"I'd hoped she was free for dinner tonight," he said. "Can you tell her I stopped by?"

"I'll pass on the message," I assured him, scooping both animals into my arms.

"Thanks." He flashed a lopsided smile before hauling in the large crate for Sammy.

I swore I heard Muumuu laugh when Cameron was on his way back to his car. The vet returned with the dog food and other accessories I'd spent a small fortune on. Nudging them into the front hall, he retreated to his red sports car and drove away.

Setting the animals down before either could inflict serious injury on me, I closed the door. Muumuu sniffed the dog accessories, then sauntered off with a swish of her tail. Sammy, mesmerized by a bag of dog treats, sat wobbling his head and drooling. I gave him a treat before shuffling to the kitchen to make a sandwich.

After I poured sparkling water over ice in a wine glass, I scooped some of Sammy's food into a bowl, and carried both out to the front porch to sort my thoughts.

Muumuu glared at us from behind the screen door. The last thing I needed was the two of them chasing each other into the street.

I sipped my drink, unable to shake the unease that had settled over me. Tilly might not have died in front of me if I'd known what to do.

Sammy put his paws on my thigh before rubbing his face against my leg. I lifted him onto my lap. Once he settled, I reached for my goblet of sparkling water. My days of partying like a rock star, despite my current state of mind, were long over.

Sammy raised his head as his body vibrated with a low growl seconds before a man cleared his throat and said, "Excuse me."

I jumped knocking over the wineglass, which broke into several pieces.

"Sorry. I didn't mean to startle you."

When he took a step closer, Sammy backed against my stomach. His fur rose like a mohawk down his back.

Tall and lean, with dark hair and a solemn expression, the sight of the man's leather jacket and tight blue jeans made my stomach lurch, and it took a heartbeat for me to recognize him. The paramedic from earlier. What was his name again?

"If you're looking for Sage, she's at the store," I told him, placing a hand on Sammy's back to calm us both.

"Actually, I was looking for you," he said, smiling and holding out a smooth hand. "Keyon Blake. I'm one of the paramedics who helped Tilly earlier."

I tried to swallow, but my mouth was dry, and my knees were too weak to hold me if I stood up. Too bad I'd knocked over the sparkling water. "What can I do for you?"

When Keyon took a couple steps closer, Sammy growled even louder.

"English Sheepdog, right? How long have you had him?" he asked. The puppy didn't seem to intimidate him in the least, although even Muumuu was more ferocious.

"Since I found him under my chair at the tea house this morning." I left out the part about upending the table and breaking the teacup. "I haven't decided if I'm keeping him."

Keyon reached out a hand to pat Sammy, who sniffed his fingers before giving him a lick of approval. "Too late. It looks like he's decided to stay."

I glanced down at Sammy who licked the tip of my nose. "Looks like."

"So, how long have you owned the vintage shop?" he asked as Muumuu hissed from inside the doorway.

"I don't. My sister owns it."

He reached out to tousle Sammy's fur. "Was Tilly there to buy or sell something?"

Wary, I told him, "She came to ask about something in the shop."

His eyes, the silver of weathered wood, met mine. "Anything in particular? Was anyone with her at the time?"

"She was alone. Why?" My dinner crept up my throat as Sammy stepped off my lap and onto the porch. When he rolled over to let Keyon scratch his belly, I scowled. *Traitor.*

"Did you check her pulse?" Keyon asked.

I shuddered. "I didn't feel one."

"Is that when you called an ambulance?"

"No, I called a minute later. After Gill came in with the groceries. He was supposed to be meeting Tilly in the shop."

Keyon raised his eyebrows. "I didn't see any groceries."

The images I'd struggled so hard to shake earlier, crept back into my head. "I put them in the fridge while I called nine-one-one. Gill started CPR and didn't want Tilly to get mad."

"You left Gill and Tilly alone to call an ambulance?"

Why was the paramedic asking so many questions? If I were Gill, I would've dropped everything to help. Unless it was my ex. Yet he specifically asked me to put away the groceries. If he'd wanted to make sure Tilly was dead, that was the ideal opportunity.

Great. Now this wannabe detective was making me suspicious. I shouldn't have chickened out of asking Tilly about the trunk the last time I was in Sweet Eden. If she didn't intend to sell her belongings, why did Gill send them to Vintage Sage in the first place?

Sammy whimpered, diverting my attention.

"Where were you when Tilly collapsed?" Keyon asked.

"Behind the counter," I told him as I glanced at my broken wine-glass. Sparkling water bubbled around the shards. "Why do you want to know?"

"I have a hunch Can you humor me?"

I pulled Sammy back onto my lap to cuddle. "I'd feel better if I knew why you were being so nosy."

"Understandable," he said, then asked, "What exactly was Tilly looking for?"

"She wanted something back that was sent to Vintage Sage by accident."

"Was she angry?"

"No, she seemed quite rational. Until she went pale. I offered to get her a glass of water, but she..." A veil of tears blurred my vision. I closed my eyes. "She collapsed and hit her head."

"Laken?" Keyon asked from far away.

"I checked her wrist for a pulse. That's when Gill came in. He..." I couldn't speak. Twice in one day.

Sammy whimpered, then licked the tears off my cheeks.

"I saw the lump where Tilly hit her head, you're not making that up. Why did Gill want you to put the groceries away?"

Did Keyon think Gill and I teamed up to kill Tilly?

"Do you think she was under the influence of something?" he asked.

Before I could respond, Sage walked up the sidewalk carrying two paper grocery bags. "What do you want, Keyon?"

Keyon took a quick step back. "I came by to make sure she's okay."

"Why wouldn't she be okay?"

He seemed at a loss for words for a minute. "Tilly San Vicente died at the vintage shop right in front of her. I was one of the—"

"I'm aware of that. "You can leave. I'll look after her," my sister said with a scowl.

"Yeah. No problem." He started to move away, then cleared his throat. "I think she needs a drink to steady her nerves."

Sage raised her eyebrows. "Is this about Tilly or you?"

He took one last look in my direction. "I just needed a few answers. Laken, I'll give you a call if I have more questions."

"You're not a cop. Leave her alone," my sister snapped.

Once Keyon was out of earshot, my sister groaned. "Why that lunatic didn't go into law enforcement still baffles me."

"I take it you know him."

My sister stormed into the house, then returned a few minutes later, minus the grocery bags. She plopped into one of the wicker chairs I'd painted a cheery blue only a week ago. "We dated one time. Only once. What did he want?"

I lifted Sammy off my legs and sat on the chair next to her before I filled her in. A minute later, she returned inside and brought out two glasses. Wine for her and sparkling water with a lemon slice for me. Muumuu wove around her bare ankles before basking in the sunshine.

Sage handed me the sparkling water, then opened a couple bags of treats to keep the pets occupied. "Why's he so adamant someone murdered Tilly?"

Tears swarmed my eyes. "Gut feeling? He didn't say. Honestly, I thought she'd had a heart attack. I swear I never touched her, Sage."

"Don't take it personally. Keyon's good at keeping secrets." She appeared to know a lot more than I'd expected. "He's the one man in Glitter Bay you need to away from."

"Besides the vet?" I asked, sipping my sparkling water. I itched to trade it for a glass of wine. "You seem to have issues with a lot of men around here."

She chuckled. "I suppose it seems that way. I've dated some of them. Keyon and I went out one night. That's how I met Jonathan."

Sage rubbed Sammy's head until Muumuu hopped onto her lap. "Did you give the puppy a name yet?"

"That's right. You haven't formally met yet. Sage, this is Sammy."

"You named this sweet puppy after your ex-husband?" she asked. "Are you crazy?"

I smirked. "He was a pain in the butt when I met him. The name seemed suitable. Did out anything else about the things in Tilly's trunk?"

She sipped her wine. "We can talk about that later. Since neither of us feels like making dinner, I'll call Pie in the Sky for a medium vegetarian, then we can go over the list and see if we can figure out what she wanted back so badly."

My thoughts roamed to Keyon. Handsome and charming, he was so polite he probably made the blue-haired ladies of Glitter Bay swoon. Good thing he wasn't my type. Not that I had any idea what my type was anymore. I sure wasn't in a hurry to find out.

Had Tilly swooned over Gill when they met? Not likely. She seemed too rigid and angry to be romantic and gooey-eyed. Since he'd married her, she must've had some redeeming qualities at some point.

After ordering pizza, Sage waved me inside before handing me a sheet of paper. "I started pricing some of Tilly's things out, but figured you'd have a better idea what they're worth."

I took that as a compliment. "A diamond bracelet and ring? I didn't see those."

"They were sewn into a little pocket inside the wedding dress. Seems like an odd place to stash jewelry. Almost like someone wanted to hide them."

The little hairs on the back of my neck rose. I'd seen one necklace that looked paste. The family Bible was old but unremarkable otherwise. More of a sentimental item.

The next item made me sit up straighter and gasp. "Wait, you found another dress? How did I not see it?"

She poured herself more wine. "It was rolled up in a velvet bag. It's black and looks like an old twenties' flapper dress covered in crystals and fringe. I hung it up with the wedding dress and will show you tomorrow."

I read every item on the list, including Sage's handwritten notes about sizes, colors, necklace lengths, and the like. Tomorrow, I wanted to check out each item before we talked to Gill.

"So, what are we doing with Sammy tonight?" Sage asked.

"What do mean?"

"He's a puppy, Laken. They pee, they poop, and they chew on things. I don't want him running amok through the house all night. Didn't Cameron suggest you buy a crate?"

I covered Sammy's fluffy ears. "It's in the kitchen. Isn't it barbaric to keep a puppy locked in a crate all night?"

"You'll thank me when you don't step in puddles or have to repair chewed furniture."

While I understood the whole crate idea was to keep Sammy out of trouble, he had other ideas. By two o'clock in the morning, my heart broke at the whimpering coming from the kitchen. I covered my ears with my pillow and squeezed my eyes shut.

Sage thundered down the stairs, then stomped back up and dropped Sammy on my bed. She closed the door as she left.

As he snuffled my face, I scratched behind his ear and whispered, "I don't know where it is you came from, buddy, but my sister and I like to sleep at night."

Sammy curled against my stomach.

"Good thing you're cute." I ruffled his fur, then lay back on my pillow. "We'll try to find your owner tomorrow."

He let out a soft groan as if to say, "if you must."

After making a few awkward adjustments to get comfortable, I closed my eyes and slipped into a restless dream. Keyon Blake popped into my head. He accused me of murder while dragging Andy and Gill behind him. A burly police officer hauled me out of Vintage Sage, then slapped glittering diamond handcuffs onto my wrists.

I awoke in a cold sweat with the feeling Keyon was right.

Tilly San Vicente was murdered.

I'd met enough dream interpreters and psychics in Hollywood to suspect her death had something to do with that trunk. In particular, the things that sparkled like diamonds. In the morning, I'd take a better look at every item. Especially the jewelry.

Chapter Five

After waking up every half hour to pry pieces of my wardrobe out of Sammy's mouth and toss him back onto the bed, I got up even more exhausted. By seven, Sammy lay across the end of my bed gnawing on a sweater from my favorite Beverley Hills boutique. I really needed to get someone to fix my closet door.

"Sammy, no." I lunged across the bed to yank the sweater from his mouth and tore even more holes in the fabric. My ex gave me that sweater when I had constant chills from chemo. Like my marriage, it wasn't worth saving. Just another faded memory from my chaotic marriage. No major loss.

"Here. It's yours now." I tossed him the scrap. I needed to break my bad habit of tossing my clothes on the floor before I went to bed. Good thing I'd hung that gorgeous gown in the back of my closet.

Rather than chew on the tattered cloth, Sammy pounced on it then curled up and fell asleep. He was a lot like my ex in that regard. I'd named him well.

Before I rolled out of bed, I decided to put up posters around Glitter Bay to see if anyone lost a dog. More specifically, a designer clothing-chomping, shoe-destroying English sheepdog. As much as I adored Sammy, the pup had no respect for my wardrobe, no matter how much it cost.

With my morning ruined by thoughts of Emery Samson, my ex, I patted Sammy's head. Time to get my sorry butt out of bed for my usual morning tea and scone.

Oh, crap.

Tears flooded my eyes as I pulled the covers over my head. The tea house wouldn't be open. Tilly was dead and Gill was in mourning. I wiped my face with a blanket. Sammy and I would have to alter our morning routine for a while.

"Why don't we go for a walk on the beach this morning?" I asked. "Then we can come home for tea and oatmeal pancakes before I go to Vintage Sage. I need to take another look at Tilly's trunk."

Before I did anything, however, I had to make posters to find Sammy's owner. Once he was safely home, we could all get some sleep.

Sammy yawned, abandoning the tattered sweater to follow me to the closet. He trailed behind me going in and out of the bathroom, back to the bedroom, then down the stairs to grab his leash. Both he and Muumuu reached the front door seconds before me.

"Sorry, kitty, you can't come to the beach." I nudged aside the grey ball of fluff and swung open the door.

Muumuu peered out at the clouds and gloom, turned up her nose, then wandered back up the stairs, probably to cuddle with Sage.

The chill in the air sent shivers over me. I suddenly missed that sweater Sammy ate last night and certainly wasn't in L.A. anymore. I grabbed a sweatshirt before we left the house.

I spent the first fifteen minutes trying to talk myself out of going home, while Sammy tromped over dew-laden grass and stopped to sniff everything in sight. Just as yesterday, he squatted in front of the tea house to do his business.

The open sign was lit, and Gill wiped the front counter. A young man with blue hair sat opposite him. I gawked. If someone I love had just died, there's no way I'd be at work early the next morning—let alone for the entire week.

Once I'd cleaned up after Sammy and tossed out his waste, I scooped him into my arms and walked up the steps of the tea house. I gawked through the French doors before Gill waved me in. The blue-haired kid shuffled into the kitchen.

"What are you doing here?" I asked, keeping a tight grip on Sammy, whose nose twitched toward a platter of sweets. "You should be home with your family."

He poured me a cup of tea. The sweet scent of Jasmine wafted toward me. "Tilly and I live upstairs. We were here more than anywhere else. She loved this place."

Had I met that Tilly? From her constant sour expression, I never would've guessed she had a sentimental side. Nor that she'd loved—or even liked—the tea house.

"As for family, I can't get rid of my grandson. He's been hanging out here all night," he said, pointing his thumb over his shoulder as a door closed somewhere in the tea house.

"If I knew that I would've brought your groceries. Were he and Tilly close?"

"Yeah. Abbie comes once a week to help us clean. Not that he's any good at it. At least we see him."

I'd never noticed the layer of dust on the antique teapots on the shelf. Never examined the greyed mass-produced artwork near the washrooms. Didn't see the coat of grime on the windows overlooking the moody Pacific. I'd seen everything through rose-colored glasses, just like when I met and married Emery.

"Do you have anyone to help you take care of things?" I asked, ducking to pry Sammy's mouth off a wooden chair leg. "It's always nice to have someone to lean on when you need to."

"My family won't be much help. My daughter disowned us, and Abbie..." He paused. "You don't need to hear all that. You have your own problems."

I scooped Sammy into my arms and stroked his head. "Tilly's death must be hard on your grandson."

"Everything's hard on that boy. He's been troubled since day one," he said, then wiped the back of his hand across his eyes. "I don't know what's going to happen. I can't run this place alone. I may have to sell everything."

"But the tea house is a local landmark."

Gill frowned. "Landmark or not, I'm an old man, Laken. I need help."

I wanted to tell him quitting wasn't an option, yet that's exactly what I'd done. I gave up my whole life and career because of my ex. What I needed was to rebuild instead of bobbing along and pretending to weigh my options.

What if one of those options involved buying the Sweet Eden Tea House?

I'd daydreamed dozens of times about moving Vintage Sage there to make use of all those great windows. Perhaps even selling tea to our customers. Sammy and I could move in upstairs, and the building would burst with life. My mind hummed with possibilities as I scribbled my phone number on a napkin.

"If you do need a hand, I can make arrangements with Sage to help you for a while."

"Are you sure you can juggle the dog and two jobs?"

"I don't do much at Vintage Sage. How hard could working two part-time jobs be?"

He chuckled. "I need to start a pot of soup."

When he disappeared into the kitchen, I turned to leave just as the front door opened.

A much older woman wearing a wide-brimmed purple hat and a pale violet cardigan over a faded red blouse took a few timid steps inside. She reminded me of Sammy when I'd first found him. Nervous and unsure.

Sammy's nose wiggled as he took a few quick sniffs and gave a low growl.

"Stop that." I held him tighter. "I'm sorry. He's never like that with anyone."

Not that I knew of anyway.

Blue curls peeked out from beneath the woman's hat. Not grey blue, but a bold robin's egg. Her gaze darted around the room like she was either searching for or afraid of something. Or someone.

Gill didn't return to greet his customer, so I took a deep breath. "Can I help you?"

"That depends." She eyed me and Sammy. "Do you work here?"

My face grew warm. "Well, no, but Gill's busy."

Her shoulders lowered an inch. "I heard a rumor that Tilly..."

I didn't know what to say but Gill certainly did.

He snarled behind me. "What do you want, Enid? You know you're banned from ever setting foot in here."

Sammy leaped from my arms and nearly pulled the leash from my hand. When he ran toward Enid growling, I pulled back the leash to stop him short. Rude, but effective until I learned how to train him.

"I'm fully aware of my standing around here." She straightened her purple hat, puffed out her chest, and stood straighter. "I heard about Tilly's passing and simply wanted to extend my condolences."

Sammy ignored the taut leash, straining to get closer to Enid's blue leather shoes.

"You don't *simply* do anything," Gill said. "What do you want?"

She pursed her pale pink lips before she asked, "Was Tilly murdered?"

His face reddened. He reached for a teacup and threw it in her direction. "Get out."

Enid stepped aside with the grace of a dancer to narrowly miss a hit to the shoulder. When the cup shattered on the floor next to her, Sammy ran behind me, wrapping his leash around my ankles.

Gill picked up another cup and drew his arm back.

"What are you doing? Stop that!" I tried to lunge toward him. Instead, I stumbled, hitting my knee on a chair. That would leave an ugly bruise.

"I'll get the broom," Abbie shouted from the kitchen.

Enid took a step forward despite the threat of more china flying toward her. "Please believe me. All I want is to extend my condolences and help."

"I know exactly what you want," he growled, "and I said get out."

I ducked an instant before he threw the second teacup, which flew past Enid's left ear and broke against a wooden chair. Her face paled beneath her caked-on makeup.

Finally, she held both hands in front of her and backed away. "You know where to find me if you change your mind."

"What the heck's going on out here?" Abbie ran from the kitchen. He paused and scowled. "Oh. It's you."

When Gill picked up a third teacup, Enid darted out the front door.

"What was that all about?" I asked, with barely had time to face Gill before the door reopened. Surely, she wasn't dumb enough to return so soon, was she?

She was. "Does this mean I'm still banned?"

"For life." Gill let the third teacup fly.

That one hit the wooden doorframe and exploded into tiny pieces. The handle skittered across the floor to my feet making Sammy bounce back.

Abbie gawked at his grandpa.

Gill stormed into the kitchen and tried to slam the door, which swung back and forth several times with harmless squawks.

Sammy let out a yelp, pawing at my legs for me to pick him up. I held him against my chest.

“What was all that about?” Abbie asked, walking toward the mess with the broom to clean up the shards.

“I hoped you could tell me.”

Once he was done, he left the tea house just as three older women came in and ordered tea with petit fours. Over the next fifteen minutes, I served four more customers and dusted the antique teapots while Sammy dozed.

“What are you still doing here?” Gill emerged from the kitchen.

“You had customers, so I sold them tea and sent them on their way.”

He closed his eyes with a sigh and said, “Go home, Laken.”

“I have to,” I told him, reaching for Sammy’s leash. “It’s time to go to work.”

Gill pulled a ring filled with keys from his pocket before leaning down to ruffle Sammy’s fur. After he’d ushered us outside, he locked the door behind us. “I need to go, too. I have arrangements to make. It seems word spread has about Tilly’s death and the vultures are circling. I had seven messages on my answering machine last night, then Enid stopped by today.”

“What do you mean?”

“At my age, a single man is fair game.”

I chuckled, then met Gill’s serious gaze. “Why did you ban Enid from the tea shop?”

"Enid Walsh is Glitter Bay's local busybody. That woman's nothing but trouble. If gossip were an Olympic sport, she'd have a warehouse full of gold medals."

"Are you sure you don't need help?" I asked. "I could look after the front counter until things settle down. I could also find out more about the contents of that trunk.

He continued walking. "Go home, Laken."

"I could run interference with the vultures. You know Enid will be back."

Gill paused. "I could use help to fend them off."

"I could help you for a few hours in the mornings, then work at Vintage Sage in the afternoon."

He gave a slow nod. "Come by tomorrow morning. We can talk then."

Once he was half block away, I coaxed Sammy toward the beach. We'd barely gone a dozen steps before a hand clapped my shoulder and Enid fell into step beside me.

"Sorry to startle you, dear," she said. "Are you new in town?"

Sammy, busy snuffling the grass, flinched and growled. Not the world's best watchdog, but he was adorable.

"I moved to town a couple months ago," I told her.

"Your puppy's cute. What's his name?"

"Sammy. I just found him."

"You found him? In the park or on the beach?"

As strange as it sounded, I replied, "Under a chair at the tea house."

Enid adjusted her hat. "Very funny. I've never had a dog. I couldn't be bothered to walk them or clean up poop. Cats are easier. Cleaner."

She'd obviously never met Muumuu.

I tugged the leash to get Sammy away from a questionable pile of rubbish, then continued toward the beach. "Nice to meet you."

She followed, sticking out her hand. "I'm Enid Walsh. I've lived in Glitter Bay most of my life and know everyone in town. Do I know your parents?"

"They live in Seattle. I'm Laken."

"And you live here with your little dog, Toto." She held her hat as we stepped onto the wooden boardwalk. "What did you say your name was again, dear?"

"Laken. Lake with an 'n.' Sammy and I are staying with my sister."

"Oh? And who is your sister?" she asked.

"Sage Miller."

Enid crinkled her nose as if she caught a whiff of something foul. "The young lady who owns Vintage Sage. We bump into each other now and again. I must say, your sister is a strong-willed young woman. I've heard her in town council meetings and wouldn't want to get in her way when she's angry."

I stepped off the boardwalk to pick up a stick. "I've never known my sister to get worked up without good reason."

Sammy, happy to be off his leash, pranced in circles until I threw the stick in the ocean. He barked and ran into the waves.

I kicked off my running shoes and wiggled my toes in the cool sand.

"Are you sure it's wise to go barefoot?" Enid asked. "You could get sick. The sand isn't very warm, even though the water looks like it's covered in diamonds."

Her mention of diamonds brought to mind the trunk and its contents. I sent Sage a quick text to remind her to leave me a copy of the list.

Sammy jumped through a few waves before forgetting about the stick. He ran toward us, then paused less than a foot away to shake off the water and grit. Enid gave a loud screech and waved her red patent handbag at him.

"Sorry. I don't know what's wrong with him. This morning, he tried to eat a table leg and two shoes. It wasn't even a matching pair."

"He chews because he's teething," she snapped as she re-centered her hat. "He is still a puppy, you know."

"Yeah, that's what the vet said." I grabbed Sammy's collar to clip on his leash. "The problem is he has a taste for high fashion and furniture. What brought you to the tea house so early today. Besides Gill?"

Her gaze flickered toward the marina as she sighed. "Writer's block."

"You're a writer?"

"Journalist. My column appears in the local paper every week. Sometimes the stories write themselves, but it's tougher when people refuse to speak to me."

People refusing to speak to a reporter? Go figure.

"What do you write about?" I asked.

"Oh, that's right, you're new here," Enid said. "I write the best gossip column in town. Well, the only gossip column in town, but that's just semantics."

Sammy yawned before speeding up and pulling me along the beach.

Enid matched her pace to mine as she added, "I'd like to share Tilly's story with my readers. Strictly as a professional courtesy, not gossip. She was a local businesswoman. Did you know she used to work in a bridal shop before she met Gill?"

"Really?" Which explained the dresses.

"You sound like you doubt me. It's my business to know these things. I am a reporter of news for inquiring minds, after all."

That was one way to put it. I tried not to be judgmental, especially since I was curious about Gill's reaction to her at the tea house. "Why are you talking to me? I didn't know Tilly that well."

"True, but I need a witness who can describe what happened in detail."

"I won't be much help. All I know is that she had a heart attack," I tugged on Sammy's leash to slow him down.

"Especially after you saw Gill throw teacups at me." She huffed. "The man has a temper, what can I say? This is my last hurrah. I plan to retire from the newspaper biz soon to write a book."

I caught sight of something black and rectangular in her hand. A cell phone? Nope, she was old school. Probably a voice recorder to get the scoop on Gill, or me. I was the ex-wife of a major—okay, B-list—Hollywood actor. According to the paparazzi, my life was fair game.

"What do you plan to write?" I asked.

Enid grinned, holding onto her hat as a gust of wind picked up sand from the beach. "A thriller. I'm fascinated with cold cases. My favorite is a local story about a sapphire and diamond necklace stolen years ago."

Startled, I glanced at her, taking my gaze off Sammy for a second. "Why is that?"

She leaned closer, then lowered her voice, "I think there's a local connection to the theft, but I can't prove it."

"That's intrigah—," I shrieked as Sammy broke into a full run, yanking the leash out of my hand. He didn't seem too eager to help Enid with her book. When he finally stopped, his ears perked forward. His full attention was focused on something ahead.

"What's up, boy?" I asked as I caught up to him.

Enid caught up to us panting and said, "I hope you're not expecting him to tell you, or we'll be here all day."

I picked up the end of his leash out of the sand but couldn't figure out what he was so fascinated with. Finally, I shrugged.

One Enid caught her breath, she asked, "How well do you know Gill?"

"I don't really. I only met Gill and Tilly at the tea house after I moved here. Why?"

"You two seem awfully chummy." She gave me a sideways glance. "Are you having an affair?"

Cheating being a sensitive subject, I yanked Sammy's leash without meaning to. He yipped and sat by my foot. "What? No. Why would you say something so awful right after Tilly died?"

Her face grew as red as her shirt. "It's nothing personal. I've known the man forever. Trust me, he's not as sweet as he seems."

"Too much information." I walked away shaking my head.

Gill used to touch Tilly's hand and did everything to make her life easier. My ex would disappear for hours on end and complain how I didn't look after things the way I used to after I got sick. Him mostly. I knew sweet when I saw it.

"Laken, are you okay?" Enid asked, placing a hand on my arm.

I flinched. "Yeah. Why?"

"You were muttering and walking so fast your poor puppy got left behind." She pointed at Sammy and the leash wrapped around my left leg.

"My mind went somewhere else. I'm okay."

"To a special man in your life?" She winked with a knowing smile.

I untangled the leash. "My ex-husband."

Enid's face brightened. "An ex? How juicy. Were you together long? Do you know where he is now?"

I let Sammy play in the grass as I ran down the upcoming movie schedule Emery had supposedly sent by accident. "Singapore, I think."

"Singapore," she said. "What's he doing there? He should be here trying to win his gorgeous wife back."

I'd already said too much. Emery had made it perfectly clear through his lawyers that he didn't want me back. I was sick, over eighteen, and didn't have breast implants or a French Riviera tan. Not a great moment for my ego, but the feeling was mutual. As far as I was concerned, the man lacked both a heart and a soul.

"Tell you what, I'll let you off the hook. For now. But only if you tell me why Tilly was in Vintage Sage the day she died. What was she doing there?"

"Why don't you ask Gill?"

"The man banned me from the tea house for life. Twice."

I smirked. "That didn't seem to stop you today."

"Like I told Gill, I simply wanted to pass on my condolences."

An odd sensation in my stomach told me Enid had planned to have a far different chat with Gill if I wasn't there. He might've thrown something heavier if she had. Keyon and Andy would've had to take her to the hospital. Or the morgue.

Checking the time, I excused myself. I had to get Sammy home, then hustle to work before Sage got worried. My plan was to study the list of contents of Tilly's trunk.

The next time I spoke to Gill, I wanted to be armed with information, and possibly more questions.

Chapter Six

Two days after Tilly's death, I took Sammy for an early morning walk. I was disappointed not to receive any calls after putting up twenty posters around town. As we walked, I was surprised to find they'd all vanished. Miffed, I went back home, then we wandered around town to staple hastily made posters to every power pole Sammy stopped to sniff. Pretty much every pole within six blocks.

He'd not only eaten a pair of my underwear that morning but also a sock or two. I bagged the evidence of his wardrobe indiscretions and tossed it into the trash bin outside the tea house.

Once again, the open sign was lit, and the front door stood ajar. I marched inside with Sammy on my hip. "Gill, what are you doing here?"

"Laken, I hoped you'd come by," he said. "Sage dropped off my groceries yesterday afternoon, so we had a chance to chat. Were you serious about helping me for a while?"

"Of course, I am. Sage went to some special yoga class last night, so I didn't get to talk to her."

He nodded. "She'd mentioned that. Seems she's happy to loan you to me for the mornings until I get things sorted out here. What are those you're packing around?"

"Posters. I'm trying to find Sammy's owner. Do you mind if I hang one by the cash register?"

"Go right ahead, then I'll show you around. If you're going to work here, you need to know where things are."

Although I wasn't sure what more there was to see, I told him, "Let me take Sammy home and put him in his crate. I'll be back in half an hour."

Gill waved a hand. "He'll be fine here. He's harmless."

"You haven't seen my wardrobe. I've sacrificed a pile of socks and underwear to the little beast."

"Guess he's trying to teach you to put your things away." Gill chuckled, then motioned me to follow. "Come on. He can play out here while we talk."

Beyond the back door, was a twenty-by-twenty-foot courtyard blocked off from the alley by a ten-foot-high, wrought iron fence. Neglected flower beds dotted with half-hidden water features ringed a cobblestone patio. Rusty metal tables and chairs lay strewn about as if a strong wind or a temper tantrum tossed them around.

"Sage never told me this was here."

"She probably doesn't know," Gill said. "Tilly looked after this garden every day until her arthritis got too bad. I didn't have enough energy to serve people inside and out by myself, even though it would've made her happy if I'd kept it up every summer."

"You used to serve tea in the garden?" I asked, keeping an eye on Sammy as he nosed around the overgrown plants and weeds.

Gill nodded. "We did. The courtyard gets the shade on hot afternoons. We were so busy all summer that we needed to take reservations for high tea."

"Why didn't you hire someone to help?"

"Hiring people costs money," he said. "Besides, Tilly didn't want just anyone taking care of her precious flowers."

Untamed rose bushes and flowers wrapped around the neglected fountains among the weeds. I envisioned metal tables draped with white linens, rosebushes in full bloom, and servers dressed in black circulating among occupied tables. If I owned the place, I would've hired a gardener regardless and turned the place into a bistro.

I reigned in my burst of excitement, then texted Sage to tell her where I'd be for the next few hours. After making sure Sammy couldn't get into mischief, I joined Gill inside and asked, "What would you like me to do first?

"How about a little cleaning?" he asked, pointing to a bucket on the counter before he opened the swinging door to the tea house.

As I filled a bucket with hot water in the kitchen sink, called out, "I wanted to ask you about that trunk your grandson brought to Vintage Sage."

Gill frowned toward the front door. "What are *you* doing here?"

I peered around his head to see a tall woman with long, black hair piled in a messy updo. She sashayed through the room, wearing a scowl, four-inch heels, and a painted-on red dress. Her makeup was flawless. She could've easily fit into one of those beautiful gowns if she didn't have the breast implants.

I turned off the water and added soap to the bucket, then grabbed a rag and went into the tea house behind the counter. No way was I missing this.

"Father." The woman stopped near the counter and placed a hand on her slender hip, as if posing for a magazine shoot. The scent of jasmine wafted through the room.

"Gabriella," Gill said, folding his arms across his chest.

"Since my mother died, I came to pay my respects."

That was the blue-haired boy's mother? Holy crow.

"You did that the last time you left home."

"Yeah, I guess in a way I did." Gabriella San Vicente let out a laugh, but her forehead didn't move. Botox?

Gill growled. "Let me guess. You're here for more money."

"My inheritance," she said, holding her hands out at her sides. "What else? You haven't given me a thing since I left high school."

"What if everything goes to me and you get nothing?"

Her painted face paled. "We both know she had bank accounts, jewelry, and owned more than half of this place. You and I are her sole heirs."

"What about Abbie?" I asked.

Gabriella scowled and backed away as if I were contagious. "What about Abbie? Who are you, anyway?"

"Laken's helping out around here until I get things settled."

Her forced smile grew so sweet it made my teeth hurt. "Laken, huh? Oh, I'll bet she's helping. By things, you do mean my mother's estate, right?"

"And funeral arrangements," he said.

"Did mom know about this one?" Gabriella asked, looking me over.

I stared. "Excuse me?"

"What are you saying?" Gill asked.

She met my gaze with a smirk. "My mother's been dead two whole days and you already have a new girl in the stable. Some things never change."

Was Enid right about Gill? While I didn't take him for a ladies' man, I had his daughter pegged. No offer to help with funeral arrangements. No sympathy. Total princess. I knew too women like her to sympathize.

"Just tell me what mom left me, then I'll go," Gabriella told him.

Gill sighed, pinching the bridge of his nose between his thumb and finger. "You'll have to ask the lawyer. I don't have any details."

"Typical." She folded her arms across her stomach with her lips frozen in a pout. "You never cared about me."

I'd seen a lot of spoiled brats in Hollywood, but this girl put some of them to shame.

"Gabriella, why don't you come back after lunch, then we can discuss whatever bug has crawled up your—"

When the front door opened, Keyon and Andy walked in. Gabriella leaned back and draped her arms across the counter. Her pout turned into a weird grin. If the men were bracelets, she would've happily worn one on each arm.

"And who do we have here?" she asked, her voice low and sultry losing the nasty tone in three seconds flat.

Keyon scowled. "I'd say it's nice to see you, Gabby, but it never is."

"Don't be a jerk, Keyon." Gabriella laughed. "I haven't seen either of you in ages. Give me a hug."

Andy shook his head. "I'll pass and take a large, black coffee."

"This is a tea house, son. We do not sell coffee," Gill spit out the last word. "If you want that stuff, go to Seattle. Take my daughter with you."

Keyon chuckled. "The only place I'd take her is out onto the ocean with an anchor tied to her neck."

Andy whistled. "That's harsh."

"That's what happens when you treat all the guys in town like toys. Right, Gabby?"

"Oh, please. Like either of you complained at the time."

Gill's gaze met mine and he shook his head.

Keyon's face reddened. "The only mistake I made was driving you home when you were too drunk to walk."

Gabriella would've fit right into Emery's circle. Her behavior was enough to make me uncomfortable, let alone her father.

"You know that's far from the truth." Gabriella leaned against Keyon's chest to give him a playful nip on the chin. "You have the hots for Laken, don't you?"

He stepped back so fast that Gabriella stumbled forward.

"What was that for?" she asked, steadying herself against the counter.

Andy turned to walk away. "Come on. Let's go grab a cup of coffee."

"We'll come back another time, Gill," Keyon said.

Once they were gone, Gabriella turned back to Gill. "Well, I suppose if you're too busy to fill me in on Mom's will, Abbie and I can visit the lawyer on our own. After that, you and I will have a little chat. I want what I've got coming to me."

She stalked out of the shop, pausing long enough to slam the door behind her.

"Oh, you'll get what's coming to you," Gill muttered, releasing a string of obscenities before disappearing into the kitchen.

Tension still swirling around me, I returned to cleaning. My mind went off like fireworks in a dozen different directions. Gabriella had a history with both Keyon and Andy. She seemed to get into as much trouble with men as Gill seemed to with women.

I glanced up. All that drama and it wasn't even eight o'clock in the morning.

A half hour later, Sage walked in. She flashed a wide grin when she saw me scrubbing shelves. "Wow. I was told you were playing Cinderella but didn't believe it."

"Who told you that?" I asked.

"One of my friends from the shelter. She couldn't believe my fancy pants sister would stoop to scrubbing teapots and counters. That and I got your text."

Fancy Pants. Sage had called me that ever since walking into the mansion I shared with my ex. Granted, my closet was the size of her kitchen and living room combined.

I shrugged. "I thought if Gill was determined to keep the tea house open, the least I could do was help."

"Where's Sammy?"

"In the courtyard out back."

Her eyes widened. "This place has a courtyard?"

Leading her though the kitchen, I opened the back door and heard my sister gasp. "I've been coming here for a month, and I never knew about it."

"Me neither."

Sammy bounded toward us letting out a series of high-pitched whines and whimpers. A doggy version of Morse code.

"Aww, the poor guy's lonesome." Sage let him jump up against her leg then patted his head. "I'll take him home for now and put him in the crate when I leave for the shop."

"Are you sure? I don't want him to be a nuisance."

"He'll be fine," she said.

Unconvinced, I told her, "Just keep the bedroom doors closed or both our wardrobes will shrink considerably."

"No feeding him T-shirts or socks. No problem." Sage laughed.

"Just keep an eye on him or you'll find out firsthand."

She shook her head. "Don't worry. I'll look after him. What's the worst that could happen?"

Once she walked Sammy home, Gill and I discussed the menu and prepped for lunch. He wasn't convinced anyone would show up, but the tea house was full before eleven. By noon, we'd run out of ham, cheese, and fresh buns from the bakery. At least there was enough turkey in the freezer to make another three pots of soup thanks to Tilly planning ahead.

I texted Sage my apologies after the lunch rush ended, then wiped crumbs off the tables, swept the floors, and pushed chairs in place. "Is lunch always so busy?"

"Nope. Everyone just wanted to gossip. Don't let them get to you." Gill counted out some bills, then frowned before closing the cash register. "I need to do a deposit. Can you stay for a few minutes?"

I propped the swinging door open with a stool. Tilly's stool. "I'll text Sage and do the dishes while you're gone."

"This isn't such a bad thing after all. I finally get out of doing dishes. He paused near the door. "I need to stop at the funeral home."

Making funeral arrangements alone wasn't something I'd look forward to. I bit my lip before volunteering to help.

He handed me a key. "We'll close early since you need to help Sage. Do you mind coming in tomorrow morning?"

"No problem," I told him.

I was nearly done with the dishes when the door opened again. "I'll be with you in a minute."

"Take your time."

My first glimpse of the man waiting made my jaw drop. Movie star handsome—and I knew movie stars—he was tall with wavy dark hair, probably lean and strong beneath his black trench coat. The same man who came into the tea house the day I found Sammy.

I wipe sweat off my face before I approached him. "What can I do for you?"

"Is Gill San Vicente here? I'd like to speak to him, please." His slight Irish accent made my knees week and I swooned.

Mimicking accents was how Emery first won me over. Spoiling me rotten was the second.

"Gill's not here."

He drummed a finger on the counter. "When do you expect him?"

"I'm not sure. He had things to take care of."

"Then I'll stop by another time," he said. "Could I get a small Earl Grey to go?"

"Sure. Do you take anything? Milk, sugar, or lemon?"

"Just hot and black."

His words were nonchalant yet sent a pleasant shiver over me. Hot flashes must be some weird left-over side effect from chemo. Was perimenopause possible at twenty-seven? Okay, I was thirty but for Emery's sake, I'd lied about my age the whole time we were together.

I made his Earl Grey tea and nearly forgot to charge him.

"Are you alright?" he asked. "You're quite flushed."

Nodding, I swallowed hard. If he only knew.

"When you do see Gill, please tell him my offer still stands."

Offer? Once he left, I realized I forgot to get his name. What was wrong with me?

As I turned, my gaze landed on Tilly's empty stool. The man in the black coat was in the tea house the morning she died. Had their conversation triggered her heart attack, or did he slip something into her tea that mimicked an attack?

I was overthinking things. Why couldn't I focus on taking care of me and leave death and suspicion out of the equation? It was just as plausible Tilly had a heart attack because of her weight, or her anxiety about that trunk.

Sending a quick text to Sage, I locked up the tea house before heading home to check on Sammy. I had questions for Gill. One was why he'd sent the trunk to Vintage Sage.

For the moment, I needed to peruse the list of contents while waiting for answers.

Chapter Seven

As soon as I got to Vintage Sage, my sister left to run some errands before going home to do paperwork. I read over the list of contents we found in Tilly's trunk and got lost in thought while I dusted until the door opened behind me.

"How's it going?" Keyon asked.

The sight of him was disconcerting. I'd forgotten about the potential for customers. "What can I do for you?"

"Sage asked me to check on you," he said, folding his arms across his broad chest. "Which is funny because I thought she'd say I was a bad influence."

"She has. Several times." Which was why saying my sister sent him made no sense.

"I'm surprised she didn't tell the police I'm stalking you."

"I asked her not to. For now."

His smile wavered like he was unsure he took me seriously. "I'm sure she'd love to see me in trouble for old time's sake."

"And what old times are those?" I asked.

Keyon walked toward me. "Ah, I finally have your full attention."

"So, now that you have my full attention, what do you want? I'm busy."

He glanced around. "Yeah, I've never seen so many customers here."

"Start talking or I'll put you to work. There's a lot to do around here."

"Like what?" he asked.

"Wiping shelves. Dusting. Sweeping floors. The list is endless."

He leaned on the counter. "It's interesting you're doing so much to help someone who'll just turn around and sell the place in a couple weeks anyway."

"Sage?"

"Gill."

"What's so interesting about that?" I tried to sound nonchalant but itched to kick him out. "I'm there for moral support."

He grinned. "Maybe. But the tea house is the perfect place to hear the gossip about Tilly's murder."

My breath stuck in my chest. Did he think I killed her? "I hadn't heard she was murdered."

"I think she was murdered," he said. "You should pay attention to the rumors going around."

Gossip was the one thing I knew a lot about. Thank you, paparazzi. The tabloids were great at getting stories wrong by the time they went to press. Kind of like the telephone game we'd played as kids.

"I need to get back to work, so if you don't mind..."

Keyon swiped the counter with one finger. "I thought Sage would be here."

"And I thought she sent you."

When he grinned, his cheeks tinged with red. "I'll leave you to it."

I'd straighten a rack of blouses before the door opened again. This time, Gabriella San Vicente peered inside. She wrinkled her nose as if catching a whiff of something disagreeable.

"What is this place?" she asked.

"My sister's vintage clothing shop." I used to be just like Gabriella when I shopped Rodeo Drive. Half a lifetime ago, it seemed. Seeing that arrogance from the viewpoint of a salesperson made me cringe.

"Quaint. Kind of cramped for a clothing store, isn't it?" She glanced at a few items without touching anything.

"Can I help you?" I asked.

"You can start by telling me where he is."

"Who?"

"My father."

I wiped my sweaty hands on the damp cloth. "If he's not at the tea house, he might be at the funeral home."

Her glare could've bored through steel. "He's making her arrangements alone. That man's not getting away with this."

"I'm sure he didn't want you to worry."

She narrowed her eyes. "Then why leave me out of it all. He just wants to do everything his way. Has he met with the lawyer yet? What's going on with the will?"

"I don't know. I didn't ask."

Gabriella toyed with the end of her long, black braid. "My mom hated me, you know. She had a soft spot for Abbie though. It wouldn't surprise me if the witch left everything to him leaving Dad and I out on the street. I'm sure that would serve us right. We've both made bad choices."

"Your parents owned the tea house together, didn't they?" I asked. "She can't give it away if it's in both their names. Only her half."

She closed the gap between us before she spoke and told me, "My dad was never good with money, which is why I'm worried. Mom kept the roof over our heads. When I was a kid, she worked two jobs. I'd hear her sewing late into the night. They separated once because of his get-rich-quick schemes, among other things. The tea house was Mom's. Dad worked for her."

If that was the case, Gill wouldn't be able to sell the tea house until the deed was officially in his name.

"Who's his lawyer?" she asked, suddenly distressed.

"No idea. He had a bunch of business cards near the phone, but I—"

"Thanks. I appreciate that." Gabriella gave me a quick hug, then burst out of the store without looking back. Maybe if I stayed on her good side, I could sneak a peek of the will when she got a copy.

At five o'clock, I locked the front door, then tidied up for the next day. Being alone in Vintage Sage was usually comforting, kind of like hanging out in an eccentric aunt's house. With each tick of the clock behind the cash register that day, reality set in.

Tilly died there. I dreaded seeing her hazy specter drift past the cash register scowling and accusing me of...

I shivered, no longer sure who to trust. My gut wasn't helping. I was so hungry I could eat both small steaks I'd put in cold water to thaw when I checked on Sammy. Hopefully, Sage had remembered to stick them in the fridge when she got home. She'd offered to help me cook them, even though she refused to eat them. I needed the iron. She was having grilled portobello mushroom.

Exhausted and hungry, I couldn't deal with any other calamities. I crossed my fingers and hoped Sammy had stayed out of mischief. I'd barely reached the front gate when my sister shrieked.

"Sage?" I sucked in a bracing breath and ran up the front steps. "What's wrong?"

My sister stood in the kitchen, hands on her hips, while Sammy gnawed on the remains of a steak. The mushroom sat on the counter with claw marks in the cap.

"Dinner's going to be late." Her face seemed ready to crack from anger.

"How did he get that?"

She pointed to a kitchen chair near the counter, where Muumuu sat looking content—or gloating. It was hard to tell with cats. "That chair was by the table when I went to my office. I didn't hear a thing until Muumuu started to meow for dinner."

"Could a puppy his size push the chair to the sink?"

"Well, Muumuu didn't do it. It's partly my fault. I forgot to put your steaks in the fridge when I got home. I've just had so much on my mind lately."

I bit my lip. "Neither of us expected Sammy to steal it."

"Or that he'd have a sidekick." Sage grimaced toward her cat.

We both looked at Sammy, who seemed unaware of the anger radiating off my vegan sister as he gnawed on my dinner. Muumuu jumped down to help Sammy lap up bits of meat.

I ran a hand through my hair. "I'll run out and grab something."

"No. You're wiped." She grabbed her phone as she headed for the door. "You keep an eye on the monsters. I'll get dinner. From now on, I don't think we can leave Sammy unsupervised unless he's in the crate."

Translation: Wherever I went, Sammy had to go. *Ugh!* Having a dog was turning into a huge headache, and I hadn't even had him a week. I was starting to see why no one had claimed him yet.

I sat on the floor next to Sammy, careful not to get anything gross on my clothes. "What are we going to do, Sammy? If you want to live here, you need to behave, or Sage will throw us both out."

Disappointed, I tossed the dog outside and the remains of the steak into the garbage, closing the screen door before I mopped the kitchen floor three times. Muumuu stood at the door and meowed. Whatever deal they'd made, Sammy seemed to have gotten the best of.

I poured a glass of sparkling water for me and wine for Sage before I went to sit on the deck. Scrubbing my face with both hands, I released a long sigh. "What a week."

Sage arrived fifteen minutes later with takeout from the Devil's Peak Tavern. At least she approved of my careful cleanup of the kitchen. After years of maid service and servants, it was nice to feel productive again. Even if it was a big adjustment.

"You must be tired. What was it like working two jobs today?" she asked over cilantro lime shrimp, rice, and cod cakes.

"You make it sound like I've never held a job before."

"Sorry, I know you've had other jobs."

I poked at a shrimp. "Just not since I met Emery. It's easy to be dazzled by expensive jewelry, trips to exotic locations, and award shows, you know."

Sage nodded. "Not to mention the hired help and designer clothing. I am jealous you've never had to worry about anything so trivial as paying bills."

Only worrying when my ex didn't come home for days or weeks at a time. He insisted he was either working late on set or running lines with a coworker. I'd believe him. Then I heard the rumors and found evidence of his many indiscretions.

"Did you get much of the cleaning done today?" she asked.

"Quite a bit at Sweet Eden, and some at Vintage Sage. I think I overdid things this morning."

Sage sipped her wine. "Did Keyon show up again?"

"Earlier. He told me you sent him to check on me."

She frowned. "Not in a million years."

"I know," I said before shoveling rice into my mouth. "He's adamant there's something suspicious about Tilly's death."

"You were there. What do you think?" she asked.

Reaching for my sparkling water, I sat back. "It seemed like she had a heart attack, but I don't have enough training to know otherwise. Maybe he has good reason to be suspicious."

"Maybe. Just don't get too close to him. He acts nice on the surface, but something about him gives me the creeps."

"You figured that out after only one date?"

Sage's cheeks reddened. "Is that what he told you? He and Jonathan have been friends since they were kids, which is how Jonathan and I met." She grimaced. "Keyon learned to never bring a girl to meet one of his buddies on the first date."

"Is that what happened?"

"Yeah. We went to see an awful action movie, then to a bar. Jonathan was a perfect gentleman and made my knees weak. I forgot all about Keyon. When he hooked up with some other girl, Jonathan drove me home."

"That's how I felt when I met Emery. Weak knees, fluttery stomach, the works," I told her. "I won't make that mistake again."

Sage raised her eyebrows. "Falling head over heels for someone or rushing to marry a rich, handsome movie star?"

"Hey! We waited six whole months."

"Which is a lifetime in Hollywood. I get it." She cracked the tail off a shrimp. "Then you got sick and grew up faster than he did, so he found other playmates."

The truth stung. I blinked back hot tears. "That hurt."

Sage gave my hand a squeeze. "I'm sorry, Laken."

I shook off her hand to take a drink. "It's okay. Emery and I are history. We all know he had playmates long before I got sick."

"And I know part of you still loves him but leaving him was for the best. You get to hang out here and heal while he causes his PR people nightmares."

"At least he's not my nightmare anymore."

"Nope. You can hide out here as long as you want and then take on the world when you're ready," she said. "Take time to think about what *you* want to do, then make a new life for yourself." She paused. "As for Sammy, I think he's moved in whether we've decided what to do with him or not."

Across the yard, the puppy let out a yip. He ran toward us shaking the toy that was clenched in his jaw.

Sage winced. "I hope he doesn't think he's bringing that thing inside."

Sammy dropped the toy near a flower bed before he started digging.

"Oh, come on," my sister groaned. "Sammy, get out of there."

I grinned, pulling the tail off a shrimp. "At least he's not dragging it into the house, and I know what I'm doing after dinner."

"Bathing the dog and locking him in his crate for the night."

As much as it pained me, it would be worth a few sleepless nights to keep some clothes in my wardrobe. Not to mention keeping both animals from destroying the house.

I bathed Sammy, then couldn't resist a peek at Tilly's gown. The sparkling stones made me smile. If I didn't know any better, I'd swear they were real diamonds.

Wishful thinking.

Money like that would go a long way toward Gill's retirement not to mention riling Gabriella up even more.

Chapter Eight

Sammy started whining the instant I closed the crate. I climbed the stairs, shut my door, and resolved to be strong. The longer he cried, the harder it was for me to fall asleep. When Muumuu began to howl outside my door, I pressed my pillow to my ears and willed them both to be quiet.

Half an hour later, Sage stomped down the stairs and sprang Sammy from puppy prison. She tossed him on my bed, then slammed my bedroom door shut.

Bleary eyed, I thought about bringing the crate upstairs as he curled up against me. When I awoke six hours later, Sammy clutched the tattered sweater between his front paws as he snoozed. I smiled, part of me glad no one had called about the posters. He was mine for now.

I took him for a quick walk before showering, then headed to the tea house. To say my stomach churned was a slight understatement. I felt like a walking butterfly hatchery after the visits from the man in black and Gabriella yesterday.

The lights were still out and the tea house silent. I took a deep breath and pulled out the key Gill gave me to unlock the door. Before I turned the key in the lock, I hesitated. What if he wanted the tea house to remain closed today?

I touched the black gemstone dangling from a gold chain around my neck. The tourmaline, a gift from Sage while during my chemo, was supposed to protect me from negativity and ground me. With everything going on lately, I could use all the grounding I could get.

Once inside, I didn't hear a sound in the building. I decided to let Sammy into the courtyard while I called Gill. The front door opened behind me before I'd reached the counter.

Sammy let out a bark as Keyon and Andy strode across the wood floor. Keyon flashed a dimpled smile before leaning to pat Sammy's head. Andy looked around with a frown. I got the impression he'd rather be anywhere else.

"Are you here for tea or to ask more questions?" I asked.

"One question," Andy said. "Why doesn't Gill sell coffee?"

"Because it's a tea house," Keyon reminded him. "We'll have two cups of tea and some of those tasty scones if you have any. What kind of tea would you recommend?"

The little I knew about tea were the things Sage and Gill taught me. Before I could speak, Andy folded his arms across his broad chest.

"Can we get out of here?" Andy asked. "The place isn't even open yet and I've got things to do. Like get coffee."

"My partner here needs to relax and enjoy a nice cup of tea before we get another call. He's been skittish for days," Keyon told me. "He needs something to help him mellow out. Something without caffeine."

My wits reappeared. "Then I'd suggest the chamomile. For you, I'd go with a new green tea Gill brought in called Dragon Well. It has a light color and flavor. I was drinking some when I met Sammy."

"Is Sammy your boyfriend?" Andy asked.

I picked up my puppy. "This little guy."

"Now there's a selling feature," he said. "Do your customers get one with every cup of tea?"

Shaking my head, I told him, "I'll talk to Gill about that as a marketing tool. I'm not even sure how I ended up with him. He kind of came out of nowhere. Since the courtyard's fenced in, Gill figured he'd be safe there and not be able to run off."

While I made Andy's tea and searched for the scones, I hoped they'd take their drinks outside.

At the same time "I handed Andy his tea, his radio crackled. "Thanks."

"There's a courtyard here?" Keyon asked. "Can I see it?"

"Later. We've got work to do." Andy tossed a couple bills on the counter.

Once he left the building, I touched the tourmaline for comfort. Grounding.

"Are you okay?" Keyon raised his eyebrows.

"Yeah, fine." I reached over to scratch Sammy's ears. "I need to take him out back."

He smiled. "I'll join you. I want to check out this courtyard."

"Don't you have a call?" I asked.

"Andy's good at making excuses. He can sit tight for a few minutes."

Not sure why Andy had to make excuses, I led him through the kitchen out the back door. "There's a lot of weeds, but the tables and chairs are in good shape and just need a coat of paint. If I pull the weeds and scrub the cobblestones, Gill could use it for a tea garden again."

Keyon looked around. "It's too bad it doesn't overlook the ocean. That would be a great draw."

"That's what I thought, but it's too much work and money to create a whole new garden out front." I stopped Sammy from digging up the ground near the garbage can in the corner.

"I doubt Gill wants to put much work into the placed at this point. I know a good landscape guy who could put in a tea garden in no time," he said, walking across the yard to the gate and jiggled the latch. "At least the gate's secure. Sammy couldn't get out of here short of tunneling under the fence."

"Don't give him ideas. The more I hang out here, the more potential I can see in this place. The building is solid and it's in a great location."

"I agree. Besides, this place could use some positive energy."

Positive energy? For a brief second, Keyon sounded just like Sage. A shiver ran up my arms.

Sammy followed us back inside, sitting near my feet as I made Keyon's tea. "Sorry, I have no idea where the scones are. It would be nice to see this place a lot busier."

When I handed him the cup, he lifted it to his nose and inhaled. Not a sniff, but a long, slow, sensuous...

Heat rose from my toes straight to the top of my head. What was wrong with me?

"Mmm. I like it already," he said, winking as he pulled out a five-dollar bill. "I'd better go make sure Andy doesn't play with the siren. Maybe after my shift we can take Sammy for a walk on the beach."

"That sounds like fun."

He turned and walked toward the door. "Then it's a date. I'll see you later."

That sounds like fun. Yikes. It dawned on me that I'd just committed myself to a date. What was I thinking? Probably that Keyon was the first man to pay attention to me since I'd left Los Angeles.

My knees seemed to melt like a bar of chocolate. I sagged toward the stool behind the counter, missed, and fell flat on my butt. Not one of my most graceful moments. Thankfully Keyon and Andy were gone, and Gill hadn't shown up yet.

Sammy licked my face. At least he didn't laugh. If dogs could laugh. I gave him a hug and had barely scrambled to my feet when the door opened again. This time, Sammy gave a low growl as Enid blew in clutching a green hat adorned with a long yellow feather to her head.

"What a blustery day today. There's a rainstorm blowing in." She shuddered visibly as she closed the door. "I figured this was the perfect morning for a lovely cup of tea to take off the chill."

Behind her, the man in black, who'd come in the day before, started up the sidewalk. He seemed to change his mind as rain began to fall. Mr. Earl Grey, hot and black. Even the thought of how he'd said those words sent a shiver through my entire body. He pulled up his collar before he turned and left. Odd. Most people would've run inside to stay dry.

"You'd better take your tea to go," I told Enid. "If Gill sees you in here, he'll throw more teacups."

Enid waved a hand. "Pish posh. That man's full of hot air."

Not from what I'd seen.

"It looks like you brought your little friend to keep you company again. Come here, you sweet little puppy." She clicked her tongue.

Sammy backed away whimpering.

Undaunted, Enid sat at the table nearest the counter, then took off her hat. The feather stood straight in the air before curling onto the edge of the table. "I'll have a cup of Earl Grey with lemon, please."

I glanced toward the kitchen door. "I really don't think this is a good idea."

Sammy sat between us and gave another low growl.

"Chop, chop," Enid said, clapping her hands. "The sooner you get my tea, the sooner I'll leave. While I wait, you can fill me in on how the old vulture died."

"Ah. Finally, the motivation." I folded my arms across my chest. "Here's the deal. I'll make you tea, but only if you take it to go before Gill comes."

Enid picked up her hat and stood. "Oh, very well. Be a dear and toss one of those lovely tea biscuits into a bag. I'll take my breakfast on the veranda. It's a bit breezy, but I'll be out of the rain."

I punched her order into the cash register knowing Gill would be livid when he saw her. "I think I saw some biscuits in the fridge. The fresh ones haven't arrived yet that I know of. You need to pay for everything first."

"Then heat it a little, please. Don't you trust me?" She stuck on her hat then rummaged through her pockets.

"Nope." I met her gaze, then asked, "How long have you known Gill and Tilly?"

Enid grimaced. "This is a small town. It's common for everyone to know everyone else. Some people just can't seem to keep their noses in their own business."

"Do you mean Tilly?"

She handed me a wadded up five-dollar bill, which seemed odd for someone who acted so prim and proper. I would've guessed she ironed her money. "It's not polite to single out any one person, but there are a few troublemakers here in Glitter Bay."

I had no doubt Enid Walsh was the biggest troublemaker around. As I straightened her bill and gave her change, I said, "You must've known Tilly well. It was kind of you to extend your condolences."

"Gill didn't seem so happy."

I poured hot water over an Earl Grey tea bag in a paper cup before I passed it to her. "His wife just died. He has a lot on his mind."

Enid raised her eyebrows. "Like what?"

"Calling family, making arrangements, those sorts of things."

"That's true," she said. "Well, I won't keep you. I'm sure you have a great deal of work to do. Heaven knows that old vulture never lifted a finger around here."

I placed her biscuit in a paper bag hoping she'd take her cue to leave. Just when I thought she'd finally leave me in peace, chair legs scraped the floor. Enid sat and then pushed the chair across from her out from the table with her foot.

"Since it's quiet and Gill isn't here yet, why don't you tell me about yourself?"

No way was I about to divulge my story to someone anyone threw teacups at. "You need to leave."

"Sit." She placed the hat with the long yellow feather on the table before sipping her tea. "I understand if you're wary after the way your boss reacted to me, but since he's not here, we might as well get acquainted."

Not sure where to start, I sat across from her not sure what to say. Lucky for me, I didn't have to say a word.

Enid nibbled on her chilled scone before saying, "I'll warn you, before Gill spills the beans, that I'm a reporter. I've written for the local newspaper practically since they opened their first office. It's not a pleasant thing to work for a someone more interested in politics than local events, but I make do."

"You told me that the other day." I looked around for Sammy hoping he'd gotten into trouble to give me an excuse to escape. I didn't want to say anything I'd regret. Just my luck, he was snoring under the table.

"You can't imagine how difficult it is to train someone who's younger than most of my hats and less absorbent than a tea bag."

"Do you enjoy your job?" I asked, making a mental note not to say anything I didn't want most of the Pacific Northwest to find out. While I couldn't stop her, I could distract her for a while.

She waved a hand. "It's not easy being in the limelight all the time, you know. The Who's Who are constantly asking me to appear at dinner parties and soirees simply to get their names in my column. Sadly, they don't want me to bring up the scandals."

"How dare they?" I chuckled. It sounded like they all knew how to keep their friends close and Enid closer. "It sounds like an exciting life."

"I used to think so. Then Tilly died," she said, leaning closer.

"What does that have to do with anything?"

Enid's smile twisted from warm to sly. "When I heard she collapsed, my reporter's senses tingled. I wondered if I was missing out on something big."

"Like what?" I asked.

"The crime beat, Laken. Cold cases and the like." She grasped my hand. "I've always been interested in the infidelities of life and never bothered with such morbid things as theft and murder. Have you ever wondered what could push a person to the brink of madness that they would kill another human being?"

Not besides my ex. I swallowed hard before asking, "Do you think Tilly was murdered?"

When she flinched, tea sloshed on the table. "Where have you been? Darling, that's been the rumor since her overweight corpse hit the floor."

"Enlighten me. Pretend I haven't heard any of those rumors." I no longer had to feign interest. The only rumors I'd heard were the ones Keyon started, and I wanted to be ready if he came up with a new theory.

"That depends," Enid said, dabbing the tablecloth with her napkin. "Were you friends with her?"

"With Tilly?"

Beneath the table, Sammy groaned.

Enid leaned forward, ready to spring from her chair. "Was that Gill?"

"Sammy. He's a noisy sleeper. He also eats shoes, so be careful." I glanced at the front door, then told her, "I only knew Tilly by name and scowl."

"One story was that Gill has mob connections and paid for a hit on his wife."

I guessed she'd started that one. "That doesn't seem likely."

"No, it doesn't." She shook her head. "He'd probably rather strangle her in person."

"Or maybe Tilly had a boyfriend and Gill got jealous."

Enid brayed like an Andalusian donkey. "You think Tilly had a boyfriend? You saw her, right? Who'd want to date her?"

"Besides Gill?" I asked.

"Good point," she said, her face reddening. "What would that man see in someone so grumpy? I'll tell you, Laken, that's one relationship I've never been able to figure out."

Was she jealous or genuinely perplexed? "I doubt Tilly was always so miserable."

She met my gaze. "Oh, yes, she was. Take my word for it."

"What are you doing here?" Gill bellowed from the front doorway with his hands on his hips.

Sammy let out a sharp bark as both Enid and I jumped.

"Hello, Gill." Enid's knuckles turned white as she clutched her napkin, yet she flashed a syrupy smile. "I simply came to pay my respects and your lovely assistant was kind enough to keep me company."

"Pay your respects, my backside." He stomped across the room, pointing his index finger at her. "You know full well that you are banned from the tea house. Laken never should have let you inside."

I rose from my chair. "I'm sorry, Gill, I—"

"Sit. You're not going anywhere. Enid will never set foot in here again, will you?"

Enid Walsh flared her nostrils as she picked up her hat and took time to arrange it on her head. Suddenly, she appeared more somber and less frivolous than moments before. Something was missing. "I've adored our time together, Laken, but I must be off. Be a dear and look me up sometime. We'll have to meet for coffee."

"She has better things to do than associate with the likes of you," Gill barked as he stormed into the kitchen with Sammy at his heels.

"Oh yeah? We'll see about that." She spun on her heel, then walked out the door.

As I picked up her abandoned tea and scone, something bothered me. Gill had banned her from setting foot inside the tea house, yet she knew exactly what Tilly did all day. If she had stalked Tilly, for whatever reason, the odds were good she'd either murdered her or knew who had.

I set the teacup and plate in the dish bin then brought it into the kitchen. "I'm sorry, Gill. I shouldn't have let her come inside."

"It's not your fault, Laken," he said, leaning against the counter. "That woman could sweet talk Sasquatch into tap dancing on thin ice."

"I guess I was just curious."

He raised one eyebrow. "From now on though—"

"I swear. I won't let her into the tea house again." I hoped that promise would be as easy to keep as it was to make. Enid seemed like a persistent, if not pushy, woman.

As Sammy wandered over to the back door to go out into the courtyard, it dawned on me what was different about Enid when she left. Sammy shook the yellow feather from her hat like a first-place trophy. If his escapade became a story in Enid's column, I'd clip and save it. Just because.

Enid was right about one thing. A light rain had blown in off the ocean.

"I need your help." Gill sat a stack of paint chips on the counter. "Gabriella had a bright idea we should paint the tea house."

My mouth dropped open. Last I heard he and his daughter didn't see eye to eye. Did Gabriella finally corner him long enough to give him a piece of her shallow mind?

"Is this the royal we where she has the idea and I do the work?" I asked. When Gill raised his eyebrows, I paused. "Sorry. Enid has that effect on me. Why does Gabriella think you should paint the tea house?"

"Some silly notion about selling the place. Making it more attractive to buyers to get better offers. I'd prefer customers over some buyer who wants to turn the place into a resort or a parking lot."

My thoughts went into overdrive. The tea house would make a great new location for Vintage Sage. While my sister couldn't afford the building, I definitely could.

I sat on the worn wooden floor to spread color swatches around me, like a peacock tail. Peach butter. Appletini. Raspberry Mousse. The colors were bold and sounded yummy. Gabriella must've made these choices rather than eating lunch. I regretted I'd never pursued a side gig in interior decorating while my ex traveled the world to make movies.

"What colors do you like?" I asked, hearing scratching at the door.

No answer. Gill had gone to let Sammy in out of the misty rain. Within seconds, twenty pounds of damp English Sheepdog puppy flew across the room and skidded across the scattered chips. As I struggled to grab him, my back hit one of the table legs full on.

"I see you two are making progress." Gill chuckled from the kitchen doorway.

I rubbed my back. "If you call scattering paint chips all over progress, then yes."

He set a few bakery boxes on the counter and asked, "Did you at least find anything?"

"Just my appetite." I struggled to sit up as Sammy spit out chips. Wet and crinkled, two chips landed on my leg.

"Gee, thanks." I picked the paint chips off my leg, then took a second look. "Whistling Wind and Thoughtful Spot. Now that's interesting."

"Why's that?" Gill helped me to my feet.

"They actually look good together," I told him, holding them up for him to see.

"Whistling Wind" reminded me of the storm clouds that gathered over the ocean right before they unloaded a downpour. "Thoughtful Spot" was a peaceful, pale turquoise, like the summer sky in the morning. Both were suitable for a spacious vintage boutique, and Sage would love them.

Gill studied both paint chips then asked, "What are people going to say when they find out a dog picked the colors for the walls?"

"Do you have a better suggestion?"

"A dog, Laken." He glared long and hard. "People will say I'm crazy."

I shook my head. "They'll say that you have a nice, peaceful place here. Why would you bother to tell them who picked the colors in the first place?

When Sammy snuffled Gill's pant leg and whimpered, Gill reached down to pet him. "Good point. It could be our little secret."

"I'm not about to tell anyone Sammy did a better job of picking colors than me."

Gill raised his thick eyebrows and chuckled. "When you put it that way, I've never liked secrets."

"Ha. Ha." Speaking of secrets, this was the perfect opportunity to ask about Tilly's jewelry. "I found something in that trunk that I wanted to ask you about."

"I'll stop by the hardware store to get paint," he said, as if he hadn't heard me. "How many cans do you think we need?"

"Gill, I really need to talk to you about—"

When the front door opened, all of our creative endeavors crashed to a halt as police walked into the Sweet Eden Teahouse.

Chapter Nine

The police had questions for Gill. I had no idea what they wanted to discuss with Gill, but I itched to find a spot to eavesdrop on them. Even though part of me wanted to put my feet up and take a serious nap.

"Is there anything I can do?" I asked, dawdling near a table.

"You go on ahead, Laken," Gill said. "I'll see you tomorrow."

I sighed, then paused near the front door to make sure I had my keys. As Gill led the officers up to his apartment, I caught the words "diamonds" and "theft." My blood seemed to freeze in my veins, I had no choice but tiptoe toward the apartment door.

"Good-bye, Laken. Lock up when you leave." Gill pulled the door at the bottom of the stairs closed between us.

I huffed really wanting to hear more. Maybe Enid and her sudden interest in cold cases would be of use after all.

Clipping Sammy's leash to his collar, I realized I had over an hour before Sage expected me at the shop. Enough time to "bump" into Enid and ask for her help. I turned the sign to 'closed', then locked the front door.

Outside the tea house, Sammy began to jump and bark. I struggled to keep my grip on the leash. "Come on. You've been so good all morning."

"That's my fault," Keyon said behind me.

Sammy shot off the porch like an arrow from Cupid's bow. He even dropped the feather from Enid's hat he'd been carrying around like a trophy since she left.

A gush of warmth spread through my body. I spun around in time to see him tackle Keyon's leg. "Sammy, no!"

"You just want to play, don't you, boy?" Keyon knelt down and rolled Sammy around on the grass. "I'll bet Laken hasn't spent time with you all morning."

I was growing concerned about the hot flashes that hit me when he was around. Good thing I had an appointment with my doctor later this month.

"Did he find the feather in the courtyard?" Keyon asked.

"Nope. That's from Enid's hat."

"That's sounds like a story I need to hear." Keyon scrubbed the top of Sammy's head. He didn't seem concerned about the police presence, which was just as well. I had no idea what was going on anyway. "Since you've both been cooped up this morning, I figured we could go for a walk on the beach."

Sammy bounced around Keyon's legs and yipped. A run on the beach might burn off some of his frantic energy, so I could get some sleep.

I stifled another yawn. "A walk on the beach sounds like a great idea."

"You look like you've had a long morning." Keyon scooped Sammy into his arms and met me at the base of the front steps. "Why don't we go for a walk, then find somewhere to get takeout? Then we don't have to leave the crazy mutt tied up somewhere."

"He's not a mutt. He's a purebred English…Wait." I paused as panic set in about the idea of lunch alone with Keyon. "This isn't a date, is it?"

"Oh, hell no." He stiffened. "Not unless you want it to be."

"Me? Nope. Just two people walking a dog."

He set Sammy down on the grass. "To be honest, I'm not looking for a girlfriend or anything. I've been burned enough."

"You and me both." I wiped my hands on my slacks. That took the pressure off.

Keyon raised his eyebrows, then whistled to Sammy, who ran around us at top speed. No matter what command Keyon gave, Sammy seemed to cooperate. Most of the time. At least he didn't eat anything he shouldn't.

Once we reached the beach, Keyon showed Sammy how to sit while he took off his shoes and wiggled his toes in the sand. Sammy sat vibrating until he couldn't keep still any longer and leaped to his paws.

I pried off my shoes, miffed that Keyon had nicer feet than I did. His toes were straight and sexy, while a couple of mine were gnarled. A couple years ago I caught Emery taking pictures of topless girls in Costa Rica. I'd kicked a rock wall and broken two toes. In hindsight, I should have kicked my ex and spared my toes.

"How do you get Sammy to listen?" I asked.

"Doggy treats," he said, reaching into his pocket. "And before you say anything, they're organic and delicious."

I clutched my shoes in one hand. "Did you taste one?"

"It says so on the label. Sit," Keyon commanded as Sammy stood against his pant leg. He pushed Sammy's backside down. Once Sammy sat, Keyon gave him a treat. "They're made from real chicken and vegetables, so they have to be delicious, right?"

The dog treats smelled good, and I was hungry. I wasn't sure if I was more jealous of Keyon or Sammy. "Do you want a sheepdog? He eats socks and underwear. Other than that, he's smarter than he looks."

"What do you mean?"

I described how Sammy, obviously encouraged by Muumuu, pushed the chair to the sink to get the steaks. "Sage was livid."

"You have to admit, he is pretty smart. Not many dogs would think of that." Keyon picked up a sand-covered stick. "Hey, you want to play fetch?"

"Please tell me you don't expect *me* to chase that dirty thing." I chuckled.

He unclipped Sammy's leash, then passed it to me. "I was talking to your dog."

"Well, that's a relief." I buried my toes in the sand while I studied Keyon out of the corner of my eye. Well-muscled and handsome, he might be worth chasing a stick for.

Keyon let Sammy sniff the stick before he tossed it ten feet away. The puppy chased the stick and stopped so fast he tumbled head over heels in the sand.

I couldn't keep from laughing.

"You have a great laugh," Keyon said with a grin. "Bring it back, Sammy."

My puppy shook the sand out of his fur, then trotted back with his tongue hanging out. The stick lay on the beach surrounded by everything he'd shaken off.

After five more attempts at getting him to fetch, Keyon threw his hands in the air. "I give up."

Sammy rolled around on the beach as if he agreed.

"How was Gill doing today?" Keyon asked.

"I didn't see him much before the police showed up." As I reached to put Sammy's leash back on, it occurred to me Keyon hadn't even asked why the police were there. I was about to comment when Sammy let out a bark, then took off down the beach. "Oh, come on. That's not funny."

"Don't worry. He won't go far."

I snorted. "You don't know this dog. He does things just to annoy me."

"He's a puppy. He wants to play."

On cue, Sammy returned with the stick Keyon threw earlier clamped between his jaws.

"See what I mean?" He grinned.

"I take it that's doggy sarcasm."

"At its best." Keyon wrestled the stick away, then gave Sammy a treat. "Good boy. You want to fetch again?"

The stick landed farther down the beach, but Sammy veered straight into the ocean. My breath stuck in my throat for a few long seconds before he leaped out of the water and nipped at the crest of a wave.

"Did the police say what they were looking for?" Keyon finally asked.

"No. Did you suggest they search the tea house?"

"They said it was a closed case," he said. "That Tilly died from a heart attack, so I should stop going to them with crazy ideas."

I knew how they felt.

"So, are you going to tell me who broke your heart?" His abrupt change of conversation caught me off guard. "Sage wouldn't say."

Sisterly love. Sage had told quite a few people about me. Except Keyon. Good she had my back when it counted. "That's funny. I swear she's told half of Glitter Bay my life story."

"Who was he?" Keyon asked.

I kept my gaze on Sammy, to avoid looking at Keyon's strong jaw and greyish eyes. "Just some guy who loved other women too much for my liking."

"He cheated on you. I find that hard to believe."

My heart fluttered. "What about you? Who broke your heart?"

"No one important."

I raised my eyebrows. "Don't tell me it was Sage."

"Heck no," he said. "Sage and I were doomed from the start when my best friend walked in on our first date. She fell for him hard. He can cope with all that hippie stuff Sage is into far better than I ever could. So, I stepped back and let nature take over."

"That was big of you." I smiled, pretending to believe his version.

"Yeah, totally out of character, according to some people."

"Is it?" I asked. "It sounds like you know what you want and won't settle."

His face reddened. "Don't let one act of chivalry fool you."

Up the beach, Sammy wrestled with a starfish.

I groaned. "He's getting filthy. Sage is going to strangle us both. I'll have to give him another bath when we get home."

"Interesting. You call Sage's house home and work at the tea house." He blurted. "Are you planning to stay around Glitter Bay longer than Sage thought?"

"She *did* talk to you about me." I tightened my grip on my running shoes. "What exactly did she tell you?"

Keyon squirmed, then whistled for Sammy. "That you were going through a rough patch and recently left a bad relationship."

That figured. "Is that why you're being so nice to me?"

"No, I—"

Sammy ran over and began to shake water and grit on both of us. I shrieked and covered my face with my arm as I hid behind Keyon.

"Oh, is that the way things are?" He glanced over his shoulder. His eyes crinkled in the corners. "You don't want a boyfriend. You want a shield from all the dirt."

My face burned as I clipped Sammy's leash to his collar. "What do you mean?"

"It was a joke." His expression softened. "What did you think I meant?"

"I need to go home."

Sammy was wet and dirty and licked my face like I was a steak-flavored snow cone.

"I have to take Sammy to the house, then go to the shop. I'll see you around."

Keyon frowned. "Okay. Sure. What time are you done work? I'll meet you later."

"Six." I wasn't so sure meeting him after work was a good idea, even if he was cute.

Sammy led the way home while I plodded behind him barefoot across the pavement. I gave him a quick bath, fed him, then grabbed a sandwich before locking him in his crate and heading for the shop.

Ever since Gill mentioned selling the tea house, my mind whirled with possibilities. We could still serve tea to our customers and make use of the kitchen as a little staff area. Our changing rooms could be much larger than the three-foot square closets the shop currently had, plus we could take advantage of the natural lighting to create displays that would draw in more customers, like they did on Rodeo Drive. While I wasn't much good at business, I knew how to shop.

By the time I got to Vintage Sage, I was so excited I blurted out my complete list of ideas to my sister in one long breath and nearly hyperventilated.

Sage took a step back. "Slow down and start at the beginning."

By the time I was done, her eyes were wide.

"Laken, I can't afford to buy that or any other building," she said. "I barely have enough cash flow to make this place work. The tea house is way out of my league."

"Not if I buy it. I could live upstairs and help you with the shop." I waved a hand around the dim little store. "It's bigger, brighter, and a way better location. We could display more of the great items you have tucked in back and get real jewelry showcases. I still have connections in L.A., you know."

"It sounds too good to be true."

"This is me, Sage. I have the money and the time. Besides, I want to do this for you. For us. If you agree, I'll talk to Gill and make him an offer. Are you in?"

My sister gazed around the dingy shop, then sighed. "What do you need me to do?"

What did I need her to do? I caught my breath. "Come with me to see Gill. If he sees we have a plan and are excited about this, there's no way he'll turn us down."

"It would be nice to have more space to display things like that crazy wedding gown that seems to eat everything around it."

"Speaking of which, where did you stuff it?"

Sage laughed. "It's still in one of the changing rooms. If I bring it out, it fills half the store. You want to try it on? I'll pay you to be my mannequin."

"I could, but I think even that would be more effective if you had more space and some fabulous windows overlooking the ocean." Time to be shrewd. Hopefully, the police were done at the tea house. "Have you had lunch yet? Gill serves soup and sandwiches."

She grimaced. "You never play fair. I've been to the tea house before, Laken, even for lunch. Why do I need to check it out right now?"

"Come on," I resorted to pleading. "I'll keep an eye on things here. You go for lunch and look at the tea house like you're moving into it tomorrow. Just a beautiful building you'd be thrilled to expand your business in."

"My failing business, you mean."

I rolled my eyes. "Sage, your store is located on a rundown street sandwiched between an abandoned building and a junk shop. It doesn't exactly say, 'Look at me.' You need a location people will want to check out, not pass by from a street away."

"Okay." She sighed. "In the meantime, can you find somewhere to put that trunk before I break a toe on it? I'll ask Gill what I should do with it while I'm there."

"Sure. Sounds like fun." Fun? What was I thinking?

Once she left, I scouted the shop to find a good spot for a trunk that could house a small body. I found one. In the back corner beneath a mannequin dressed in a genuine nineteen-twenties flapper dress. It was the best I could do.

Even empty, that bloody trunk was heavy. I settled for dragging it across the store with my knees bent and my butt sticking out. I managed to get the trunk to the front of the counter when it caught on a floorboard. I tumbled backward and fell flat on my butt. Not one of my most graceful moments.

As I was about to get to my feet, something beneath the counter caught my eye. I picked up the slender piece of plastic and frowned. I'd been in enough hospitals and doctor's offices to recognize the cap from a needle when I saw one. I tucked the plastic syringe cap into my pocket.

Unhooking the trunk from the rogue floorboard, I hauled it to the far end of the shop. As I started to set a pair of antique lamps on top of it, I paused. A little voice in the back of my head told me to see what my sister had left inside. The lid opened with a creak. Empty, except for a small piece of paper stuck in the bottom. When I pulled on it harder, the entire bottom panel of the trunk popped out.

My jaw dropped. "What the...?"

Did Gill have any idea the trunk had a false bottom?

I set the thick cardboard aside and found an assortment of yellow newspaper clippings beneath. I sifted through them one by one and realized they all related to a jewelry heist in July nineteen seventy-nine. The photo of the stolen necklace, a large dark stone surrounded by diamonds, triggered a memory. I'd seen that necklace, or at least one similar, before, but I couldn't remember where.

Sitting back on my heels, I recalled Enid mentioning a cold case she was fascinated with. A fabulous sapphire and diamond necklace that was stolen years earlier. Sammy had distracted me after she'd confided she thought there could be a local connection, then we'd parted ways. Did Gill have something to do with that heist?

Tucked beneath the pages was a small, black velvet pouch. I opened the pouch as my heart raced. Empty. Not a surprise. I would've dismantled the necklace and sold the stones individually to create a new life somewhere no one could find me.

Somewhere like Glitter Bay.

Chapter Ten

I spent the rest of the afternoon searching for information on Sage's computer, while there were no customers. I didn't come across anything different than what was in those newspaper clippings and still couldn't figure out where I'd seen that necklace before. All I knew for sure was the crime was never solved.

What if Gill had bought the tea house using money from the stolen diamonds?

Maybe he and Tilly fought, and she threatened to turn him into the police, which was certainly a motive for murder. Except for the fact, according to Gabriella, it was Tilly who owned the tea house.

Had the syringe cap I found been there for a long time, or had Andy dropped it while helping Tilly? I pulled it out of my pocket and rolled it around in my fingers not wanting to think about Gill injecting his wife with who knew what.

Frustrated, I took the pieces of jewelry out of the trunk to examine them one by one. The lone bracelet bore a thumbnail-sized sapphire cut in the shape of a glittering heart. The diamonds that adorned the rest of the piece looked more like Swarovski crystals. The combination was breathtaking. Yet, as someone who'd seen and worn million-dollar jewels, the piece seemed more like a prop on a movie set.

My shoulders stiffened and I whispered, "A movie set."

That was when I took a closer look at the bracelet. Aside from the fact the original sapphire weighed about seven carats, it was identical to the replica for the Heart of the Ocean, the fictional necklace used in the movie *Titanic*.

"No way." I clutched the bracelet in one hand as I reached for the keyboard to search for Heart of the Ocean, which was based on the Hope Diamond. "Three versions were created. The original resides in James Cameron's office. That's where I saw it before. The second is in the possession of the J. Peterman Company."

I wrote the name down to search later and continued.

My heart raced as I scrolled down to the third version. The Asprey and Garrard Necklace. Asprey and Garrard were commissioned to create an authentic Heart of the Ocean necklace and set a one hundred and seventy-one carat, heart-shaped Ceylon sapphire in platinum, then surround it with one hundred and three diamonds. The "heart" was in fact a large inverted pear-shaped sapphire with a slight cleft. It sold at auction for twenty million dollars.

"Wow." I rubbed my eyes to make sure I'd read that right. "Where is it now?"

Scrolling down farther, I saw it was "Unavailable for public viewing," according to the website. Did that mean the owner wanted to stare at it alone all day or did someone steal it from what had to be a top-notch security system? Not likely since the robbery occurred long before the movie script was even a notion. Not to mention if someone had lost a trinket like that the news would be splashed all over the Internet.

I took a deep breath and started my search over. This time, I used key words from the yellow newspaper articles. Necklace. Jewelry heist. Hope Diamond.

If the Heart of the Ocean was a fictional recreation of the Hope Diamond, chances were it wasn't the only necklace of value made in the cursed stone's image. Only one, an equally impressive version of the Heart of the Ocean with an actual heart-cut sapphire, leaped off the images page. It looked exactly like the one in the newspaper clippings.

How could Gill or Tilly have obtained a gem of that caliber and manage to keep it a secret from everyone in Glitter Bay? Granted, this town wasn't nearly as status frenzied as L.A., but someone would've noticed. Enid came to mind.

When I spied Keyon outside the shop, I placed the clippings in a large envelope and stuffed it in one of the drawers. I still wasn't sure I trusted him.

"Hey, Laken," he said, walking into Vintage Sage. "Quiet here today?"

I shut down the computer. "Hardly. I haven't had much peace until now. Sage will be glad I finally sold that fake mink stole she thought was so hideous."

"I'll bet you're hungry then."

"Famished," I told him, leading him outside before locking the door.

"Do you like Italian? I know a place that makes great seafood fettuccini. It's conveniently close to a store that sells kiddie pools."

I raised my eyebrows. "How do you know who sells kiddie pools?"

"A friend of mine is a single mom with two small kids. I bought one for them last summer. Where to first?"

"Since you know where everything is, why don't you lead the way?"

Keyon's charming smile returned. "Sounds good."

"Why did you try to convince the police someone murdered Tilly?" I asked. "She had a heart condition, you know."

"It's just a hunch. I don't have any proof."

"Maybe I can help." I pulled out the small plastic cap. "I found this under the counter."

Keyon frowned. "A cap from a syringe? Andy gave Tilly a shot when we got there. It's not like him to leave anything behind, but I suppose it's possible."

His answer unsettled more than reassured me, especially when he stuck the cap in the front pocket of his khakis. "I'll ask him later. Why don't you check out the kiddie pools? I'll order dinner and grab some wine. Red or white?"

"Get whatever you like. I don't drink."

Keyon's cheek twitched. "Sparkling water?"

"Perfect." I flashed a smile before heading to the shop next door.

"Can I help you?" A lanky man in a blue dress shirt towered over me the instant I paused near a stack of colorful plastic pools. He had to be at least six-foot-eight.

I tried not to let his height intimidate me. "I'm looking for a pool for my puppy."

"What breed?"

"English Sheepdog."

"Lady, you'll want a way bigger pool than the ones you're looking at," he said.

I stared. "He's only a couple months old."

The salesman burst out laughing. "Right now. By the time that dog's fully grown, you'll be able to saddle him up and ride him around town."

"You do know there are other places in town I can buy a pool."

"I'll gladly sell you one," he told me. "Just make sure he doesn't eat it. At that age, he's still teething and will chew on anything."

Teething explained the loss of the wide assortment of socks and sweatshirts to my furry new roommate. "How do I stop him from eating everything I own?"

The sales associate sold me the pool, treats, a doggy toy and a book on how to train my dog. Only after he'd bagged my purchases, did I remember I had to get everything home. Kind of like shopping with Emery on Rodeo Drive.

"I hope you got a deal on all this stuff." Keyon appeared at the checkout, carrying a plastic bag and a bulging paper bag that smelled heavenly.

"Apparently I need all this stuff for a dog I have no intention of keeping." I sighed. "If I ever do find his real owners, they're in for a big surprise."

He looked mildly amused. "If you need anything else, I could go rent a truck."

"Very funny."

Once we got to Sage's house, I handed Sammy a rawhide bone to chew on while I filled the pool with water. He watched from a distance then crept closer and hung his head over the side to drink the water.

Keyon laughed from the back porch, where he'd set the table with our dinner and two wineglasses. "Just toss him in. He'll figure it out."

"That sounds so mean." I lifted Sammy into the pool. The water came to his belly.

"Why? He runs into the ocean without a second thought."

Sammy stuck his nose in the water, then sneezed before he splashed around.

"See, he's fine," Keyon said. "Come eat before the pasta gets cold."

"You seem awfully at home here." I sat across the table.

"Jonathan and I have been friends for years. I come over when he's in town."

The way Sage talked about Keyon I was surprised he'd ever set foot in her house. Jonathan or no Jonathan.

I savored a few bites of pasta before asking, "What makes you sure Tilly was murdered?"

"Besides a strong hunch?" He met my gaze over his glass. "Gill's behavior when Andy and I arrived. Why do you think he asked you to put his groceries away? So he had time to inject her with something that stopped her heart."

"No way" I fumbled my fork. "He was nowhere near Vintage Sage when she died. How would he know whether she collapsed or not?"

Keyon twirled a forkful of pasta. "Maybe he tampered with her medications. Something else you said bothered me."

"What's that?"

"Did she clutch her chest or her arm when she fell?"

"No. She just collapsed. I've heard women feel heart attacks differently than men do, though, so it still could've been a heart attack." I sat back and frowned. "Who'd want Tilly dead? I know she wasn't the most pleasant person, but she must've had *some* redeeming qualities."

"There's a story going around that she chased someone out of the tea house with a butcher knife, then she tripped and broke her ankle."

I speared a cream-covered shrimp. "Why would she do that?"

"Dunno. That was way before my time," Keyon said. "I heard my dad tell the story when I was a kid."

"Who did she chase?"

"No idea. It's probably just one of those local legends."

More gossip. I bit my lip and glanced to where Sammy leaned over the edge of the pool. "But if there's a grain of truth, it could be motive for murder, right? Who would know the truth?"

"Besides Gill?" He shrugged. "Talk to Enid Walsh. I'll bet she has dirt on everyone in Glitter Bay."

"Then why don't you ask her?"

He grimaced. "Do you know what it's like having someone over twice your age flirt with you, especially when they're crazy to begin with? It's creepy."

"I thought you'd be used to women flirting with you." I laughed. "I'm sure you've rescued a lot of little old ladies eager to express their gratitude."

Keyon cleared his throat. "One or two. I don't want to talk about them, though."

I met his gaze over my drink. "Then tell me about the girl who broke your heart."

"Or that." He reddened.

What–or who–was he trying to hide?

Long after Keyon left that night, Sage applied hot pink nail polish to her toenails, then sat back to take a sip of peppermint tea from the mug I'd painted during my last visit here a couple years ago. The same summer my ex shot a movie in Spain and frolicked with some starlet barely past puberty.

"How was your date?" Sage asked.

My face warmed as I clutched the pink mug studded with a rhinestone heart she'd painted for me. "It wasn't a date. Keyon had more questions about Tilly."

"What was it then?"

"More of an interrogation." I sighed and placed a hand on Sammy as he slept peacefully in the oversized chair beside me. For once he wasn't chewing on clothing or furniture. I was determined to savor the moment.

"Duly noted." Sage smirked.

Muumuu stretched beside her.

"Did he tell you why he thinks Tilly was murdered?"

"No, but I'm starting to think he's right." I watched the flames dance in the fireplace. "But I found a syringe cap under the shop counter. Keyon mentioned Andy gave Tilly a shot while they worked on her and maybe he dropped it, which is possible, but..."

Sage leaned forward. "But what?"

"But he thinks Gill sent me out of the room to put away the groceries so he could inject her with something to stop her heart. The thought sent a flurry of shivers over me. I longed for the warmth of the fluffy pink blanket on my bed.

"Are you okay?" my sister asked.

I'd seen enough mystery movies of the week to know where to start. "Do you know who had a grudge against Tilly?"

Sage stared. "This is a small town, Laken. A lot of people didn't like her much, but I doubt anyone wanted her dead. Don't get caught up in Keyon's delusions. He's cute and has great abs, but he's not second date material."

"You think Keyon has delusions?" My stomach churned.

"And great abs. You missed that part." She laughed, which made me smile. "All I know is he tends to get caught up in some crazy ideas sometimes."

I clutched the tourmaline pendant around my neck. "Murder is crazy?"

"Being sick, then kicking your ex to the curb left you vulnerable. I know you're a grown woman, Laken, but..."

"But you're worried about me." My hands shook as I tried to push the negative thoughts out of my head. I placed one hand on Sammy's back as he moaned in his sleep.

"Of course, I am. You're my sister."

Not the answer I wanted to hear, but confirmation my internal radar was still skewed when it came to men. I needed to focus on taking care of Sammy and me. The worst part was, I knew even less about dogs than men.

"Did you get a chance to talk to Gill yet?" I asked.

"Yes and no."

I raised my eyebrows. "What does that mean?"

"It means I went to the tea house like you asked, but I'm not comfortable about talking to Gill about buying the place so soon." She sipped her tea. "Not that I don't like the idea of moving Vintage Sage there. I just think it's too soon to bring it up."

"Speaking of Tilly, I found something interesting in her old trunk today."

Sage frowned. "How? It was empty."

I stifled a yawn. "I dragged it to the far end of the shop to stash it under those lamps in the corner for some ambiance. Anyway, I opened it to make sure we hadn't forgotten anything and found a paper stuck in the bottom. When I pulled on it, a false bottom popped out."

"You found a hidden compartment?" she asked, her eyes wide.

"Yeah. It was full of old newspaper clippings. Something to do with a jewelry robbery fifty years ago." I rubbed my eyes. "I'm not sure why someone saved them, but they are interesting. I would've brought them home, but that's when Keyon came in. I tucked them in a drawer for now."

"Okay." My sister was looking at her phone and didn't seem all that interested.

"I'm sure they're nothing important." I shrugged, then asked, "What do you know about Enid Walsh?"

That got her attention. "Did you finally meet that old busybody? Honestly, she can't keep her nose out of anybody's business."

"I'm sure I'll be seeing a lot more of her at the tea house with Tilly gone." I paused and let out such a loud yawn that Sammy flinched. "What should I do?"

"About Enid or Keyon?" she asked.

"Enid. For now."

"Lock the front door," she said. "Enid's a local legend. If there's gossip, either true or made up, she's the first in line to pass it along and ruin people. Be careful what you say around her. For your own sake."

My stomach slithered into knots. Enid could fill her weekly column for the next five years if she discovered who I really was. I needed to watch what I said, so she didn't have a reason to search for me on the Internet.

If she hadn't already.

Chapter Eleven

I had another long, restless night to think over Sage's concerns while wrestling my belongings from Sammy's jaws. If I learned nothing else, it was not to leave my clothes lying on the floor.

Early the next morning I trudged behind Sammy for a walk along the beach before we headed to the tea house. I stuck fresh cut flowers from the peony bushes into bud vases on each table and hoped Gill had a miracle tea to perk me up. Between Sammy's nighttime antics and Keyon's murder theories, I wasn't getting much sleep lately.

I filled a kettle and plugged it in to boil, then searched the fridge for a bar of butter to slice into quarter-inch pats while I tied a faded apron around my waist. The entire time I mumbled about the day ahead.

Gill emerged from the door that led up to his apartment. "Is that you, Laken?"

"Good morning." I slammed the fridge.

"Doesn't sound like it's such a good morning." He placed a tea bag in each of two cups, unplugged the kettle, and poured some over each bag. "Everything okay?"

I slumped onto a stool at the counter and breathed in the scent of Darjeeling. "Sammy's eaten half my wardrobe, I've hardly slept in days and Keyon still thinks someone murdered Tilly. Now he's trying to convince me."

The second Gill paled, I wanted to take back my words.

He sat across from me with his cup and told me, "I said that out of grief. My wife died of heart failure. At least, that's what the doctor said. Since he's the medical professional, I believe him."

I closed my eyes and caught a whiff of lemon from his Earl Grey. This was one flowery tea tin of worms I should've left alone. "I know you've heard the rumors."

"I have, and I'd ask you not to repeat things you know nothing about, young lady."

"I'm sorry. You're right. I should keep my nose out of things." Tears swarmed my eyes, and I fought the impulse to run out the front door. "Some people say you have an eye for the ladies."

"You talked to Enid," Gill said with a grimace.

"Gabriella mentioned it yesterday."

"A man can look. That's not a crime."

I fought to keep focused but my thoughts strayed to my ex. "You're right. Looking isn't a crime. If you don't act on the attraction."

He tilted his head before he asked, "Do you think I cheated on my wife?"

"What?" I'd meant Emery, not Gill. "No."

Rather than blow his top, he released a slow breath. "I get it. I know about your ex, Laken. Sage told me when you first came to town."

My sister hadn't kept her big mouth shut after all. I clenched my jaw.

"Not all of us are like that." He placed his warm hand on mine. "I stayed faithful to Tilly for a lot of years. and she was faithful to me. End of discussion."

Something about his wording bothered me. He'd stayed faithful to Tilly for "a lot of years." Had he been unfaithful in the past? Hanging out with Keyon was making me paranoid. "I'll go open the doors."

He gave my hand a squeeze. "I really am glad you're here. I couldn't keep this place going alone."

"Since I hang out here all the time, I might as well earn my keep." I pulled my hand from beneath his, then went to open the front doors. As I let in the morning air, I took a deep breath. "Looks like another beautiful day."

Gill brought out a damp cloth. "Could you wipe the tables and chairs? They don't take long to collect dust out there."

While I cleaned, I ruminated about what I'd said to Gill. He needed a friend not another doubter. I returned inside to finish my cold tea and decided to let him know what else was on my mind.

As Gill came out of the kitchen, we spoke at the same time. "I've been thinking.".

I chuckled, setting my empty cup in the bin to wash later. "About what?"

Gill avoided meeting my gaze. "Would you consider buying the tea house?"

Good thing I didn't have anything breakable in my hands. "Would I what?"

"Hey, Gill," a young man opened the front door. The morning delivery from Sweets and Treats arrived before we could continue the conversation. Gill helped the delivery man carry several boxes into the kitchen to check over our order of fresh scones and tarts for the day.

Just as the kitchen door swung shut, the man in black strolled toward the counter. "Let me guess. He's still not here."

"He's busy in the back. Did you want to wait?"

He gave a nod and handed me a business card. "Earl Grey. Hot and black. Please."

A hot flash swept over me as I poured his tea and stuck his card in my pocket. He gave me a five-dollar bill, then waved off his change as he left. Before I could strike up a conversation, more customers came into the tea house.

Funny how, after being such a shopping diva, I enjoyed serving people, learning more about tea and meeting locals I might not have met if I didn't work at the tea house. Once the tea house grew quiet once more, I realized the man in black had already left.

My mind began to wander. What had Sage told Gill about my life in Los Angeles? If she mentioned the divorce and settlement from my ex, it would explain why he suddenly wanted to sell me the tea house.

"Laken." Irritation colored Gill's voice.

"What?" I met his gaze as he stood next to a tall young man with blue hair. The same young man who'd brought Tilly's trunk into Sage's shop. Abbie San Vicente.

From the frustration on his face, he'd probably called my name a few times.

"Sorry. I was thinking about something."

"Nothing along the lines of murder, is it?" Gill asked.

"It's not. I promise." I took a deep, calming breath. I'd just stepped into the kitchen when the cash register dinged. I glanced out in time to see Abbie pull out a twenty.

The day Tilly died she'd confronted Gill about taking money from the cash drawer. I guessed he'd been covering for Abbie, who stuck the bill in his pocket and followed his grandpa out to the porch.

As the two men spoke in low tones, I wiped off the counter with every muscle in my body twitching to confront the kid. I placed an empty platter on the counter and looked back in time to see Abbie stomp down the front steps. I untied the well-worn apron and hung it behind the kitchen door, then grabbed my purse with every intention following him while Gill straightened a shelf near the entrance.

"Where are you going?" Gill asked.

I glanced out the front window, not wanting to lose sight of Abbie. "I... Uh..."

He handed me some cash from his wallet. "Could you pick up some milk and cream while you're out? The cartons in the fridge have expired. I forgot to grab new ones."

Since I hadn't looked inside the grocery bags the day Tilly died, I had no idea what he'd bought. "No problem. I'll take Sammy for a walk."

"You can't bring him in the store, so you might as well leave him here," Gill told me. "He'll be fine."

I took off down the stairs toward the sidewalk like there was a sale at Prada. A shiver ran down my back as I kept glancing over my shoulder the entire way. I caught sight of Abbie near the bakery. He headed into the hardware store, then directly to the paint section. After selecting three cans of spray paint, he paid with the twenty before leaving the store.

I put on my sunglasses as I left a half minute behind him trying to appear casual. Until I walked into a shopping cart and knocked over a potted plant. Classy.

Lucky for me, Abbie didn't go far. He carried the paint to a run-down garage a couple blocks from the marina, then stuck a key in a shiny padlock and pushed open the door. After putting the shopping bag inside, he propped the weathered blue door open with a piece of metal and disappeared inside.

I paused in the doorway and peered over my sunglasses until my eyes adjusted. My quarry—Abbie—stood several feet away near a kid's bike.

I took a deep breath before I entered the garage. "I want to know why you stole money from Gill."

Abbie sucked in a sharp breath as he spun around. "Geez, lady, you scared me half to death. Don't you have anything better to do than follow me around?"

"I saw you sneak money from the till and use it to buy spray paint." I placed my hands on my hips to appear menacing. "Are you one of those punks who go around spraying graffiti on everything? You know I could report you."

"For what?" He pulled on a thick chain and raised the garage door. Dozens of bicycles of assorted colors and sizes came into view.

"Did you steal all these?" My stomach flipped.

Abbie folded his arms across his thin chest. "What about me makes you think I'm a criminal?"

Mostly a nagging gut feeling combined with his blue hair. Call me crazy. "I know you took money from the teahouse, and you probably stole those bikes."

"For your information, I scavenge the garbage on trash day to recycle broken and discarded bikes for underprivileged kids." He picked up the bag from the hardware store.

"Sure, you do. How long have you worked on that story?"

Abbie took off his sweatshirt, revealing a dozen tattoos on his arms. The tank top beneath was covered with paint splotches of every color of the rainbow. "About eighteen months now. I started doing it as part of my probation and realized I was good at fixing things."

A bit sheepish, I asked, "What were you on probation for?"

"I painted some artwork on an old garage."

"You vandalized someone's property."

He leaned against a workbench. "All I did was add some color to an old eyesore to make it look better. The judge didn't see things from my perspective. They tore that old garage down anyway, so I don't see why what I did even mattered."

I took a closer look around his shop. Handmade cards and posters drawn by kids hung on the walls above shelves filled with assorted spray paint colors, bicycle parts and fresh, white filter masks. In one corner of the shop sat a rusty motorcycle missing several pieces.

"You fix motorcycles?" I asked.

He shrugged. "A guy I know said he'll teach me. He gets me old bikes and parts from police auctions. He's good friends with the cops in town, so don't mess with me."

"Oh yeah? Who is this guardian angel? Maybe I've met him."

Abbie raised his eyebrows. "If you want to talk to him about getting a rad bike, I've got his number. He's a paramedic. Keyon Blake."

My face warmed at the mention of Keyon's name. I pointed to the childish artwork on the wall to hide my embarrassment. "Are these from the kids you built bikes for?"

He smiled. "Yeah. Some are foster kids. Some are kids who spend lots of time in the hospital. I also build bikes for kids whose parents can't afford one."

I read a few of the cards. "You do the painting and repairs for free?"

"Like I said, I want to do some good." Abbie's face reddened.

"So, is this why you took money from the cash register?" When I faced him, I caught the flicker of a shadow in the doorway.

"Gramps and I made a deal. He gives me money for paint and stuff, but only if I stay out of trouble. If I get so much as a ticket, the deal's off."

"I take it your grandma wasn't in on the deal."

Abbie rubbed his chin. "Gramps said he'd take care of everything. I think he liked seeing her flip out when the books didn't balance, though. She was a real control freak."

Recalling how angry Tilly became seeing Sammy the day I'd found him, the control freak label fit. It bothered me Gill never let her in on his deal with Abbie.

I dug into my purse. "I'd like to help you out."

"That's not necessary. I do have a real job. I just don't get many hours right now. It gives me more time to build bikes, you know."

"You don't have any pink spray paint. Little girls love pink." I pulled out a fifty and stuck it in his hand. "And glitter. All girls love glitter."

Whether he planned to spend the money on paint or drugs didn't matter. I wanted to help someone doing good for others. I left the garage smiling before he could argue.

"That's it?" Enid practically pounced on me the instant I left the garage. "You followed the kid to a dingy garage, then handed him money? Is that all you plan to do about that menace?"

I held up a hand. "Don't you dare say a word to anyone."

"Why not? A hundred bucks says he fills those bike frames with drugs and ships them to South America." She clutched my arm so tightly that my hand paled to white. "If we caught him stuffing packets of cocaine into the frames, we'd get a huge reward."

She'd also have a great story and Gill's grandson would go to prison.

"I'm sure that seems like a great idea for your column, but Abbie rebuilds bikes for underprivileged kids, not drug cartels."

"So, he says." She sniffed. "I'm not the bad guy here, Laken. That boy is."

As a headache dug its talons into the base of my skull, I faced her. "Is there something you wanted besides to ruin my day?"

Enid huffed, folding her arms across her chest. "While I don't like you working with that con artist, you're in a great position to help."

"What con artist? You mean Gill?" The hairs on the back of my neck quivered. "Help you do what?"

"First, convince him to lift my ban at the tea house."

"The man threw teacups at your head. Next it could be saucers or teapots. I have better things to do than clean up every time you set foot in the place."

"Pish posh." She waved a hand. "It's all for show. If Gill was alone, he would've welcomed me with open arms."

I doubted that. "I need to stop at the market. Gill needs milk and cream."

"I saw the man in the black coat was back. The developer. What did he want?"

Developer? I remembered the business card and dug it out of my pocket. "Do you really have nothing better to do than spy on me?"

She snatched the card from my hand. "I do, but you're far more interesting. Is this the company that hunk works for? If this is his card, he's had a lot of surgery."

"What do you mean?" I took the card to read the raised black print. "Cash Enterprises. That has to be his company."

"Not bloody likely. Did you see the name on the card?"

"Pricilla Cash, CEO. Interesting."

Maybe I should have a chat with the man in black after all. At least I'd be able to find out more about this Pricilla Cash while I had access to the computer at Vintage Sage that afternoon.

Enid finally released my arm, leaving angry red marks behind. She narrowed her eyes. "You think Gill killed his frumpy old wife, don't you?"

"What?" I stared.

"Come on, Laken. Give me something juicy to write about in my column. Tragic death, sex and scandal fetch the highest ratings."

I rubbed my forehead. "There's nothing of the sort going on, so don't go stirring up trouble."

"Tilly's dead, Missy. Trouble's already stirred up." Enid poked her finger against my collarbone. "I smell something in the air."

"Yeah, salt and dead fish. We're next to the ocean," I pointed out. "There are no leads and there's no juicy story. Abbie's off the suspect list, so leave him alone."

"*Moi*?" Enid snapped back as if I'd slapped her. "Why would I harass the boy?"

"Why indeed. How's your book going?"

The fight seemed to drain out of her into the sand. "Awful. The collection of columns will be easy, but I need something juicy and the whole murder mystery idea with the woman falling dead in a dusty shop has so much potential."

Then it hit me. She couldn't finish writing her book or her column until I solved the mystery. I itched to ask if I was the sleuth in her novel, then I realized she was. Enid Walsh, senior detective. At most, I was her dopey sidekick.

She sighed dramatically. "For now, I'll go with plan B and publish my old columns."

"Have fun with that. I need to get back to work."

"See you later, honey." Enid smiled. "I have a zillion questions for your boss and I'm sure you'll be as keen as me to hear his answers."

Thankfully, she abandoned me outside the market and beelined toward the Devil's Peak Tavern, the pub that stood on a high cliff and overlooked the ocean.

I returned to the tea house to hear Gill shout, "Get out of there!"

My stomach lurched. "What did he do now?"

Gill sputtered, pointing out the door. "That."

I stuck the cartons in the fridge before pushing between Gill and the doorjamb. Sammy stood on a mound of trash, his fur matted and caked in dirt, tea leaves, stale biscuit crumbs and who knew what else.

When I groaned, he wagged his tail, then rolled on the cobblestones in more garbage from the large metal can.

"Sammy, what did you do?" I needed to either stick him in the crate or find someone brave enough to puppy sit.

Gill ground his teeth so hard I heard the crunch from three feet away. "Maybe you should take him home."

"Right after I clean up his mess."

"Good idea. The last thing I need is a health inspector to drop by and see this mess."

I tied my apron, then grabbed a pair of gloves and a fresh garbage bag. As I muttered under my breath, I picked up moldy food with one hand and pushed the stinky dog aside with the other. My stinky dog, who licked my face when I bent down. His breath was rancid.

"I don't know what you ate, but you'd better not get sick in Sage's house." I picked up a piece of wilted lettuce. "Gill trusts me to help in the tea house and you to guard the courtyard. How could you do this?"

Sammy rubbed his nose with one paw.

Instant pangs of guilt gnawed at my stomach. As I pulled eggshells out of his clumped fur, I regretted suggesting we add egg salad sandwiches to the lunch menu. I scratched his wet, gritty ear glad I'd worn the gloves.

"Once I get this tidied up, I'll take you home for a bath."

He scampered toward one of the flower beds to add another layer of ick.

"What else would you do?" I asked, picking up rotting food and napkins. As fast as I cleaned, he burrowed into the remaining garbage.

"Uh-uh. No more treasure hunting for you. You're in enough trouble as it is. Let me finish, so we go home."

Sammy sat near the bowls of water and food I'd put out earlier. If food wasn't his motive, what was? I tried to keep one eye on him as I cleaned the yard.

As I started to stand the garbage can upright, Sammy dove straight into the bottom. I tipped it on its side, then fished him back out. "Aren't you dirty enough?"

Sammy gave a yip, then backed out with a rectangular packet of newspaper. I swore he paused to flash me a smile.

"What did you find?" I asked, taking the packet from his mouth.

I unfolded the newspaper to reveal a syringe that fit the plastic cap I discovered. If someone *had* murdered Tilly, the syringe and the cap might be the proof the police needed. It couldn't hurt to have someone check them for prints, even though they'd likely only find Gill's since the can was close to the tea house. Not many people would enter the courtyard to throw out trash since there were garbage cans all over the neighborhood. Not unless they were planting evidence.

"Good job, Sammy." I patted his head. "We need to show this to Keyon."

I rewrapped the syringe and grabbed a plastic bag. With no other needles in the garbage, finding this one seemed suspicious. I needed to ask Gill about the syringe. After I tidied up the yard, I put a heavy rock on the garbage can to keep Sammy out while I stuck the syringe into a bag to take home.

"Hey, Gill," I called out. "I'm taking Sammy out the back way. Do you need anything before I go?"

No answer. I spotted him out on the front porch talking to someone hidden by the wall. Whoever it was made Gill angry enough to turn a deep shade of crimson. Finally, he growled, "Don't show your face around here again."

Someone wearing dark clothes turned and left. Gill blocked my view as he stomped inside and slammed the door behind him.

"Is everything okay?" I asked.

"Don't worry about it. Just go clean up your dog." He flicked something off my apron. "And while you're at it, change your clothes and take a shower. You look like you rolled around in garbage too."

"Kind of." I winced. "Is everything okay?"

He grabbed a cloth and wiped the already pristine counter. "I'll see you tomorrow."

My thoughts turned to the syringe. "Gill, was Tilly diabetic?"

He raised his eyebrows. "Why do you ask?"

"When my dad had a heart attack, the doctors discovered he was diabetic." I tried to appear nonchalant. "He had to take insulin and watch his diet."

"I'll see you tomorrow, Laken," he repeated.

Hint taken. "I'll see you tomorrow morning then." As I untied my apron, I stuck my hand in what I hoped was a blob of butter. I wiped my finger with a napkin, then washed my hands under hot water in the sink. "I'll wash the apron."

"I'd appreciate that," he said. "Just one more thing. My grandson may be misguided, but he's no killer."

"Abbie?" I tried not to squirm under his scrutiny. "No. I saw him take some money out of the register. I thought I'd talk to him privately, so I didn't upset you. He told me about the bikes."

"He and I have an understanding." He turned away. "See you tomorrow."

I walked into the kitchen, grabbed another plastic bag and shoved the apron inside. Over the past couple days, my Coach purse had become a doggy bag filled with treats and toys—and now evidence of some sort. I dug out the leash, then headed into the courtyard.

Sammy lay in a patch of sunshine. Just my luck he decided to let the gunk from the trash dry on his fur. Not my kind of conditioning treatment, but he seemed content. He wouldn't be so happy when I had to pull out the chunks in the bathtub later.

"Come on, boy." I snapped on his leash. "Let's take you for a swim before we get anywhere near the house. Sage will strangle us both if we get her furniture dirty."

Sammy trotted toward the back door of the tea house, but I tugged him toward the gate. He whined and took a side step. After a little coaxing, I got him into the back alley. It seemed he'd had more fun digging in the trash than I thought. We'd barely reached the beach before he strained at the leash again. I let him run though the water to wash off the smell while I kicked off my shoes. The waves cooled my tired feet.

"Hey." Keyon jogged toward me. Sweat zigzagged down his flushed face and his T-shirt clung to his torso. "I thought you were at the tea house this morning."

As I admired the ripple of muscles in Keyon's legs and torso, I forgot about Sammy and our *eau de garbage* scent. How was this guy still single and why was he hanging out with the likes of me?

"Laken?" Keyon asked. "Are you okay?"

"I just realized how bad I smell." I glanced around for Sammy, who'd found a starfish. At least it wasn't a crab, which reminded me of Tilly. I dug out the bagged syringe. "Actually, I'm glad to see you. Is this one of yours?"

He ran a hand though his damp hair. "I don't do drugs."

"In your line of work, I hope not," I told him. "I meant is this the type of syringe you guys use in your kits?"

"It looks like the ones we use at work, but how should I know? They're widely available. People buy them for insulin and so on." He took the bag to study the syringe through the plastic. “Where did you find this one?”

“In the trash bin at the tea house. Sammy chose to dine a la carte today. I should move that bin outside the fence if Sammy’s going to hang out there.”

“That would be a good idea, except for the raccoons.” He held out the bag. “Do you need this?”

A gut feeling made me say, “Yes.”

Keyon seemed reluctant to return the bag. “What are you going to do with it?”

I didn’t have a clue right then, but I held onto it like it was a life preserver. “Did you work today?”

“Day shift tomorrow.” His gaze remained on the plastic bag in my hand. “Was Tilly diabetic? That would explain the needle.”

“Gill wouldn’t say. Sammy knocked over the garbage can and made a huge mess.” I paused. “I wasn’t sure how to bring up the topic without sounding nosy, but I mentioned my dad discovered he had diabetes after he had a heart attack.”

He wiped away the sweat racing down his forehead. “You do realize a used syringe is a biohazard. Either you or Sammy could’ve been jabbed. You’d be concerned if it was caught in Sammy’s fur.”

“Yes, but we didn’t and he’s fine. We both are.”

Keyon wiped his forehead. “You and I know that, but Gill doesn’t. The point is either of you could’ve been jabbed. That would give you a legitimate reason to ask questions.”

I sat in thoughtful silence. “Because then I’d need to know what the needle was used for and who used it. Just in case.”

“Now you’re catching on.” He wiped something off my nose. A small gob of mayonnaise he then smeared on the only clean spot on my shirt.

I hugged my stomach. "You want me to lie to Gill. That seems awfully devious."

"It is." Keyon used the bottom of his T-shirt to wipe his face. His washboard abs shone with sweat. "Sometimes you need to be a bit devious to get what you want."

"I'm not that kind of person." I forced myself to look away from his washboard abs, not sure if I meant devious or desperate.

"You have to be more straightforward to get answers," he said.

"With Gill? I agree."

Keyon placed one hand on my shoulder. "And with me."

Yikes. Another hot flash. I wiped my palms on my pants and whistled to Sammy. I needed a cold shower before I said anything stupid. If only I hadn't given Keyon the syringe cap, we could share our evidence with the police to support the murder theory.

"I'll let you know what I find out from Gill," I told him.

"Sounds good." He nodded toward Devil's Peak Tavern. "I'm going to finish my run and take a shower. Maybe I'll see you later."

The long-neglected parts of me hoped so.

Chapter Twelve

Jonathan sat on Sage's front porch by the time I got there. He smirked while I carried Sammy up the sidewalk but was gracious enough not to double over laughing. He even offered to give Sammy a bath while I cleaned up. I shampooed three times, then settled for colorful yoga pants and a baggy white shirt.

Around five-thirty, Sammy barked at the front door. The doorbell rang seconds later. When I opened the door, my breath caught in my throat.

Keyon, dressed in khakis and a pale blue shirt, stood on the front step with a bottle of sparkling water in one hand and a bouquet of colorful daisies in the other. "Hi."

"What are you doing here?" I asked.

"I was invited." Keyon held out the bottle. "Here, I know you don't drink wine."

My face grew warm. "That was thoughtful. Thank you."

Jonathan placed his hands on my shoulders from behind. "Oh, good. Keyon's here. I thought I'd have to man the barbecue alone."

"Not a chance." Keyon's gaze remained locked with mine.

"You want a beer?" Jonathan pulled me out of the doorway to let Keyon enter.

Sage came from the kitchen, wiping her hands on a tea towel. “Since when has Keyon ever refused a drink?”

“I’d love a beer. It’s been a rough week. I could use a distraction.” Keyon handed the daisies to Sage. “Thanks for inviting me.”

I gathered inviting him wasn’t her idea.

She grimaced. “Alcohol is a distraction?”

“Some days.” Keyon pecked her cheek. “Dinner with friends is a better one.”

Sage flared her nostrils but didn’t reply.

Jonathan dropped an arm around Keyon’s shoulders and walked him to the kitchen. “Maybe getting things off your chest will help.”

“Maybe,” Keyon said, glancing in my direction. Was I a part of his rough week?

“We’ll take Sammy outside,” Jonathan said. “He and Keyon can run sprints across the yard to burn off some steam.”

Keyon growled. “I’m not that cranky.”

“You will be after I tell you about my week,” Jonathan told him, opening a can of beer. “I’ve got some news that’ll make you jealous.”

If Jonathan had big news, I hadn’t heard about it from Sage. When I glanced to my sister for a clue, she bowed her head and finished making the potato salad. Something was up. I guessed she’d only just heard Jonathan’s news, too.

“What’s going on?” Keyon asked before they reached the patio doors.

“I’ve been offered a job in L.A. as personal trainer to a couple movie stars on the set of a big action thriller starring Emery Samson.” Jonathan grinned.

My heart skipped a beat. “Are you serious?”

Keyon laughed. “Dude, that’s awesome.”

“Yeah. Awesome,” Sage muttered.

I didn't know what to say. My sister hated the bustle of Los Angeles as much as I did, for the same reasons I did. Emery Samson was a huge one of those reasons. "Are you taking the job?"

"He'd be crazy to say no," Keyon said, patting Jonathan on the back. "An offer like this doesn't come along every day. Emery Samson is big league."

Sage snorted.

I scowled as I folded my arms across my chest and nodded toward my sister, whose eyes were filled with tears.

Keyon winced. "Oh."

"Of course, I am." Jonathan gave my sister's a squeeze. "It's no big deal. I'll fly to L.A. Monday mornings, then come back every Friday night."

I wanted to laugh at his naivete. Hollywood rarely took weekends off, especially while shooting on set when the conditions were right.

"And I told him he's crazy," Sage said. "We only see each other a couple weekends a month as it is. Nothing would change. He'd just live farther away."

The tension in the kitchen threatened to squeeze the breath out of me until Jonathan led us to the deck to eat. Sitting next to my sister, I'd hoped we could change the conversation, sit back, and relax for a while.

Keyon blew that notion before I'd even filled my plate. "Tilly San Vicente died."

Jonathan raised his eyebrows. "Tea house Tilly?"

"She had a heart attack inside my shop," Sage said, reaching for a baby carrot. "Laken was minding the store when she collapsed."

"Tilly was overweight and had heart problems," Jonathan said. "No surprise there."

"Actually—" I started.

"No, it's not a surprise." Sage snapped before Keyon could bring up his theory.

I picked at my potato salad while Jonathan steered the conversation toward politics and the upcoming election. With my thoughts still on the Sweet Eden Tea House, I asked, "Do you guys know Gill's grandson?"

"Abbie?" Sage asked. "What's he done this time?"

I thought fast. "Nothing I know of. I've only seen him a couple times. I just wondered what kind of guy he is."

Keyon snorted. "Do you mean is he dumb enough to kill his grandma? I doubt it."

Jonathan chuckled. "If he's anything like his mother, he is. Wait, who said anything about Tilly being murdered?"

"No one." Sage chomped a baby carrot as she glared at Keyon. "Gabriella's not so bad. She's just not cut out for small town life."

"And hooks up with every man in her path of destruction," Jonathan said.

A female version of my ex.

"You don't know her very well, do you, Sage?" Keyon asked.

"And you do?" Sage asked.

"Whoa. Change of topic before tempers flare." Jonathan held up a hand. "You all need to tell me how great the steaks are."

When no one else spoke up, I speared a small piece of meat. "You did a great job, Jonathan. I can't remember the last time I had such tender steak."

"Well, if you ask me," Keyon said, "Gill has the most to gain from Tilly's death. Besides, he was the first person to bring up murder."

Jonathan shook his head. "Seriously? The woman had a heart attack and suddenly you think she was murdered. If that's the case, Gill also has the most to lose if he gets caught."

"But what if someone wanted to make it look like he killed her?" Sage asked. "He could still lose everything without proof. People would boycott the tea house and his business would go under."

Keyon reached for a piece of broccoli. "What about Gabby and Abbie? I could see Gabby framing him."

I took a deep breath, then asked, "What about Enid Walsh?"

"Sorry, Laken." Jonathan laughed. "Enid doesn't have the common sense of a gopher. I'm sure she's so happy to be rid of Tilly she'll write columns out of spite."

Keyon chuckled. "Personally, I think Gill got tired of putting up with her. That woman scared the hell out of me every time I set foot in the tea house."

I'd heard enough. "Do you want to know what I think?"

"Laken," Sage warned.

"Keyon's accused Gill," I said, "but there's one other suspect he hasn't considered."

"Who?" Keyon asked.

"The man in black," I blurted out.

My sister froze.

Jonathan narrowed his eyes. "You think Johnny Cash killed Tilly?"

I stared. "Why would you say that?"

"He's the only man in black I can think of."

"I meant the man in the black trench coat who came to the tea house a few times to talk to Gill."

"What did he say?" If Keyon were a dog, his ears would've turned toward me.

Jonathan sat back. "What does he look like?"

Not sure who to answer first, I blew out a breath. "He heard about Tilly's death and extended his sympathies, then said to tell Gill the offer still stood."

"What offer?" Keyon asked.

I shrugged. "I guess he figured Gill knew what he meant."

Sammy groaned beneath the coffee table.

Sage tapped her foot on the floor like she'd downed a pot of coffee. "The guy's probably some developer swooping in on an opportunity. I doubt he had anything to do with Tilly's death. Besides, you don't have any proof she was murdered, only wild speculations."

Keyon frowned. "There is proof."

"No. There's not," Sage told him, her voice growing louder. "If you keep sucking my sister into believing your crazy delusions, you're going to get her into trouble. I'm telling you, Laken, stay away from Keyon. He's a loose cannon."

Keyon's face reddened. "I'm not delusional."

"Neither am I." Miffed, I folded my arms across my chest.

My sister shook her head. "Laken, I know what you've been through. I was there. You get swept off your feet by men with crazy agendas and are shocked when things don't work out."

My face burned. "I know what I saw, and I know what I found. Keyon's no more delusional than I am."

My sister closed her eyes. "I'm not saying you're delusional, you're..."

"Gullible," I finished. "I get it, but I'm not stupid."

I stormed inside the house and headed for the stairs.

Sage caught me halfway up, then dragged me to the living room. She sat next to me on the couch and whispered, "You need to calm down. The last time you got this worked up, you ended up in hospital again. Is that what you want?"

An uneasy silence surrounded us.

"Sammy found a syringe in the garbage at the tea house," I told her.

In my haste to get to the shower earlier, I'd dropped my purse at the bottom of the stairs. When I brought it to the couch, my hands shook so badly that I nearly dumped everything on the carpet. "I found a cap under the counter while I was cleaning. Sammy found the syringe wrapped in newspaper in the garbage can."

Sage took out the bag with the syringe. "Where's the cap?"

"I gave it to Keyon, but I kept the syringe. At first, I thought the paramedics left them behind when they worked on Tilly, but I found the cap under the counter at Vintage Sage and the syringe at the tea house."

My sister tucked her legs into the lotus position. "Maybe Tilly had a medical condition and needed injections."

"I thought of that, but Gill wouldn't tell me. Why wrap the syringe in newspaper?"

Sage blew out a breath. "Maybe he or Tilly wrapped it so no one would get hurt."

"If she used them on a regular basis, they would've had a sharps container for the needles." I hesitated. "Keyon told me there are drugs that can mimic a heart attack."

"Did you go online and check?"

"Not yet. I had no idea what to look for."

"Just ask him or Andy to give you a list of drugs you could research," she said.

When Sammy jumped on the couch between us, I rubbed the top of his head. "What if her death's related to something in that trunk? She must've saved the articles about the jewelry heist for a reason."

"Have you gone to the police yet?" Sage stuck the bag into my purse.

"No. Keyon thought we should do more digging."

"That's odd." She stroked Sammy's back until Muumuu sauntered between them. "It's not like him to be cautious."

"Maybe he's scared."

Sage hugged a throw pillow. "Or maybe it started as a ruse, but now that you've found proof, he's not sure what to do."

"Is it safe to come inside? Jonathan poked his head in the doorway and asked. "We cleaned up out here."

My sister placed her hand on my thigh. "You good?"

"I'm fine. Just need some rest." I folded my arms across my stomach.

Jonathan strode across the room to sit in the armchair. "Laken, we want to know what this man in black looks like."

Keyon sat to my left on the couch. "Maybe I've seen him."

I thought Sammy growled in his sleep, but it was my sister who snapped, "Enough of this nonsense. I'm going to wash the dishes and put on some coffee."

"I'll help." I jumped up, accidentally tapping Sammy's nose with my hand.

Keyon pulled me down by the back of my shirt. "Sit. I want to hear more."

"Cream or sugar?" I bounced to my feet so fast my head spun. The world seemed to turn midnight blue. "Oh wow."

"Laken!" Sage wrapped her arms around me as she forced me onto the couch. She turned to Keyon and Jonathan, "Will you two leave her alone? She's not well."

"I'm fine." I grew even dizzier with my eyes closed.

"You're not fine." My sister growled again. "You've been pushing yourself too hard and need some rest. Less than four months ago you were in the hospital doing chemo."

Keyon's mouth opened. "You were what? Why didn't you tell me?"

"It's in remission." I hugged my arms around my torso.

Sage huffed. "She doesn't like to make anyone worry. She didn't even tell me she was sick until she passed out and crashed her car into a tree."

"And now I'm stronger and work for both you and at the tea house," I reminded her.

Sammy curled up between me and Keyon.

"Yeah, it's funny how things work out," Sage said.

Keyon turned to Jonathan. "Did you know Laken was in the hospital?"

"I didn't just meet her yesterday, bro," Jonathan said.

"You knew for the last two months that Laken was staying here and never bothered to tell me?" Keyon asked. "Or that she'd been in the hospital."

"One month." Jonathan corrected. "Actually, I helped move from—"

"Portland." Sage snapped. "You didn't know her anyway, so what's the big deal?"

Jonathan stared into his wine. He knew everything about my illness and my ex, who he planned to work with. I hoped he'd keep his mouth shut. At least until I knew Keyon better.

Good gravy, what was I thinking? I wasn't interested in getting to know any man a little better, especially one who triggered knee-weakening hot flashes. My heart was still a cluster of sharp shards. Finding Sammy had helped.

Keyon had a long list of suggestions of what I should eat, drink and do to heal. While I'd heard them all before, I stared when he suggested yoga.

"Have you actually ever been to a yoga class in your life?" Sage asked.

Jonathan laughed. "He used to date a yogi. Old habits die hard."

“In other words, yes.” Keyon grimaced. “I’ve trained for years.”

Sage seemed intrigued. “I didn’t know that.”

He snorted. “You don’t even like me. What makes you think I’d tell you?”

Sammy’s head bobbed. He yawned and went back to sleep with his head on my thigh. Scattering garbage in the tea garden all day followed by a walk on the beach had finally worn him out. Now if only he’d sleep through the night.

I walked Keyon to the front porch while Sage and Jonathan went into the kitchen. From the tones of their low voices, I guessed they were arguing about his new job and the fact he would be working with my ex.

Keyon paused on the top step. “Cancer, huh? Did you do the chemo or did Sage drag you to a shaman healer who made you drink green sludge?”

“What do you mean by that?” I asked.

“Look, I’m a paramedic and not a believer in natural medicine. It wouldn’t surprise me if she made you sleep with crystals and drink gross concoctions to help you heal. We both know she’s like that.”

“You seem to know her better than I thought.”

He grinned. “Just not well enough that she’d tell me her cute sister was in town.”

Cute? My face warmed. “Well, now you know.”

“Yes, I do.” Keyon took a step closer. His breath, sweet with mint candy, warmed my face as he gazed into my eyes. “The question is, what are we going to do about it?”

As he drew near, I leaned against the railing. My knees grew weak, and I thought I’d stop breathing when his lips brushed mine. I fought the urge to kiss him back.

Not that he gave me the chance.

Keyon Blake walked into the night leaving me to mull over possibilities.

Chapter Thirteen

I sipped from a large mug of English Breakfast tea while I gazed around the Sweet Eden Tea House. In my mind's eye, I visualized where we'd use the paint colors Sammy picked out. Blue on the walls. Greyish brown on the counters and shelving. A crisp coat of white for the veranda and wicker furniture. A pale yellow similar to the siding on the tea house to coat the peeling wood furniture inside.

All we needed was to make a list of supplies to freshen up the place.

The second the man in black strode through the front door, he derailed my train of thought. Derailed was a bad choice of words. More like sent my happy plans careening into an overgrown ravine of suspicion. His black trench was coat draped over one arm and he seemed much less menacing wearing a light grey suit with a purple dress shirt and silvery tie. While his hair was lightly salted with grey, his face was smooth and unlined, like he rarely ventured out of doors.

"What can I get you, sir?"

"It's Bryan, actually," he said. "You seem very businesslike today. To what do I owe the brusqueness?"

I yawned, rubbing my face with one hand. "Sorry. I didn't get much sleep last night. I have a puppy that insists on eating everything besides his food."

"At least he's getting his fiber." Bryan chuckled.

"That's what I keep saying. Anyway, Gill's not here," I told him before he could ask. In fact, Gill had left for the bank only a couple minutes earlier.

He draped his coat over a chair at a table near the counter, then narrowed his eyes to study me. "Yeah, I saw him leave. I feel like I know you from somewhere."

A knot formed in my stomach. "I have been here a lot lately. I keep passing along your messages to Gill, but he's a busy man."

"No," he said. "From somewhere else. What's your name?"

From the tabloids most likely. I frowned as the knot doubled in size. "I'm Laken."

"Have you been to Seattle recently?"

Although I'd been there dozens of times to shop with Sage and Mom, the less he knew about me, the better. "Not recently. I thought you were from Portland."

"I live in Seattle, but I'm on the road a lot for work." His expression softened, his dark eyes cool and emotionless. "You'll have to come visit sometime. I could take you sightseeing. You'd love the view from the Space Needle."

I'd been there and done that. Emery and I took a trip to the top of the Space Needle long enough to capture a single, obligatory photo before he threw up. My ex was deathly afraid of heights. He'd only open his eyes to ham it up for the camera the instant his bodyguard yelled, "Say cheese." After that, we shoved him back into the elevator and back to ground level.

"Are you okay?" he asked. "You went a bit pale for a second there."

"I'm good, thanks. What can I get you?"

He averted his gaze and became businesslike, as if he'd crossed some invisible boundary. "A large Earl Grey and a raisin bran muffin with a side of butter, please."

"Hot and black." The words rolled off my tongue so fast I couldn't stop them.

He raised his dark eyebrows, then smiled. "I guess I have been here a lot lately."

My face burned as I turned away to prepare a tray. "You wouldn't have to if Gill was actually here when you showed up."

"Funny how that works," he said. "It's like the guy's a psychic. He seems to sense when I'm walking through the front door."

I rolled my eyes upward. Since Gill lived upstairs, he could leave whenever Bryan or Enid showed up. "He's a busy guy since his wife died."

"Gill must have been devastated. I heard she died in a local shop."

"My sister's vintage clothing store," I told him. "I was behind the counter."

"I'm sorry to hear that. You seem like such a sweet lady."

Was he hitting on me or trying to get information on Gill?

"I mean that sincerely. I've spoken to a lot of people around Glitter Bay, and you're one of the nicest so far."

Likely because I wasn't one of the people whom he'd approached about buying up my livelihood. I rang in his purchase before I reached for a plate for his muffin. He paid with a credit card then handed me another business card with his name, Bryan Cash.

"That reminds me, you left someone else's card the other day. Who's Pricilla?"

"Pricilla? I guess I left the wrong card. It was supposed to be one of mine. Hers must have been in my pocket for someone else."

For Gill, I guessed. Mistakes happened all the time. "Who's Pricilla? Your wife?"

Bryan met my gaze. "My mother. She started the development company before I was born and has built an empire. She's one of those people you do not say no to, which is why people like your boss avoid me like I'm contagious."

"That would explain it." I itched to run to a computer and do some digging.

"I'm serious about taking you sightseeing," he said. "Any time you want to get out of Glitter Bay, give me a call. I'd be happy to show you around."

Flustered, I stared as he walked toward his table, not sure if I should kick him out or find out what he was up to? Curiosity—as usual—won out. Gill could be in deep trouble if this guy was a developer bent on taking over the tea house.

"I don't know when Gill will be back." I heated his muffin, then set it on the tray and added a pat of butter.

His phone rang as I poured the hot water into a small teapot. He scowled, then shook his head. "Wow that woman's persistent."

"Is everything okay?" I asked, setting the pot next to a dainty flowered teacup, which matched his shirt. That the tiny teacup didn't suit him in the least made me chuckle.

"Business," he replied. "I've been receiving e-mails and phone calls from some nosy reporter ever since I came to town."

Enid Walsh. I nearly dropped the tray as I picked it up. "How come?"

He sat back as I placed the tray on the table. "Rumor has it I'm scouting sites for a new hotel-slash-restaurant-slash-night club."

"That's a lot of slashes. No wonder rumors are flying." I placed the plated muffin in front of him. Any one of those things would bring a huge injection of money into Glitter Bay. I could see why reporters would hound him.

Correction, one reporter.

"Are you in town to scout sites?" I hovered as I waited for an answer.

He poured milk and sugar into his teacup, then met my gaze, his eyes as brown as the chocolate chips in the cookies from the bakery. "Honey, my name is Bryan Cash and I work for a company called Cash Enterprises. We're a multimillion-dollar corporation that buys and develops investment properties. Why else would I be here?"

"The scenery? The ocean air? Stories of pirates and buried treasure?" I glanced toward the front windows in time to see Enid lower her camera. "Oh, no you don't."

Bryan turned in time to see her bury the camera into her bag. "Who is that?"

I didn't answer. As Enid clomped down the front steps and made a dash for the sidewalk, Bryan and I followed. He was faster than both of us.

He ran past me and practically leaped down the stairs to clamp his hand around her arm. "Who are you?"

"This is Enid Walsh," I told him, gasping for breath. "The nosy reporter who's hounding you. She just took a picture of you."

He studied Enid with her purple windbreaker, lime green leggings, and bright blue hair before leaning back slightly. "You're a reporter?"

"Yes, I am," she huffed. "Do you have a problem with that?"

He raised his eyebrows. "You look more like you should be knitting tea cozies in an asylum than skulking around taking snapshots of innocent people."

"I wouldn't exactly say she was skulking." I tried not to laugh.

Enid gawked. "Buddy, if you're innocent, I'm Tinker Bell. With everything I know about you already, I could call the cops and have you locked up for life."

"Maybe you'd better let Tink go before she makes a scene," I suggested.

He released his grip and straightened his suit jacket. "And what is it you think I've done, Ms. Walsh?"

"I don't think, Mr. Cash." Enid tapped her temple. "I know."

Bryan tightened his jaw. "And what is it you think you know?"

"That you're a slimy developer who wants to tear this place down to build a ten-story glass and metal monstrosity full of condominiums."

"Hotel rooms, actually." He seemed amused. "Go on."

She jabbed him in the chest with her gnarled finger. "With a heated pool and a spa, no less. Big city people will come from everywhere and ruin our quiet little town."

"Yes, and they will also eat in your restaurants, shop in your quaint little stores, and sail their yachts into your cove," Bryan pointed out. "You're right. What a dumb idea to bring more money and wealthy people into town. Ms. Walsh, do you realize your little town of Glitter Bay could become the next Martha's Vineyard? You'd have the rich and famous coming from all over the world to see the sights and play in the ocean."

Including my ex-husband and all his movie star friends. I hated the idea already.

"It'll never work." Enid placed her hands on her hips and widened her stance.

"Why not?" Bryan asked. "What do you have against someone wanting to create a more dynamic future for Glitter Bay?"

She huffed. "We have tourists now. They toss trash in our streets, want things we don't offer, and cause trouble."

"Can we take this inside, guys?" I asked.

"No. I'm banned," Enid reminded me.

Bryan grinned. "Well, I'm not, and I'd like to finish my breakfast."

"Enid has a point. We all know what's going to happen." I stepped between them, with my back to Enid, hoping she wouldn't do anything stupid. "You'll buy up all those quaint little shops you say you like so much, then tear them down to build your playground for the rich and famous. Do you know how many jobs you're going to take away from the people who built this town?"

Bryan met my gaze. "Do you know how many new jobs we'll create? By building one hotel alone, we'd employ at least a hundred and fifty people."

"But at the cost of how many local businesses?" I asked. "People like you think you're saviors. You want our way of life, then turn it into exactly what you're trying to escape from in the first place."

Enid patted my back. "You tell him, Laken."

I suddenly realized she'd taken several pictures of me glowering at Bryan. With each push of her finger on her camera button, she grinned wider.

"Cut that out," I snapped.

"Oh, don't mind me," Enid said, clicking her camera once more.

The object of our ire turned to face her. "Look, lady, if you're looking for a news story, pull out your notepad. I have a few things to reveal to the people of this town."

"That you're leaving?" I asked, folding my arms across my stomach.

"Nice try, sweetheart. I'm not leaving Glitter Bay until I get what I came for."

Enid lowered her camera. "Yeah, we know. To make a deal with Gill for the tea house. Once you get that the rest of the Glitter Bay merchants will fall like dominoes. Or so you think."

Bryan flared his nostrils before he stormed back into the tea house. Seconds later, he appeared with the flowery purple teacup, his trench coat, and his muffin. He pushed Enid and I both aside, then paused and said, "Thank you for the tea. Laken. If you see Gill, please let him know I'm serious about my offer. He needs to stop blowing off our meetings, or he will regret it."

For someone so eager to give his side of the story to the media—well, Enid—he was in an awful hurry to escape us both. Maybe he expected someone else to stand up to him, rather than a blue-haired old woman and a skinny, red-headed supermodel. Okay, ex model. Scratch the super.

"I think he likes you." Enid's mouth hung open as she stood next to me. "Aren't you going to stop him?"

"He'll be back."

"How do you know?" she asked, taking one last photo as he stalked away.

I headed back up the steps. "He took one of Gill's teacups. I doubt he'll take it far, although he does seem like the vindictive type. He might want something in exchange."

She followed me up the steps, pausing on the front porch. "For the teacup? I wonder if he likes older women. He's good-looking for a troublemaker. I could be a cougar. Maybe I should catch up to him and hear what he has to say."

"Go right ahead. I'll be happy to never see him again."

"Me? Nah. I'm old and frumpy. I doubt I could catch up."

Frumpy wasn't a word that came to mind when I thought of Enid, especially when I protested her taking Bryan Cash's vacated seat. He'd left a wadded napkin on the table next to a five-dollar bill.

She nudged it to one side and set her camera on the table. "If we dressed you in a short skirt and high heels, I'll bet you could get close to him." She wiggled her eyebrows. "Very close."

"Not a chance." If Tilly was murdered over Bryan's idea to turn Glitter Bay into a playground for adults, the whole development could be reason enough to kill for again. There was still one thing that bothered me.

"How much do you think Gill could get for the tea house and property?"

"Why? Are you planning to save up your tips and buy it?" She held Bryan's tip out to me. "I know a few local realtors. I'll make some calls and find out."

"That would be helpful, thanks," I told her, grateful she'd given up on the short skirt and high heels idea.

Then Enid chuckled and said, "We can shop for skimpy dresses and knock-'em-dead shoes when you're done work today. One of us must be able to turn that ultra-conservative's head."

Before I got sick and lost weight, I was Emery's arm candy. I'd bought dozens of those outfits back in Los Angeles to impress Emery's Hollywood friends and peeve his fans. Most of those outfits were either in storage or in the trash after I had a meltdown. Picturing Enid in any one of them was enough to make me queasy.

"I'll pass," I told her, careful to slip Bryan's business card into my pocket. "I have to get ready for the lunch rush, and you'd better leave."

"Where's your boss? Why isn't he here to help?"

I smirked. "If he was, you'd be ducking plates and cups."

"True enough. I should leave before he shows up."

Once she left, looking both ways before darting out the door, I studied Bryan Cash's card. He'd written a phone number on the back, probably his cell phone number. If that creep thought he could get to Gill through me, he was mistaken.

I stuck the card in my pocket and got to work.

When Gill still hadn't arrived by one, I texted Sage that I'd be late. If I showed up at all. At one-thirty, I made myself an egg salad sandwich and brewed a cup of rooibos, an African red tea. I sat outside at my favorite table and struggled not to close my eyes. The strange morning had left me ravenous and in need of a catnap, but the little old ladies Gill called the Hens came in every day at two. I wasn't about to abandon him.

Luckily for me, he arrived five minutes later, waving as he went inside.

"I'm glad you made all those little sandwiches for the Hens for later." Gill set a bowl of turkey noodle soup on the table a few minutes later before sitting across from me. "They'll appreciate them."

I smiled. "I figured you and Tilly did things like that for them anyway."

"Nope." He crumbled crackers into his soup and said, "Up until now, those nosy old biddies only came here once a month. Tea houses aren't cool enough for the young folk. They hang out in coffee shops, so the Hens are thrilled they get the place to themselves."

"Ah, so that's the attraction."

"Not entirely," he said. "Now that Tilly's gone, those old nags smell fresh meat. Before long, they'll start to bring their single friends."

"What do you mean?"

He slurped a spoonful of soup broth, leaving the noodles behind. "Seriously? Laken, I'm a widower with my own hair and teeth."

So much for my appetite. I was sure Gill was a fine catch if you were into the older, grandfatherly type, which I wasn't. I picked up my cup to distract myself with the light tobacco scent of the rooibos. "Is that why so many people are suddenly customers?"

One corner of his mouth curled upward. "You met my wife. She was mean to everyone. Most of all her family."

My fears confirmed, I asked, "Why?"

"Tilly got jealous when women came to check me out. When she got mad, she'd pout and make soup. We sold a lot of soup." He motioned toward me with his spoonful of noodles. "Not only are the old biddies back, but men can't walk past this place without stopping to meet the new woman in town."

"Me?"

"I'm surprised you didn't notice," Gill said. "I'm not delusional, Laken. People had several good reasons not to like Tilly."

"You mean like Enid?" I asked.

He continued to eat but said nothing.

"I'm sorry. Whatever happened is none of my business." I stood and picked up my plate. "Do you need me to stick around? Sage's shop is quiet, so I can wash the dishes before the Hens show up."

"Sounds good. Are you gonna eat that?" Gill asked, pointing to the other half of my sandwich.

"Go ahead."

He picked up the sandwich and took a mouthful. "For the record, Enid's a troublemaker who causes more misery than a hurricane. That's why she's to never set foot inside this building while I'm still walking this earth. Got it?"

I didn't bother to mention Bryan's visit either. "Got it."

After rummaging through my bag for Sammy's treats, I joined him in the garden where he lay curled on one of the weathered tables in the sunshine. "Get down before Gill sees you. He's already in a bad mood."

Sammy yawned before he hopped onto a chair, then to the cobblestones to stretch. He strolled toward me, his fur dusty, and then paused to sniff the air.

I couldn't smell anything.

Then Sammy licked my fingers. The silly dog had distracted me long enough to grab the treats right out of my hand.

"Outsmarted by a puppy. That's just great." I scratched his dusty head. "Don't tell Gill or he'll hire you to replace me."

Sammy yipped, then nipped at my ankle.

I sat on the cobblestones to let him crawl onto my lap. His soft baby fur was warm from the sunshine. Soon the tea house's shadow would cool the gardens and he'd become more active. Both the gardens and garbage cans would be fair game.

"Maybe Sage is right, Sammy. Maybe I'm making Tilly's death into something it isn't." I buried my face in his fur for comfort. He smelled of roses...and dirt.

"Oh no." I scanned the plants around the garden.

At the far end of the yard, he'd dug a hole beneath one of the rosebushes with large red blossoms. I needed to fill it in before Gill noticed. It was odd how he'd dug holes all over both the courtyard and Sage's yard to bury bones but always filled them in. Why not this one?

I lifted him off my legs and stood. As if he'd read my mind, he raced ahead and barked. Something reflected the sunshine as it lay in the mound of dirt next to the hole. Afraid of finding another syringe, I used a stick to unearth a small vial with a few drops of liquid remaining.

Scooping Sammy into my arms, I ran to the kitchen for my cell phone and a sandwich bag. I took three pictures before flipping the bag inside out to cover my hand when I picked up the vial.

"Anectine," I read aloud then sealed the bag before scrubbing more dirt out of his fur with my fingertips. "Why would someone bury an empty vial in the rose garden rather than put it in the trash? I have no idea what this stuff is, but Keyon will know what it's used for."

I fumbled for my phone as a heat wave surged through me. The last time I saw Keyon, we'd nearly kissed. Maybe a little distance between us was better than summoning him to examine a vial when I could find the answer elsewhere.

An empty vial, a syringe and a cap. How could I find out if the vial and the syringe both contained the same drug?

While Keyon might know someone in a lab who could help, Sage had a not-so-secret admirer in the vet clinic who'd do anything for her. I prayed my sister would convince him to help.

Dealing with this mystery would've been easier if I'd met a cute cop instead.

"Laken?" Gill called through the screen door. "Those nosy old women are here. Can you take care of them while I step out for a while?"

I gave Sammy a hug. "Sorry, buddy, the Hens are here. I'll sneak you some ham once I get them settled. They'll probably leave half of everything on their plates anyway. From what I hear, they're still watching their girlish figures, even at eighty."

Sammy whimpered and pranced when I reached for the doorknob.

"I'll be back soon. Just stay out of trouble, okay?" I stuck the vial and my phone into my bag, then washed my hands in the kitchen sink.

Gill had given each of the Hens one of my handmade menus before he disappeared. The four women chatted endlessly but never caused trouble. I'd seen them in the vintage shop countless times.

Ursula wore her flowing white hair to her waist. Her wrists adorned with a dozen different bangles and her legs invisible beneath gauzy skirts. An artist by trade, she usually had multicolored paint flecks on her skin.

Carol's heart-shaped face was framed by a straight orange bob. I guessed she and Enid used the same hairdresser. She wore yoga pants and baggy tops everywhere.

Margaret and Joanne were identical twins. Petite with tight little white curls and bright pink lipstick, they both wore thin cardigans over their high-collared blouses. I hadn't figured out how to tell them apart yet.

I took their orders and retreated to the kitchen amid a flurry of questions about where Gill was, how he was coping, and when he'd be ready to date. The entire tea house rang with peals of laughter, something I'd never heard while Tilly manned the counter. It was refreshing.

As I portioned sandwiches and desserts onto china plates, I caught snatches of conversation. Enid's name popped up several times, as did Gill's and Tilly's. I realized that if anyone knew the real gossip around Glitter Bay, it would be the Hens.

Since I had dozens of questions, I decided to get to know them better. Maybe I'd finally figure out which twin was which.

Chapter Fourteen

After meeting Enid and Tilly, I no longer assumed anyone in Glitter Bay was sweet or charming. I approached the Hens with caution. "How's lunch, ladies?"

"Perfectly lovely, my dear." Ursula pushed a handful of hair back over her left shoulder. "You must tell me where you got such delicious ham. The kind I buy is too salty and dries out my lips."

The twin who stashed napkins and sugar packets in the pocket of her blue sweater snorted. "Everything dries your lips, you old shrew. You've had chapped lips since high school, when you started to date the entire football team."

"Margaret." The twin in the white sweater, who must be Joanne, admonished her. "Don't be so awful. Ursula has a condition, you know."

I raised my eyebrows. "What kind of condition?"

"Don't mind her, love. She thinks being an artist is a mental disorder." Ursula said as she lifted her teacup.

"Speaking of mental disorders," Carol said. "Have you seen Enid's new hairdo?"

Margaret sneered, then asked, "Don't you two use the same hairdresser?"

I hid my smirk beneath one hand.

Joanne laughed. "If Enid's hair were any bluer, she could hide in a robin's nest."

"Definitely not." Margaret shook her white curls. "That woman's head is more the size of an ostrich egg."

"Maggie, I thought you and Enid were friends." Carol said.

Ursula clapped a hand over her mouth to keep from spitting out her mouthful of tea. "Now be nice, you two. Enid Walsh might be a troublemaker, but she's nobody's clone."

"Did you say clone or clown?" Margaret asked, eating half a cookie in one bite.

Carol was the first to object. "Just because you are the least fashionable person I know, Ursula, doesn't mean you have to stick up for that lunatic."

Ursula burst into raucous laughter. "Lunatic? Look who's talking, Ms. Valium."

"I will have you know—"

Hoping to break up a fist fight, I stood next to their table, not sure if they were seven or seventy, and asked, "What do you all have against Enid Walsh?"

"Aside from the fact she makes up every story she writes in that gossip column of hers?" Margaret asked, peering at me over her teacup. "Absolutely nothing."

Carol raised her thin eyebrows. "She didn't have to make things up when your husband had an affair."

"What married man hasn't had an affair?" Margaret asked as she reddened.

Ursula flashed a smile. "Not my Charlie."

Margaret scowled. "Your Charlie is dead. Who knows what he's up to in the afterlife? The poor guy's probably busy making up for lost time."

"I do," Ursula replied. "I talk to him every morning in the garden."

Joanne huffed. "I'm sure you do. How's your puppy doing, Laken? Gill told us all about the little dear. He's an English Sheepdog, isn't he?"

"Yes, and he's growing fat on a steady diet of underwear and socks," I told her. "Any ideas on how to stop him from eating my clothes?"

Margaret grimaced. "Clean your room and don't leave them lying on the floor."

"I don't." I gasped. "He's like a short, furry magician. He gets into my dresser at night. Why did you say Enid makes up everything she writes in her column?"

Carol stood and pulled a fifth chair over to their table. "Oh, darling girl. Sit."

Margaret frowned. "Don't talk to her, she fraternizes with the enemy."

"Laken's young and new in town," Carol said, wagging a finger. "She needs us to set her straight about the negative influences around Glitter Bay before she gets caught in the crossfire."

I took a quick glance outside to make sure I hadn't teleported into a war zone, then asked, "Which negative influences are those?"

Ursula offered me half of her shortbread cookie, but I declined. "Our Enid loves a good story, especially one she can embellish. A group of us even signed her up for a creative writing class to channel her creativity in a more positive way."

Carol nodded. "We thought if she got a chance to learn from a real writer, she might see the difference between reality and fantasy."

"And did she?"

Joanne sipped her tea. "Nope. If anything, that course made her even more incorrigible. She went from half-baked truths to full-blown lies."

"Has anyone ever sued her for libel?" I asked.

"Libel?" Margaret groaned. "No one reads her column anyway, and the few people who do usually have bigger problems to worry about."

Joanne gasped. "Do you think Tilly got upset with her again, so Enid did something awful to her?"

"Huh." I tapped one foot on the floor while I thought. "If no one takes her seriously, that might put her in a great position to get away with murder, don't you think?"

"Murder? Enid?" Ursula asked as her brown eyes grew wide. "You can't be serious. Her pen is far mightier than anything else she could ever wield."

Carol shook her head. "She might have a razor tongue, but she's not a killer. Even if she and Tilly did have a love-hate relationship for many years."

Margaret gave her friend's arm a quick slap of her teaspoon and said, "Hush. Carol. There are some things a lady just doesn't talk about."

Ursula laughed. "Good thing we're not ladies."

I chuckled, surprised by her reaction. "I thought you were all such good friends."

"Oh, we are, darling." Carol patted my shoulder. "But good friends also keep each other in line. As you can see, neither is easy."

"Well, since you ladies seem to know everyone in town, I wondered if you know someone by the name of Pricilla Cash?" I asked.

The Hens glanced from one to another amid a flurry of shrugs until Ursula finally shook her head and said, "I don't believe I've heard that name before. Does she live in Glitter Bay or is she one of those pesky developers who sniff around looking for a bargain?"

I glanced toward the front door. "I think she's a developer."

"Oh, really? Where did you hear about her?" Margaret asked, raising her brows.

"Someone left her business card on a table. I just wondered if anyone knew who she was or had met her." I flashed them a smile, then stood. "I'll let you enjoy your tea. Just give me a shout if you need anything."

I wandered into the kitchen to do more cleaning yet stayed within earshot. As I listened to them chatter for a few more minutes, I was amazed by the leaps in conversation from grandkids to classic cars to sex. Full out, bawdy stories, nothing ladylike at all. My face burned. Eventually, talk shifted to Gill and, just as he predicted, how soon he'd be interested in dating and what they'd like to do to him. That was when I searched for earplugs.

During the next lapse of silence, I approached the table and asked, "How well did you all know Tilly?"

Joanne leaned closer before lowering her voice. "Well enough to know she didn't like Enid or her son and refused to let either of them set foot in the tea house."

"Enid has a son?" My heart fluttered.

Ursula raised her eyebrows, then looked me over. "Don't tell us she hasn't tried to set you up with her handsome, still-single son, Andy the paramedic."

Andy? I frowned. "I didn't realize she was married."

Margaret smirked. "Enid Walsh was never married that I know of. Nor will she tell a living soul who Andy's father is. Not even Andy, so I've heard."

I kept one eye on the clock as I waited for Enid to return. If we did go shopping, this would be a trip to remember. What other secrets was she keeping?

A pang of guilt swept over me. Who was I to judge? I had more secrets than most of Glitter Bay put together.

Keyon showed up at quarter to five.

Enid still hadn't reappeared.

I let Sammy inside to say hello, disappointed I'd have to interrogate Enid about Andy some other time.

"I'm glad to see you," I said, forcing a smile. "Enid's coming and I need a buffer."

"Oh yeah?" He slipped Sammy a treat. "Why is Enid coming here?"

"Do you know Bryan Cash?"

He flinched enough that I noticed. "No. Why?"

I set a chunk of leftover ham on a plate to keep Sammy occupied. "He's the man in black I mentioned at dinner. Turns out, he's a developer from Portland looking to buy property, so Cash Enterprises can turn Glitter Bay into a resort playground town."

Keyon frowned. "By property, you mean the tea house, right?"

"Among others. From what he told us, it sounds like he wants to buy up most of Glitter Bay," I told him, sitting in the same seat Bryan had occupied that morning."

"Us?" Keyon slid onto the chair across from me. "Was Gill here?

"Enid." I debated telling him about her snap happy camera finger but hoped the newspaper would never publish her photos. Not without good reason. "Do you think many people around here would sell to a guy like that?"

"If he offered enough money, I'm sure most would jump at the opportunity," he said, tapping one finger on the tabletop. "I could think better with tea and a scone."

"They're not fresh."

Keyon smirked. "I just ended a twelve-hour shift. Even if they tasted like cardboard, I'd still eat them. Besides, I wouldn't want Gill to think I'm loitering. Where is he?"

"He had an appointment," I told him, getting up to make tea, so he couldn't tell if I was lying or not. "Probably to wrap things up with Tilly's estate so he can figure out what to do next."

"If he was smart, he'd sell this place and retire. Maybe you should think about buying it. You could turn this place into a great little restaurant."

I set two, day-old scones onto plates. One for Keyon and one for Sammy and placed them on the table. "Except, then I'd have to deal with guys like Bryan Cash by myself."

He shook his head. "I could run interference for you."

"You'd really want to take time off work to sit here and wait for him to show up?" I filled a silver tea ball with a scoop of loose Oolong tea. "I find that hard to believe."

Keyon took a scone off the plate then took a bite. Instantly, Sammy sat at his feet to beg. "You're right. Why don't we set up a meeting with this guy and—?"

"And what?" I asked, pouring boiling water over the tea ball. "Tell him we're not happy with his plans to take over Glitter Bay so he should hop on the first pirate ship out of town? I'm sure that'll work."

"Something like that."

I studied him from the counter while his tea steeped. "Why are you so hung up on me buying this place?"

Keyon shrugged. "It's already become Sammy's second home, and you can't tell me you don't enjoy serving tea and cakes to the regulars. I've seen you in action."

Carrying his tea to the table, I sighed. “I can’t help but wonder what Gill would do if he didn’t have something to get out of bed for every day.”

“True.” He raised one eyebrow. “But what if the tea house is tying him down? What if he longed to travel the world but stayed for Tilly’s sake?”

“I hadn’t thought of that.”

Keyon sipped his tea. “If you don’t make an offer soon, it may be too late. Your buddy Cash will shell out a fortune to tear this place down and put up a fancy hotel.”

I narrowed my eyes. If he’d never heard of Bryan Cash, how did he know what Bryan was prepared to do? Maybe it was simply a good guess. After Tilly’s funeral, I needed to have a serious talk with Gill. I hoped Bryan had enough class to wait that long before he did the same.

Until then, I had some research to do.

Chapter Fifteen

When Gill hadn't returned by five o'clock, I locked up and headed over to Vintage Sage, in time to catch my sister before she locked up.

"Can I borrow your computer?" I asked, flashing my sweetest smile. "I want to check out a few things."

"Like what?" she asked.

I pulled out the folder of newspaper clippings I'd stuck in one of the drawers. "To find out what the deal is with these."

She rifled through them, then met my gaze wide-eyed. "Are these the clippings you found in Tilly's trunk?"

"Yeah. Do you think they're the reason she wanted that trunk back so badly?"

"It's possible. Maybe she knew something about the heist."

I folded my arms across my stomach and blurted out the thought I'd pushed off all day, "Or she had something to do with it."

Sage looked down at Sammy, then back to me. "Now that I doubt. I'll take him home, so he doesn't eat any merchandise while you do research."

"He's had a busy day digging up Gill's courtyard, so he'll probably just sleep anyway."

"Still no call from his owner?"

I shook my head. "No. I've put posters up a couple times. Someone took them down. Whoever lost him doesn't seem to want him back."

"Uh-huh. He probably ate all their socks and undies." She gave me a hug, then walked Sammy home.

I locked the door behind them before turning the computer back on. There were a few things I wanted to check on and needed to make a list to keep my thoughts straight.

Number one, was to find out more about Pricilla Cash and Cash Enterprises.

The second one, was to learn about Anectine, especially since I wasn't sure how much I could trust Keyon. Handsome or not.

Thirdly, I wanted to go through any stories I could find about the diamond heist. Was there any way Tilly was linked to it?

I started with the simplest item on my list first. Anectine, also known as succinylcholine chloride, was normally used to relax muscles before medical personnel begin intravenous fluids. It had a half-life of one minute, so it wasn't traceable in the body once administered. People who took Digoxin, which Tilly might have taken, were at risk if Anectine was injected and could suffer abnormal heart rhythms or cardiac arrest.

Then I read a line that sent a chill over me.

Succinylcholine chloride worked by keeping muscles from contracting. Muscles used to breathe and move. Could someone have injected her after her heart attack to insert an IV? Could that be what killed her?

Since Keyon had stopped trying to resuscitate her, there was no reason for any intravenous medication, was there? No reason for anyone to inject her with anything, including Anectine.

Someone rattled the shop door. I glanced up as Enid waved through the glass. Rather than ignoring her, I walked over to the door, pulled down the shade, then went back to work. She knocked a handful of times before leaving.

Pricilla Cash's entire life was detailed online. A wealthy socialite who'd not only come from money but made millions of her own, her image was splashed all over both the Seattle and Portland society pages. She had high cheekbones and a cold stare, no matter what group she posed with. Her stylist had cut her hair in a silver bob that did little to soften her perpetually angry look.

Wherever she appeared, Bryan stood at her side like a grown-up version of a purse dog. He was movie-star handsome in a tuxedo but reportedly still single, although I was sure he could have his pick of any woman he wanted. Instead, he paraded his mother to society events. From the pictures, she appeared to be a couple inches taller than him and as thin as a model.

Speaking of models, I recognized some of the women Bryan did pose with on his social media sites. I'd worked with many of them. When I realized I'd strayed to chasing down the wrong Cash, I refocused. Yes, he was cute, but I was after information on Pricilla, not Bryan Cash's dating history.

Pricilla Alexandria Cash, aged sixty-seven, was the widow of the late Jorge Danforth-Cash, who took her last name after the wedding ten years earlier. Husband number four. Most of Jorge's information was the usual resume of the idle rich. Nothing of interest aside from a passion for horseracing. He was little more than arm candy.

I rubbed my eyes before clicking one more link. The screen filled with the same images I'd found on the newspaper clippings in Tilly's trunk. The sapphire and diamond necklace was stolen from Pricilla's family. Although she was only eighteen at the time of the heist, Pricilla was the sole witness.

My jaw dropped. Somehow Tilly San Vicente and Pricilla Cash were connected by that robbery, but how?

Someone knocked at the door once more.

"Go away, Enid." I printed off the information about the Cash family and the stolen necklace to peruse later. My eyes already burned as I yawned and checked the time. Sage would be wondering what happened to be.

Whoever was at the door knocked again, then rattled the doorknob. My sister would've let herself in. When the noises stopped, my gaze rested on the table where Tilly hit her head. I typed in Tilly San Vicente, but only articles about the tea house came up. It was like she had never existed anywhere off that stool. No social media. No new stories aside where her name popped up in several of Enid's articles. Not in a nice way.

If only I knew her family name. I tried to search for a wedding announcement for her and Gill. Old newspapers. Anything. No luck. I did find Abbie's birth announcement. Abbott Gill San Vicente born to Gabriella San Vicente. No father named.

Gill's family was starting to baffle me.

They had so many secrets that I wasn't sure where to look next. Finally, I blew out a breath and grabbed the envelope that held the information I'd printed along with Tilly's newspaper clippings. Somewhere inside were the dots I needed to connect.

It was already nearly seven o'clock by then. I'd searched for an hour and a half and was just as confused as when I started. Maybe dinner and a bubble bath would clear my head. Tomorrow was Tilly's funeral. If there was a connection between Tilly and the Cash family, one or more of them might attend. I'd have to keep my ears and eyes open.

I printed off an image of Pricilla Cash at a recent society event. No one with her presence could hide in a small town like Glitter Bay. I'd recognize her the second she set foot in the funeral home.

If she bothered to show up.

Chapter Sixteen

When I awoke the next morning, I stretched and nearly squashed Sammy when I rolled over to check the time. Seven-thirty. Sage must've brought him to my room during the night, yet I hadn't heard either of them. The long days in the tea house and working at the shop had taken a toll. Sammy had probably slept next to me all night. There was no newly destroyed clothing to suggest otherwise.

I wiggled a few inches away, with every intention of crawling out of bed to let him sleep. He closed the gap within seconds, then moaned. I curled a protective arm around him. Sleeping in on my day off wasn't such a bad idea since I'd worked far more hours than I should've. I needed rest. I closed my eyes and began to drift into a state of total relaxation. As my body seemed to float above the earth, images swam through my mind of Emery, Sammy, Keyon, Sage, Gill, Tilly...

Today was Tilly's funeral.

"Crap!" I sat up so fast that I nearly knocked Sammy off the bed. Reaching for the clock, I gasped. The funeral was at ten, and it was already nine thirty. How had I fallen asleep for another two hours?

No time for a shower. I tried to crawl around Sammy, but he blocked my path.

"You don't want me to get out of bed, do you, boy?" I asked, then rolled onto all fours to climb over him. As my feet hit the floor, so did his. Right in front of mine. I tripped over him and fell.

"I have to go," I told him. "Gill needs all the support he can get."

Sammy licked my face, then lay next to me with his sad eyes gazing up at me.

"Stop it."

"Laken? Are you okay?" Sage knocked at my bedroom door. "Who's in there?"

I crawled over to open the door. "Just Sammy."

"Oh." She was already dressed in her funeral best and carried a pair of black two-inch heels in one hand. "Are you almost ready to go? I don't want to be late."

When I opened the door all the way, she gasped. "Are you trying some scary new grunge look? I love the teddy bear pajamas, but the hair needs more gel."

"Ha. Ha. It's called bedhead." I ran a hand through my unkempt hair. "I slept in. Give me five minutes and I'll be ready to go."

"Five hours maybe." She walked away, laughing. "Hurry up. Keyon's here."

I groaned. "Great. Just who I didn't need to see this morning."

"Maybe not, but he's in the living room, so get dressed." She glanced back. "If you're not down in five minutes, I'll send him up to get you."

Sammy, the traitor, followed my sister downstairs.

"Can you feed Sammy and put him in the crate? I'll be right down."

"Yeah, sure."

I shut the door, then glanced around my bedroom. Four minutes and thirty-five seconds later, I made my appearance wearing a touch of makeup, a sleek black dress, and a metallic grey wrap I'd bought for an awards show I never attended. I grabbed the pair of matching grey heels with the least bite marks on them before I made my grand entrance.

"It's about time," Sage huffed. "Keyon, did you put Sammy in the crate?"

"He's in. Is Laken ready yet?" He asked, wearing a scowl. His anger faded when he noticed me on the staircase. "Oh. You look nice."

Sage looked me up and down then walked out the door. She didn't seem to appreciate my superpower to transform from bedhead to Cinderella in five minutes. Not a skill I was born with. Emery had brought directors, producers and studio executives home so often that miraculous wardrobe changes and transformations became second nature.

"I thought for sure you drove something with two doors and more power." Sage headed to the rear of a four-door blue car.

Keyon opened the front passenger door. "I do. I borrowed this to impress you."

She met my gaze before climbing into the back. "Nice."

"Looks like you're my copilot, Laken," Keyon said.

I buckled my seatbelt still deep-down tired. I closed my eyes and didn't force them open them until the car slowed. Keyon pulled into the parking lot of a small, white funeral home shaded by large elm and birch trees. The car barely came to a stop before my sister bailed out and disappeared into the building.

Keyon placed his hand on mine. "Are you okay?"

"I'm fine." I pulled my hand away to unbuckle my seatbelt.

"It can't be easy for you to be here today."

"It's a funeral. It won't be easy for anyone." I got out of the car and straightened my dress while my hands shook.

He walked around the car. "I just meant you were there when she—"

"That's why I need to be here. I don't want anyone to think I'm guilty."

"Do you think people will say you killed her?" he asked. "I don't believe that. I doubt anyone else will either."

Good to know he was on my side.

He placed my hand on his forearm while we walked toward the front door. Outside the weathered wooden doors, he paused. "Um, Laken?"

My breathing grew shallow, my vision swam, and my stomach fluttered.

"Are you sure you're okay?" he asked.

Nope. I was on the verge of a panic attack. "Uh-huh."

"Then could you please not dig your fingernails into my arm?" He patted my. "My hand's going numb."

I released his forearm to reach for the brass door handle, glad I hadn't had time for breakfast. My stomach churned. "I guess I'm a bit on edge."

"That's an understatement." He turned me to face him. "Take a couple deep breaths. We're here for Gill, remember?"

"I don't see a lot of cars here," I whispered.

"You did meet Tilly, right?"

Despite the empty parking lot, the funeral home was packed. According to the sign in the lobby, this was the only service planned for the day, so I assumed the current visitors were either here to support Gill—or to make sure Tilly was dead and gone.

Everyone seemed to glance our way when we walked in. Most of them had come to the tea house since Tilly's death. Some to extend their condolences, others to verify the of rumors floating around town.

Goose bumps raced up my arms as I muttered, "I shouldn't be here."

"You'd feel worse if you left," he said.

Someone tapped my arm. When I turned, Margaret asked, "Are you the cheap hussy who killed Tilly?"

"What?" My mouth dropped open as wide as my eyes.

Keyon cleared his throat. "No one killed Tilly. She had a heart attack."

"Don't be so rude, Maggie," Joanne, her twin, put an arm around her and said, "This is the young lady from the tea house."

Margaret huffed, "Oh, I remember all right. Then last night I found out this cheap harlot killed our Tilly."

"How did I kill a woman nearly three times my size?" I asked.

"You don't even know how you killed her?" Margaret asked as her blue eyes widened. "Some murderer you are."

Keyon steered me away before I said or did anything I'd regret. "She's fishing."

We made our way to where Gill and Abbie stood near a couple bouquets of flowers and a video screen that displayed a slideshow of Tilly's life on continuous loop. I pushed Margaret's accusations out of my head. As Keyon and I approached, Abbie nodded, then sauntered away. I didn't see Gabriella anywhere.

Gill smelled like rye and soap as he greeted me with a warm hug. "Laken, I'm glad to see you. Thanks for coming. I wasn't sure if you'd be here today."

"We're friends, right?" I gazed at the plain white urn standing next to an eight-by-ten photo of Tilly. Cranky as usual. "That's a nice picture. Too bad she didn't smile."

Gill flashed a sad smile. "I don't think that woman ever liked having her picture taken. Maybe on our wedding day and when Gabriella was born, but that was it."

"Why is that?" I asked.

"Some people are too self-conscious," Keyon said. "When cameras were invented, people were convinced they could steal souls."

"Judging by all the selfies on the Internet, that phase has passed," I told him, watching the slideshow for a few minutes.

In the dozens of pictures of Tilly that came up on the television screen, she didn't crack one smile. The more photos I saw, the more I understood that deep down Tilly San Vicente wasn't a happy person. Not necessarily angry, but possibly more depressed and frustrated than anything. What had happened to make her so sullen?

I was about to look away when a photo caught my attention. Two women and two men sat on an ocean dock. Tilly was much thinner and prettier when she was young. A much younger Gill had one arm around her waist and the other across the shoulders of a stunning blonde.

The blonde wore large, dark sunglasses and had a movie-star smile. She also had huge diamond earrings, a matching necklace, and what had to be a two carat blue stone on her ring. Beside the mystery woman, sat a man who resembled a young Sean Connery. Kind of like Bryan Cash. Was Pricilla a part of their past?

"Hello, Laken," Enid said. Her voice sent a shudder over me, and I took a quick glance around for objects within Gill's reach. "It's nice to see you here."

"I'm here for moral support," I told her.

"I'll bet you are." Enid raised one penciled-in eyebrow. "How convenient that you saw Tilly die and now you work with her widower."

So much for friendly conversation. The gossip columnist lunged for my jugular. Was she serious or trying to appear impartial? Enid wasn't the only elderly woman giving me a dirty look either. I seemed to have a target on my back.

"Leave her alone, Enid," Gill growled.

Keyon raised a hand. "Enid, can you give us a minute? We were discussing details for this afternoon."

"Oh, yeah?" She smirked. "What's this afternoon?"

Gill cleared his throat. "The reception."

"Yes. Of course. I'll see you there."

"I'd rather you didn't," he said.

I nudged Keyon and whispered, "And you thought I was being silly."

Gill scowled. "I'll bet that nitwit was the one who spread all those rumors."

My breath seemed stuck in my chest. "What rumors?"

"You haven't heard?" Gill snorted. "People are saying all kinds of things about us."

"About us? Like what?"

He placed a hand on my lower back to steer me away from eavesdroppers. "That you and I are lovers. We killed Tilly so we could be together."

I sputtered. "What kind of sick mind came up with that?"

Gill shot me a disappointed look that made me feel stupid for asking.

"Enid." I covered my eyes with one hand. "Why would she say that?"

"Notoriety." Keyon grimaced.

"That woman's already notorious," Gill reminded us.

I frowned. "Here I thought she wanted to be my friend."

"The word friend isn't a part of her vocabulary unless she wants something," Gill said. "She's a snake and you're best off keeping as far from her as possible."

The door opened and Gabriella walked in fashionably late to her mother's funeral. At least her ensemble was semi-appropriate. A fitted black dress that skimmed her knees and revealed less cleavage than usual, black four-inch heels, and a black hat with a veil over the top half of her face.

Keyon outright stared at Gabriella who made her way through the crowd toward us. His jaw clenched and he muttered, "Sorry for your loss, Gabby."

She ignored him and gave Gill a hug. "Sorry I'm late. Did I miss anything?"

"I didn't expect you to be on time anyway," he said.

The instant Keyon left Gabriella pulled Gill close. "Bryan Cash came to see me this morning, which is why I was late."

Gill frowned. "We'll talk after the reception. I have no idea why they want that place so badly, but this nonsense has to stop."

I hesitated, waiting until Gabriella went to greet mourners before asking Gill, "Who owned the tea house before you bought it?"

He shook his head. "I don't remember the guy's name. He died years ago, though. Natural causes, in case you have an itch to find another so-called murderer."

I winced as someone asked us all to join in the chapel.

The only person showing any real emotion was Abbie, who blew his nose and wiped his eyes several times. Since few in the community could find nice things to say about Tilly, only Gill and Gabriella spoke. Everyone else sat in silence until the brief service ended. With no burial and the reception at the tea house, no one stuck around any longer than necessary. The funeral home was empty within ten minutes.

"Where's Keyon?" Sage asked. "We're going to the tea house for the reception."

"I'm not sure. I lost him in the crowd."

"We'd better find him, or we're walking," she said. "I'm heading to the bathroom first. I'll be right back."

"I need some fresh air. I'll wait outside." I began to push the side door open as my sister walked away. I'd barely opened it a crack when I heard voices on the other side.

"You had one job to do," a man growled.

I shrank back, leaving the door open enough to hear. Ten feet away, Bryan Cash glared at someone hidden behind the door. I hadn't seen him at the funeral. I tried to peer around the wood without giving myself away but didn't have much luck.

"I'm taking care of things." Another man said, his voice vaguely familiar.

"Stop getting sidetracked. Just finish the job so we can get out of here."

"Consider it done."

"We'll see." Bryan walked away to his car.

I let the door close softly, then leaned against the wall. My heart did a cha-cha while I struggled to figure out what I just heard. I'd barely gathered my wits about me when the front door opened. I clutched my chest.

"Are you two coming?" Keyon asked. "I've been waiting in the car for ten minutes."

"In the car?" I stared.

Sage stopped next to me as he said, "Yeah. I told you I had a message from work and needed to check in. That I'd meet you in the car."

Odd. I didn't remember him saying anything before he walked away. My mind seemed to wander a lot lately. What was wrong with me?

This time, I sat in the backseat and gazed out the window as he drove to the tea house in silence. I didn't feel up to any sort of conversation. I shuffled up the sidewalk toward the tea house, already dreading the stares I'd endure and wished we could skip the reception all together.

"Wow." Sage stopped in the doorway. "I can't believe this many people fit inside the tea house. It's bigger than I thought."

Food and people already filled the tea house. I spotted Gill with Ursula and Joanne at the counter near a gigantic urn of coffee. As I wove through the crowd, I became aware of someone following close behind. When I stopped, someone ran into me from behind.

"Oh, sorry, dearie," Enid said, patting my back.

I spun around and grabbed her by the arm. "What are you doing here? If Gill sees you, he'll create another scene."

She shrugged. "Do you really think he'd throw things with all these witnesses?"

"He's done it before," I reminded her, steering her toward the door.

"I came to pay my condolences, so that's what I'm doing," Enid said, spinning out of my grasp. "Whether he wants me here or not, he needs to give me some answers."

When she tried to push past, I refused to budge. "Answers about what?"

Enid scowled. "I want to know why Gill killed his wife."

I didn't notice we'd become the focal point in the room until the accusation left her mouth. Silence fell over us like a bucket of confetti. Near the buffet table, Keyon covered his eyes with one hand. Sage's jaw went slack.

"Oh, come on, people," Enid said, hands on her hips. "You can't tell me no one else thought the same thing."

Margaret approached us, scowled, then put an arm across Enid's shoulders. "I did."

"My wife had a heart attack," Gill shouted, lumbering across the room as though someone had waved a red flag. "And I will not have either one of you spreading malicious gossip under my roof."

"Are you asking us to leave?" Enid asked, taking a step toward him.

"No, I'm telling you to get the hell out of my store or I'll call the police. Don't let the door hit you on your way out."

Margaret smirked and folded her arms across her chest. "You go right ahead and call the police. We have evidence."

I gasped. "You do?"

Enid's eyes grew wide, and she asked, "We do?"

"Yup. Show them, Enid." Margaret huffed. "You said you had proof Gill killed the old witch, so whip it out."

Gill's nostrils flared. "Get out right now or I'll see both of you behind bars."

Enid cleared her throat before she muttered, "I said I thought he killed her. Big difference, Maggie."

"This isn't the time or place," I told them, fighting to keep my voice calm even though I shook inside like a scared bird.

"Laken has a point." Enid shifted as her gaze darted around the room. "Come on, ladies, let's go back to my place to regroup."

Margaret placed her hands on her hips. "I didn't come to that ninny's funeral for nothing. There are rumors going around, and I demand to know the truth."

Gill's face grew darker by the second. "If you don't get out of here, I'm going to throw you out."

"Come on, Maggie. We have better things to do." Enid grabbed Margaret's arm.

"Damn straight," Margaret replied. "We need to go through that evidence you found. If Gill won't talk to us, the police will."

I closed my eyes as they left the tea house. Truth was, I did have mounting evidence. I just didn't know who it incriminated. All Enid had so far were photos of me arguing with Bryan, which she'd likely find a way to use against Gill.

"You attract some interesting people." Bryan stood next to me.

Oh, great. "What are you doing here, scavenging?"

"Gabriella asked me to stop by He flashed a smile. "I thought appearing at the reception was in better taste than at the funeral."

Sage put an arm around me. "Let's get out of here."

When I glanced back to Bryan, he was gone. I searched the crowd but didn't see him. Had I imagined him? "What about Keyon?"

She pointed to the back corner, where Keyon stood deep in conversation with Gill and an older man. "He won't even notice we're gone."

"What if Gill needs help cleaning up?"

Sage grimaced. "Then he would've asked you to stay. You need to get some rest, Laken. It's been a long week, and you have dark circles under your eyes. The cleaning can wait until tomorrow."

I followed my sister through the crowd, pausing to look back when I closed the door behind me.

Keyon, still engrossed in discussion with the two men, flinched when Gill shook his head and walked away. Whatever their conversation was about, Gill was done listening and Keyon didn't look happy.

"I have a huge favor to ask," I asked my sister as we walked home.

"Forget it. I told you not to get involved with him."

"Who?"

"Keyon," she said. "I refuse to run interference, so don't ask. Tell him you're not interested."

The problem was part of me was interested, just not the part that did the rational thinking. "Remember that syringe I found? I need someone to run tests to tell me what's inside."

"I don't know any psychics."

"I was thinking more like someone who has access to a lab." I hesitated. "Like a vet."

She shook her head. "Oh no. I will not ask Cameron Dale for a favor. He's flirted with me ever since I moved to Glitter Bay and applied for a job at the clinic. I'm tired of fending him off every time I turn a corner."

"I'll come with you." I grabbed her by the shoulders. "I'm the one who will owe him a favor, not you. I just need to know if the liquid in the syringe is the same as in the vial I found."

Her face paled. "You never told me about a vial. What's in it?"

"Anectine. Sammy dug it up in the courtyard of the tea house. I need to know what's in the syringe before I take it to the police."

Sage closed her eyes for a second then sighed. "Cameron's a vet. What does he know about human drugs?"

"Probably just enough." I glanced back to the tea house. Still no sign of Keyon, which was good. "All he has to do is test them and tell me if they're the same."

"Why don't you just take it to the police?"

"Because I want proof before I go to them," I told her. "Even with solid suspects, if I can go in with a smoking gun, so to speak, they'll listen."

She shook her head, then resumed walking. "Okay, but first I need to change. I don't want Cameron to think I'm coming on to him."

"Don't worry. I'll do the talking. You and Sammy are just my way in."

Sage groaned. "You're going to involve Sammy in this?"

"He found the vial and Cameron is a vet. I'll tell them Sammy ate something he shouldn't have. That'll get us past the receptionist."

"That's an awful idea."

"Do you have a better one?"

I let Sammy out into the backyard while I changed. The entire time, Sage ranted about how much I owed her for having to make nice with Cameron.

"Why do you hate him so much?" I asked. "He's a good guy and he likes animals."

My sister stopped muttering long enough to stare. "Are you serious? He's so...He's just... He's an idiot." She growled and turned away.

"Oh. Well, that clears that up," I chuckled. "I'll get Sammy."

"For the record, I still think this is a bad idea."

I rolled my eyes. "Then do it for Gill. I need answers, and this is the best way to get them. Are you coming with me or not?"

"If I say not, you'll be made at me." Sage followed me out the door but remained quiet all the way to the vet clinic.

As agreed, she let me do all the talking. Once in the examination room, she stood with her arms crossed like a sullen child until Cameron walked in. Suddenly, she fidgeted with her hair and found a poster of a dog's anatomy fascinating.

The vet halted in the doorway and sucked in a sharp breath. Any air of confidence he had before entering the room was gone. "Sage."

I glanced from one to the other before clearing my throat. "Hi, Doctor Dale. Laken Miller. You remember Sammy, don't you?"

His gaze still hadn't left my sister. The room suddenly felt crowded and hot.

"Of course, I do, Blake." He closed the door and scratched Sammy behind the ears. Call me Cameron. What can I do for you and Sammy today?"

I didn't bother correcting him for mangling my name. Instead, I pulled out the bags with the evidence Sammy had found. "I need a favor. Can you test the liquid in this syringe to see if it's the same as what's in the vial?"

Suddenly I had Cameron's full attention. His mouth dropped open and he stared at me with the widest, bluest eyes I'd ever seen. "Can I what?"

"You heard her," my sister said, snapping out of her pout. "Laken needs these tested and to get the results as soon as possible. She's trying to catch a killer."

"Are you a cop?" Cameron asked me.

Sage shook her head. "Laken thinks Tilly San Vicente was murdered."

"And this syringe could be the smoking gun?" Cameron blinked like he had something in his eyes. "That is so cool."

"Not really," Sage muttered.

"I love a good mystery." He grinned. "So, all you need is for me to run tests on the syringe and the vial? Sammy's okay then?"

"Sammy's fine," I told him. "He was just an excuse to get in to see you."

"I'm flattered. I mean, that's good." Cameron took a paper bag out of the cabinet in the corner. "Stick the stuff in here. I'll put a rush on this."

I sighed in relief. "That's great. Thanks. Make sure to bill me for the lab fees. Just don't throw out the vial or the syringe."

"I will. Uh, won't," he said. "Maybe you could do something for me in return."

Sage whimpered.

Even though I had the same sense of dread, I replied, “Name your price.”

Cameron rubbed the back of his neck. “When I do get the results, will you go out to dinner with me to talk about them?”

“Me?” I gasped.

“Laken?” Sage’s mouth fell open.

He shrugged. “Why not? Maybe dinner at Devil’s Peak Tavern?”

“I guess so. Sure.” While his request wasn’t what I’d expected, Sage was off the hook paying the price for my favor.

“Great. I’ll call you once I get the test results.” Cameron stuck the bag in the pocket of his lab coat then handed Sammy a doggie treat. “Take care. It was nice to see you.”

Once Cameron walked out of the examination room and closed the door behind him, Sage let out a squawk. “What the hell just happened?”

“I asked your not-so-secret admirer for a favor, and he asked me for a date.”

“Unbelievable.” My sister left us in front of the vet clinic and stormed off toward Vintage Sage.

Sammy and I headed for the beach. A date with the vet was the last thing I’d expected. On the upside, he could teach me more about taking care of Sammy. Too bad I had no idea how long the tests would take. I hoped I wasn’t getting in over my head.

Enid fell into step beside me, wearing a bright blue hat with a wide ribbon that had a pink feather tucked into it. The hat was the same shade as her hair. “What did Pricilla want? I saw you talking to him at the tea house.”

I wished she’d go away but told her, “His name is Bryan today.”

"Huh. Do you think he's having an identity crisis? Maybe he's one of those transgender people or something."

"His mother is his boss, and they happen to have similar business cards. What do you want, Enid? I thought you said your piece at the reception."

"I did," she said. "I'm lucky I didn't end up wearing an ugly flowered teapot for a hat. I should have worn a veil over my face."

"Trust me. He'd know it was you, even if you wore a bag over your head."

As Enid walked away, she froze and turned to face me with the tip of one finger beside her mouth and a grin on her face that reminded me of the Grinch when he had awful ideas. "I just had a thought."

I knew it.

"Why don't you buy the tea house, so everyone's safe to go inside?"

Had she spoken to Keyon or Bryan? Not possible. Unlike Gill, they'd run when they saw her coming. "Why don't I what?"

"You and I could buy the tea house together. How hard could it be to run the place? I could wait tables and make tea. When things were quiet, I could work on my columns. You could work on...whatever you do."

Her ulterior motive suddenly became obvious. She could get fodder for her gossip column without ever leaving the building.

"I'll think about it," I told her. "No promises."

"That's all I can ask."

I rolled my eyes skyward and shook my head. Teaming up with Enid would never happen. Ever.

Sage texted me around four and asked if I'd close the shop for her at five since she had errands to run. I locked Sammy in his crate, then meandered to the shop in time for her to rush out past me carrying a big purse that had gathered dust on the shelf for ages.

With the gut feeling she was up to something, I wandered through the shop until my gaze fell on Tilly's trunk. Something about those gowns nagged at me. I wanted to take a closer look at the glittering stones that adorned them but the lighting in the shop wasn't the best for examining crystals. I'd need some place brighter.

My hour at the shop dragged. I spent more time surfing the Internet than working, but by the time I left, I had a plan.

Sage had a great light in her office that she used if she needed to make repairs on jewelry or other items in the store. With any luck, she'd be out late, and I could sneak the gowns home to inspect. She'd likely want to strangle me when she found out.

I locked the front door, pulled down the blinds, then entered the changing room. The wedding gown and flapper dress hung in garment bags. The thought of being attacked by the wedding gown again unnerved me.

It was a tight squeeze to get the garment bags, me, and my purse through the cluttered hallway to the back door at the same time, but I managed. Slipping out the back way, out of sight of Enid and everyone else, I smuggled them home via the back alleys.

Luckily, Sage wasn't home when I got there. I half dragged the gowns up to my closet and tucked them in the back. Of course, I'd have to tell my sister I took them Perhaps by then I'd figure out what bothered me about them.

After dinner, Sage and I cleaned up, then read Tilly's old newspaper clippings. We tossed ideas around about what she had to do with the trunk and diamonds.

"It's possible someone stole the necklace and removed the stones from their settings," she said. "But then what?"

I shrugged. "If they tried to sell loose stones, someone would've reported them."

Sage nodded. "They might've reset them."

"But what about the sapphire?" I asked. "No one would dare to recut it. Not to mention all the gems were various sizes and shapes."

"Either way, they'd be difficult to sell without someone noticing." Sage said. "I need to do some paperwork. You need anything?"

"No." I yawned. My head hurt and I was no further ahead. "Oh, yeah. Can I borrow your craft light?"

My sister stared. "You're doing crafts now? Do I know you?"

"I'm turning over a new leaf."

"Show me what you're working on."

I hesitated, then admitted, "I brought Tilly's gowns home."

Sage scowled. "I knew it! Bring them to my office."

Sammy followed me up the stairs and bounced around my feet when I opened my closet and pulled out the black garment bags. As much as I wanted to be right about the glittering stones on the gowns, I didn't want Tilly to be a thief. Gill and his family had enough to deal with. On a whim, I also pulled out the beautiful gown I'd dreamed of wearing on a red carpet and the jeweler's loupe from the top drawer of my dresser.

When Sammy followed me into Sage's office, she shook her head and nudged him into the hallway. "Nuh-uh. If you're right about those gowns, the last thing we need is your dog taking samples. He stays out."

"I'll give him some food to keep him occupied," I told her.

By the time I took Sammy to the kitchen, then returned to Sage's office, she'd stripped both dresses of their black outer shells and had hung them on either side of the closet door.

"Not that I think you're crazy, but what makes you think those stones could be the missing diamonds?"

I met her gaze. "Enid commented on how Tilly was an amazing seamstress. If she was that skilled, she could've sewn the unset diamonds onto one of these gowns, which is why she wanted that trunk back so badly."

My sister gazed at the gowns in awe. "For real? How are we supposed to know for sure? It's not like we're trained jewelers."

Holding my loupe in my hand, I shrugged. "I asked a jewelry designer I modeled for to show me how to tell the expensive stones from the knock offs. The loupe was a gift from him, so I could practice."

"Just when I think I know everything about you," she said with a grin. "How are you going to get a good look at those stones?"

I unfolded the loupe to reveal the magnifying glass. "Turn on your craft light and I'll figure that out."

After a couple attempts, I ended up getting Sage to hold the gowns beneath the light while I used the lens, which had a standard magnification of ten times, to examine every stone on the bodice of the wedding gown. Not satisfied, I checked them all once more before I finally sighed.

"Nothing," I admitted. "They're all fake."

Sage glanced toward the closet door where the flapper dress and the blush gown hung. "We're not done yet."

"Yeah. It's just I was so sure they were on here."

She stuffed the tulle skirt of the bridal gown into the closet and reached for the flapper dress. "We'll do yours last, okay?"

"Sure." I nodded.

Was it possible Tilly San Vicente had sewn the stolen diamonds onto my blush, two-piece halter-style top? I focused on the task at hand and examined everything that sparkled on the flapper dress.

"They're fake, aren't they?" Sage asked.

"Yeah."

She grinned. "One left."

My hands began to sweat and shake. "What if...?"

"If those diamonds are real? We talk to Gill. He can decide what to do."

My sister hung the flapper dress in the closet with the wedding gown and handed me my blush gown. She stuffed every inch of fabric inside before closing the door and facing me. "Let's do this."

I wiped my hands on my shirt, then resumed my position. By the fourth stone, my heart was racing. My legs grew weak after the tenth sparkler. "Sage?"

"They're real?"

Meeting her gaze, I nodded. "Maybe you'd better keep this one in your office closet. Just in case Sammy gets any ideas."

"Uh-huh."

I knew exactly what she was thinking. That blush gown was worth more than her entire house. I doubted she'd get much sleep that night. Nor would I.

"Now what?" she asked.

"We put them back in the bags and pretend we aren't sitting on a stash of stolen diamonds for tonight."

Sage smirked. "Yeah. Right."

The doorbell rang just as we got all three gown into their respective bags and locked inside the closet for the night.

Sage shook her head. "Don't answer it. I don't want to talk to anyone. I'm going out back to meditate."

After five more persistent rings, a glass of water for me, and several barks from Sammy, I opened the door and stared.

"Gabriella. What are you doing here?"

Hair tousled and eyes glazed, she pulled a black pashmina tighter around her shoulders. "May I come in?"

My gut instinct was to send her back to wherever she'd come from—Portland, the depths of hell, whatever. I was tired so curiosity won out over sanity. "Sure. What's up?"

"This is where you live?" Gabriella stepped inside and wrinkled her nose before she glanced at Sammy, who instantly stopped barking and hid behind me. "I wasn't aware Glitter Bay had slums."

"My sister was right. I shouldn't have opened the door. Good night."

Gabriella raised a tanned hand. "No, Laken, wait."

I braced, ready to shove her back out onto the street if she made one more nasty remark. "You're sucking up all the positive vibes in the room."

"You sound just like your hippie sister." She rolled her eyes.

Not sure that was a compliment, I gave her one last chance.

Gabriella took off her pashmina to reveal too much cleavage beneath very little black dress fabric. No wonder she had her pick of men in Glitter Bay, probably including Keyon. She clutched the pashmina in one hand and licked her lips.

"I wanted to talk to you about my father," she said, trying to sound sultry but slurring more than she probably realized.

"Gill? What about him?" I tried not think about Keyon romping with the sex goddess in front of me.

"I want you to stay away from him," she whispered. "My dad may be an old man, but he doesn't need your help any more than Abbie and I do."

I didn't recall offering my help to either of them to begin with. "Are you trying to say I have no business working with Gill at the tea house?"

She twirled a strand of black hair around her index finger. "That's exactly what I'm saying. Women like you are just after his money."

Was this woman flirting with me, or trying to get rid of me? I couldn't help but laugh, which startled Sammy. He ran up the stairs.

"What type of woman do you think I am?" I asked.

"A gold digger."

"I see." I raised my eyebrows, more than mildly amused. With the amount of money my ex had forked over, I was the one who needed to beware of gold diggers, not Gill. She could've found out from someone else in town—Enid—or from the Internet, the way Keyon had. "Gabriella, I'm not interested in your dad in that way."

She went from smug to appalled in three seconds. "What's wrong with him?"

"He's old enough to be my grandfather," I reminded her. "Besides, his wife just died and he's grieving."

"So?" Her eyes widened as if she genuinely didn't understand the problem. A heartbeat later, she flashed a sly smile. "Maybe you just don't like men. Do you?"

"What?" I took a step back.

Gabriella touched her finger to my lips. "It's okay. I know you're divorced. I'll bet you'd rather be with a woman who can make your body hum."

I reached past her to open the door. "Lady, you are messed up."

"Me?" She huffed. "You're the one living with some hippie in a backward town instead of living the high life in Europe or New York. Honey, you and I could take this world by storm."

"That hippie is my sister and you've obviously heard about my ex. Money isn't everything, Gabby. There's more to life than dollar bills."

She draped her pashmina around her bare shoulders. "Yeah? I know how to ruin women like you, princess. Keyon Blake will never look at you again once I'm done."

I had no idea what she was talking about and was afraid to find out.

Gabriella sashayed down the front steps and toward a black car parked in front of Sage's house. Rather than climb into the driver's side, she opened the passenger door. As the night air swept up my bare legs, I caught sight of the man in the driver's seat.

Bryan Cash.

Chapter Seventeen

My phone rang early the next morning. I didn't dare open my eyes more than a crack as I answered with a groggy, "Hello?"

Gill's voice was raspy. "Meet me at the tea house.

"Is everything okay?" I asked, but he'd already hung up.

Curious, I rolled out of bed and got dressed. Skipping breakfast, I snapped on Sammy's leash, and went to see what was going on. On a whim, I tossed the envelope of newspaper clippings and a small bag of dog food into my bag.

As I got closer to the Sweet Eden Tea House, I noticed the porch furniture in disarray. A table overturned. A couple chairs broken and repainted in neon colors. Graffiti spraypainted on the yellow siding along with some obscure design I'd seen somewhere around town.

The front door stood wide open.

Heart pounding, I scooped Sammy into my arms and ran up the steps, shouting, "Gill? Where are you?"

"Over here." He sat on the floor against one of the tall stools near the front counter. Blood crusted the side of his face from a cut near a dark lump on his head.

I picked my way across the room, careful to avoid glass shards and debris. Once I reached Gill, I crouched to examine the lump rapidly turned a frightening purple. "Are you okay? Do you want me to call an ambulance?"

"I'm fine. I just can't believe someone would trash the place. Even my apartment's a mess."

Sammy squirmed in my arms. He wanted down, but the floor wasn't safe. Instead, I peeked out the kitchen door. The courtyard sat untouched. My stomach churned. Either the vandals had no idea it was there, or the graffiti and damage had a darker purpose that just to cause a nuisance.

"What were they after?" I asked, returning inside to help Gill to his feet.

"I'm not sure," he said, shaking his head. "I heard noises late last night. When I came down to see what was going on, someone hit me from behind. I woke up to this."

I couldn't imagine how he felt. "This might sound weird considering everything, but did you know what was in that trunk Abbie brought to Vintage Sage?"

He stared for an uncomfortable moment, then sighed. "A bunch of old clothes. When Tilly asked me to bring it down from the attic, I didn't think twice about getting rid of it."

"Without asking her?"

"Yeah. She was furious. That could be what triggered her heart attack." He paused. "Did you find something interesting inside?"

I pulled the list and a second sheet of paper out of my purse. "A wedding dress and a couple other gowns, as well as a bunch of jewelry. Sage and I assumed it was fake."

Gill raised his eyebrows. "You don't think so anymore?"

Unfolding the photo of the necklace, I held it out to him. "Have you seen this necklace before?"

He shook his head and asked, "Was it in the trunk?"

"Someone created their own version of the Hope Diamond with a heart-shaped stone that was stolen nearly fifty years ago. I couldn't get many details about the robbery, except from some newspaper clippings I found in a hidden compartment."

"Tilly hid them there?"

"That's how it looks."

"Do you honestly think my late wife had something to do with a jewelry robbery fifty years ago?"

Regretting showing him the photo, I explained, "I'm not sure what to think. The stolen necklace was owned by the Cash family. The same Pricilla Cash who wants to buy the tea house." I glanced around at the broken china and overturned chairs. "From the look of things, they'll go to any lengths to get it back."

"Cash," Gill growled. "That punk kid of hers keeps pushing me to sell. They've been pestering us for years."

If Pricilla thought Tilly was involved with stealing part of her inheritance, maybe she began to pour on the pressure. It would explain both Tilly's heart attack and the vandalism of the tea house.

Rather than get Gill even more worked up, I told him, "The jewelry is paste."

"That's a relief."

"It's possible someone replaced the rhinestones on the gowns with ones removed from the necklace. I have no idea what happened to the sapphire, though. It would've been tough to pawn or hide."

Gill took another look at the photo, then rubbed his face with one hand. "If you're right about this, I might have a couple ideas."

He motioned for me to follow him up to his apartment.

The stairs were steeper than I expected. Bright and spacious, there was a quaint balcony closed off by French doors off the living room and a small kitchen near the flight of stairs. Perfect for one person.

Cozy for two. I was awed to see such an incredible view of the ocean and beach.

Gill pointed to a large, dirty fish tank in one corner. "That's one place the thieves didn't look. Tilly was militant about cleaning it and never let me help. She'd also never let me near her sewing cabinet. She kept it locked anyway."

I wove through the upended furniture and torn bedding obstacle course toward the fish tank and crouched to examine the stones in the bottom. None resembled a shiny blue sapphire, not even in size but it was hard to tell since no one had cleaned it since she died. I'd need to get my hands wet to do a thorough search.

As I rifled through the murky stones, I noticed a small, algae-covered treasure chest tucked into the corner behind the air filter. It seemed too obvious yet remained undisturbed. Reaching through the bubbles, I removed it carefully. The little chest was heavier than I expected. Was there a one hundred and seventy carat gem inside?

I held my breath, using one of my fingernails to pry it open. When I emptied the heart-shaped sapphire onto my palm, I gasped. It looked exactly like the one in the photo. "It's beautiful."

"Holy mother of pearl," Gill whispered. "Is that what you think Tilly stole? It must be worth a fortune."

"Last I read, it was valued at about twenty million dollars. At least that's what a similar one sold for at auction."

"And it's been in her bloody fish tank the entire time."

"Looks like. Who else could've known it was here?" I asked.

"If I didn't, I doubt anyone else did," he said. "I don't know, Laken. I can't see my Tilly involved in something like a theft. I've known her since I was twenty-two, for crying out loud."

"Some people are really good at keeping secrets." Just not my ex.

“What do we do with it? If someone’s after it, I don’t want that thing under my roof let alone in the fish tank.”

My heart thudded against my ribs as I closed my hand around the stone. “I can hang onto it for a while, if you’d like. Just until we sort this out.”

Gill nodded so vigorously he reminded me of a plastic hula girl on a dashboard. “Take it. Between the police and this mess… I really don’t need the headache.”

I sat next to him still holding the blue stone. “While we’re on the topic, I have to ask you about a weird rumor I heard.”

He snorted. “You of all people know not to have faith in rumors.”

“I know, but this one’s so crazy, I had to ask. Did Tilly ever chase anyone out of the tea shop with a butcher knife?”

“People still talk about that?” he asked.

My eyes grew wide. “Then it’s true? What happened?”

“Pricilla Cash happened. She showed up a few years ago. She and Tilly had a big argument, but I have no idea what it was about. Tilly chased her out of the tea house waving a butcher knife. Her foot slipped off the last step and she fell, snapping the bone just above her ankle. Geez, I hadn’t thought about that in years.”

“It sounds like Pricilla’s family has wanted the tea house for a long time.”

“I’m not so sure that’s what they argued about,” he said. “Tilly and Pricilla knew each other when they were young. They had a big fight and hadn’t spoken in years.”

“Are you up there?” someone called from the lower kitchen.

I reached for a lamp that lay on the floor. “I’ll get rid of them.”

“Relax. It’s Abbie.”

When the tall, blue-haired boy ran up the stairs to the apartment, I dropped the stone into my purse.

"Dude, you good? What happened?"

Gill rubbed his lump again. "Someone trashed the place. Would you do me a favor and call the police?"

"You didn't do that yet?" I asked.

Abbie took out his cell phone, told the operator what happened, then asked for medical attention for his grandpa. The kid wasn't as bad as I thought.

I took the opportunity to walk around the apartment while Gill took a deep breath.

Near the sliding glass doors sat an antique oak cabinet with a sewing machine on top. I ran my fingers over the light layer of dust settled on top. Memories of my grandmother teaching Sage and I to sew drifted through my mind.

I opened one of the top drawers and was surprised to see a sketchbook. Without thinking, I flipped open the cover, startled to see painstaking drawings of dresses and gowns. Enid had mentioned Tilly worked as a seamstress. If she was as highly skilled as it appeared, she might've been able to sew unset diamonds onto a gown.

"Cool place, huh?" Abbie stood behind me. "Grams never even had to leave the house. She got out of bed, hobbled down to work, then crawled back up to bed. Gramps did the shopping, ran the errands, and dealt with customers. All she had to do was sit on her stool and rake in the money."

"Maybe you shouldn't say things like that in front of your grandpa," I suggested.

"He's used to it. He says those things all the time."

Abbie helped Gill to his feet before I followed them down the stairs. In the tea house, Gill reached for one of the chairs and sat back down. Sweat beaded on his forehead.

"I'll go out front to meet the police," I told them. What if they wanted to search me or my purse? How would I explain the gigantic blue sapphire?

After taking photos and statements, the police left. Abbie and I helped upright most of the furniture, then I called Sage to tell her I wouldn't be at the shop. My call went straight to voice mail. As I hung up, I noticed a text message and two missed calls from my sister.

Just as I texted her back, my phone rang. Sage sounded out of breath. "Laken? I need you at the shop. It's an emergency."

"I'm at the tea house. Someone broke in and—"

"They trashed Vintage Sage, too," she said, her voice catching as if on the verge of tears. "It's a mess."

As I hung up, I met Gill's concerned gaze. "They broke into Vintage Sage, which means they knew about the trunk. Abbie, can you stay with your grandpa? I need to go."

He waved a paint-speckled hand. "No worries, dude. Can't serve tea without cups anyhow."

I walked Sammy out the courtyard into the alley and ran most of the way to Vintage Sage. My sister, her hair in a messy bun, paced in front of her shop wearing yoga clothes and gnawing on her already short thumbnail. One officer tried to question her. Another checked out the crime scene. Broken lamps. Torn clothing. The glass display case shattered.

"Did they take anything?" I asked, pulling her into a hug.

"Tilly's stuff and her trunk are gone. Those dresses..." Sage burst into tears.

"I brought those home yesterday, remember?"

She sobbed as Sammy stood against one of her legs whimpering. "You didn't take the trunk, did you?"

"It was too heavy."

"At least most of her things are safe."

"What about Tilly's jewelry?" I asked, unable to tell her about the sapphire in front of the police officers.

She flashed a quick smile. "Great minds think alike. I brought most of it home yesterday to photograph it before I had it appraised. Not that I doubt you, but Gill needs the help."

Once the officers were out of earshot, I whispered, "Doesn't this seem odd? Both the tea house and your shop were vandalized, yet all that's missing so far is the trunk."

"That we know of." Sage folded her arms across her stomach. "We need to talk to Gill later and find out what he knows."

"I asked," I told her. "He has no idea what's going on and can't see Tilly taking part in a robbery any more than we could. We did find something interesting though."

My sister's eyes grew wide. "You did?"

The police officers walked out of Vintage Sage and explained how there were far too many prints on every surface to get any good ones. They were sorry there was nothing more they could do. We just needed to keep our eyes open for missing items and invest in security cameras.

"I can't afford that," Sage said. "There's so much merchandise to repair and replace."

I gave my sister a hug as the officers shrugged and returned to their cruiser. "Come on. We might as well start cleaning up."

She shook her head and whispered, "I just want to go home."

I couldn't agree more. Whoever broke in knew about the stolen necklace, and Tilly's trunk. Did I say something to the wrong person or were the thieves involved in the original theft?

Immediately, Sammy began to snuffle around the shop.

"This isn't your fault," Sage said, closing the door behind us. "I blame Tilly. I'm calling a medium to get her out of here."

Raising my eyebrows, I wasn't sure if my sister was in shock or had lost her mind. "What do you mean? Tilly's dead, Sage."

She picked up a tissue box. "I know that. Since she died here, so she's haunting the place until we solve this mystery."

"You're getting a little woo-woo for me," I told her. "I'm not so sure banishing her to the other side is the answer."

When Sage sat on the floor with a deep sigh, Sammy trotted over to sit on her legs. "Do you have any other bright ideas?"

Pulling down the blinds, I reached into my purse and handed her the sapphire. "This was in Tilly's fish tank."

"It's huge! Is this from the necklace?" she asked.

"Yeah. I think it's one of the things they were after in the tea house. I didn't tell Gill about finding the diamonds, not yet."

My sister handed it back. "What are we going to do with it all?"

I wrapped the stone in tissues before I returned it to my purse. "I told Gill I'd take care of the stone. The less he knows, the safer he'll be."

"You hope."

Nodding, I echoed, "I hope."

Chapter Eighteen

We left most of the mess for the next day, too mentally worn to focus. Sage announced she had a migraine and went to her room for a nap. While no one was watching, including Sammy, I stuck the sapphire in the bottom of the garment bag with the wedding gown.

I needed time to think. Grabbing a notebook, I sat on the front step in the sunshine with a cup of herbal tea. I had so many questions that had to wait until Gill and Sage got through the worst of their shock. Dealing with a police investigations would be difficult. None of us knew what we were caught up in.

Taking a slow breath, I closed my eyes to meditate, listening to the birds and the ocean until I heard footsteps. Then Sammy whined and moved from my right side.

Keyon walked up the sidewalk while Sammy rolled around on the grass with his squeaky toy. "Hey, what's going on? The tea house was closed, so I dropped by the store, but it was locked."

"Somebody ransacked Vintage Sage and destroyed our inventory. They also hit the tea house. Gill's got a nasty lump on his head and has to close to clean up and restock."

He raised his eyebrows but didn't seem surprised. "Any idea what they were after?"

"Not a clue." It wasn't a total lie.

Keyon watched Sammy play with his toy for a couple minutes. "Looks like someone's having fun. Maybe we should set up a kennel for him in the backyard, so he can get some fresh air and exercise while you're at work."

Just like that he'd changed the subject. I played along. "You want me to leave Sammy alone? He's just a baby."

"You could hire a pet sitter or find a doggy daycare," he suggested.

My defensiveness surprised even me. "Sorry. I'm worried about everything that's going on. Gill and Sage have a lot to deal with and I'd rather keep Sammy close."

Keyon nodded, then reached out to take my hand. "Why don't I take you out for dinner tonight? Somewhere nice where you can relax and forget about all the craziness. Sammy can keep Sage company. It's a win-win."

I had so much to do. Figure out who wanted to trash both Vintage Sage and the Sweet Eden Tea House, help Sage and Gill, clean up after Sammy, wash my hair...

Did I really want to take the chance of falling into another relationship?

"Tell you what, I'll keep an eye on Sammy. You go change."

I glanced at my yoga pants and green T-shirt. The one Sage told me brought out the red in my hair. "What's wrong with what I'm wearing?"

He smiled. "It's not classy enough for where we're going."

"Qualify nice."

"A sexy dress. Shoes that don't lace up." He ran a hand through my hair. "And be sure to brush the tea leaves out of your hair."

"I knocked over a jar of loose chamomile leaves. I thought I'd shaken them all out. I should take a shower."

"Or you could go steep in a hot bath." Keyon chuckled. "Tell you what, I'll overlook the tea leaves and dust bunnies for today, just put on something nice."

I fluttered my eyelashes. "Oh, good. The tea leaves will come in handy if we run into a fortune teller."

He clapped his hands. "Chop, chop. Move it, lady, I'm starving."

"I glanced at Sammy and asked, "Can you take him in the backyard for a minute?"

"Consider it done, milady," Keyon said with a bow, then met my gaze. "Go slip into something more comfortable."

My face burned as I hurried up the stairs. What was I thinking? If Keyon Blake wanted more than an occasional dinner companion, he'd have to move along. I wasn't interested. Much.

I tapped on my sister's door. When she didn't answer, I sent her a quick text to tell her I was going out. I hoped she'd understand my choice was due to morbid curiosity.

As I opened my closet door, I let out a groan. My teething puppy had a taste for expensive, designer clothing and wasn't discriminating. Any pieces of clothing I'd left lying on the floor were now the most expensive rags I'd ever owned. Some outfits, once in pristine condition, resembled costumes for a ritzy zombie apocalypse movie. Something Emery would star in.

Tattered seemed to sum up my new wardrobe. Trashed casual. My gown from the Oscar awards two years ago. The full-length leather car coat Emery bought me in Italy on our honeymoon. My leopard print stilettos my ex loved. What was left of them now wasn't fit for chew toys. Why had I bothered to keep them?

I rifled through the clutter to find something cute, but not too sexy. And without teeth marks. It was my own fault for not closing my closet door.

A long, blue dress with a slit up the side of one leg? Too much skin.

The hot pink dress with a plunging neckline and bare back? Too little fabric.

A green, mandarin-collared halter dress that revealed my pasty shoulders and knees? It had to do.

I could suggest a shopping trip to Portland to restock Vintage Sage – and my closet. Maybe I'd convince my dad to look after Sammy. I could always bribe him with pizza, which Mom never let him eat due to his cholesterol levels.

I dressed, applied a quick touch of makeup—eyeshadow, mascara and lip gloss—then strapped on a pair of satin shoes and grabbed a pale pink pashmina. On the way down the stairs, I heard, "Sammy, stop that. Laken's going to throw us both outside."

Setting my purse and wrap near the door, I asked, "What's going on?"

Both of them froze in mid tug of war to look at me. Keyon let go first and Sammy ran under the table with his trophy. One of Sage's oven mitts.

"Here I thought you'd put on some jeans and a nice shirt," he told me.

I shifted uncomfortably. "You said sexy. I can go change."

"Don't you dare. You look amazing. I'll just have to take you somewhere nicer."

When my ex flattered me, he always had an ulterior motive. With Keyon, I had no idea what to expect. "Let me put Sammy in his crate, then we can go."

As I reached for Sammy, Keyon's hand collided with mine. Our gazes met and we pulled our hands back like nervous schoolkids.

"Sorry," he said, his face red. "Let me take care of Sammy. I don't want him taking a bite out of your dress, especially since it looks so good on you."

I ran my hands over the soft fabric of the skirt, not sure how to react. "Thanks."

For fifteen minutes Keyon struggled, chased, and got fed up with trying to wrestle Sammy into his crate. Finally, I tossed a couple dog treats inside. Sammy abandoned the oven mitt as he trotted into the crate.

"Your dog hates me."

I laughed. "Like you said, he's just a puppy. He loves to play."

"There's a difference between play and torment, you know?"

Ignoring the whimpers from the crate, we left the house. Was this what parents went through when they left their kids with a sitter? I should've stayed home to look after Sage rather than leave Sammy with her.

What if he choked on one of his treats?

What if he caught his paw in the wire door?

Worse, what if he ate his way through the wire bars and wrecked Sage's house? I'd never hear the end of it. My breath quickened. I should cancel dinner to help my sister.

"Laken, are you going to be present mentally or just physically?" Keyon asked, then paused. "That sounded wrong."

I tightened the pashmina around my shoulders. "I never thought I'd become so neurotic about having a dog in such a short time."

He draped his arm around my shoulders as we walked past the tea house toward the Devil's Peak Tavern. "He'll be okay. It's not like we'll be out all night. How's Sage doing? Did the police finish at the shop yet?"

"Yeah. There were too many fingerprints to bother dusting."

"That's too bad."

A tall man strode into the tea house. Bryan Cash. With Gill weakened by the burglary, this was an ideal time for the shark to circle back in for the kill. Fingers crossed Abbie was there to help. Why would Gill have left the door unlocked? Unless he was expecting someone to show up.

"Who's that guy?" Keyon asked.

"Bryan Cash. The man in black. He's been hanging around since Tilly passed."

"Wow. She hasn't even been dead a week yet."

"What do you mean?"

"Glitter Bay's a magnet," he said. "This whole town sits on prime real estate. If a developer got his hands on the tea house, he'd level it to make way for ocean front condos and make his investment back in no time."

I gritted my teeth, fighting the urge to bulldoze in and interrupt their meeting. Maybe I'd talk to Gill after my dinner date.

Date.

Suddenly the notion of going for dinner frightened me more than the concern Bryan Cash and his family had set their sights on Glitter Bay. Or that someone had searched both the Sweet Eden Tea House and Vintage Sage. Were they looking for the necklace, or trying to scare us all into selling? That made no sense. Sage didn't own her building.

As Keyon and I settled at a table near the fireplace, I spied Cameron Dale across the room with a woman. I hadn't heard from him about the vial and syringe yet. Maybe I'd call him tomorrow. While I'd done some research, I still had questions a paramedic could help with.

Once we had our drinks, I asked, "Can I talk to you about something?"

Keyon crossed his forearms and leaned on the table and met my gaze over the flickering candle. "What do you want to know, beautiful?"

If that's where his mind was at, this conversation was about to go off the rails in a big way. "What do you know about a drug called Anectine?"

His smile faded. "Here I thought you were going to ask something personal. Where did you hear about Anectine?"

I wasn't sure how much to tell him. "Sammy found an empty vial and I was curious what it was."

"Was he rummaging through the garbage again?"

My palms grew damp as I glanced around in case a server was on imminent approach. "He dug it up from under a rose bush. Have you heard of it before?"

"I suppose you think someone planted the vial at the tea house."

Since I hadn't specified which rosebush he'd found it under, my stomach slithered into a knot. Anyone could sneak into the courtyard to bury it since Gill didn't have surveillance cameras, which would be a problem figuring out who ransacked the tea house. Same for Sage. Lots of privacy.

I pretended I hadn't noticed his faux pas. "That's the most likely scenario. I doubt Gill would bury evidence in his own backyard to make it look like he's being framed. His fingerprints would be all over anyway."

"Unless he wore gloves," Keyon said.

That was possible. My mouth dry, I took a sip of sparkling water. "How would someone get their hands on that stuff?"

Keyon shrugged. "Syringes are easy, but whoever got the vial would need access to the drug. Anectine isn't something you can buy over the counter."

"What is it exactly?" I played dumb to see how much he'd tell me.

"A brand name for succinylcholine," Keyon said. "Laken, if Tilly was murdered, that vial you found could be the smoking gun. We should take it to the police."

"What do you mean?"

He met my gaze. "You haven't done any research, have you?"

"Between Sammy and helping Sage and Gill, I haven't had time." I waited for my nose to grow a couple inches to give me away. "Why? What is it?"

"A single injection of that stuff can mimic a heart attack in someone like Tilly who was both overweight and in poor health," he said, then took a swig of his beer.

"How long would it take to act?"

Keyon shrugged. "There wouldn't have been enough time for someone to give her the injection and hide the evidence before she collapsed. You would've seen the killer."

Unless they'd done so in plain sight later. I kept that gem of an idea to myself.

The server brought over a basket of warm biscuits and a plate of butter flowers. She flashed a smile at Keyon. "Your dinner will be here shortly. Can I refresh your drinks while you wait?"

I considered ordering a glass of wine to calm my nerves, but I needed a clear head, especially if Keyon tried to kiss me again, or Enid showed up.

"No, thank you. There's no rush for the food." Keyon flashed her an easy smile.

Rush. The word seemed to smack me in the forehead. Once the server left, I leaned toward him. "So that vial might not have anything to do with her death. What would happen if someone injected her with it while she was in cardiac arrest?"

He seemed to hesitate. "Andy did give her a shot when we arrived."

"What would Andy have against her?" He hadn't even made it onto my suspect list.

"Aside from her attitude?" he asked. "I doubt they even knew each other. Besides, he's a coffee drinker."

I sipped my water. "Either way, I'd better bring the vial and syringe to the police. They might not believe me, but at least I can give them what I think is evidence."

He shook his head. "I doubt it would help. I'll bet you a steak dinner the killer wore gloves and probably threw them away later."

"Then maybe Sammy and I need to keep digging," I told him with a sigh.

As I set my glass on the table, Keyon took my hand. His warmth sent a jolt of electricity through me. I flinched and tried to pull away, but he held tight. "This is my fault. If I hadn't gone on about Tilly's death being suspicious, you wouldn't be caught up in playing detective."

I cleared my throat. "Sage told me to ignore you, but then I found things that—"

Our server returned one more. This time, she stood next to Keyon. "Your dinner will be out soon. Can I get you anything else?"

Was it my imagination, or was she flirting with him right in front of his date?

"Everything's fine, thanks." Keyon held my gaze.

"Can I get you another drink?" she asked.

"Sure." He handed her his empty beer bottle. Once she'd walked away, he said, "You're right. Things do point to someone murdering Tilly, but I don't like you getting involved in with something that could get you killed. You've been through enough."

Killed? Now I did need a stiff drink. "Because I've been sick?"

Keyon gave my hand a squeeze and smiled. "Sick. Divorced. Homeless."

Technically, he was right. I had no home of my own. If I bought the tea house, I could move into the upper level, but where would Gill go?

As my ears filled with tears, I pulled my hand away and sat back, averting my gaze. "You've lived in Glitter Bay for a while. Do you know Pricilla Cash?"

Our food arrived before he could answer. The server asked, "Would you care for some freshly ground pepper?"

"No, thanks." We both shook our heads.

"Parmesan?"

Keyon seemed to force a smile. His voice sounded strained as he said, "We're good. No, thank you."

I dove straight into my seafood pasta, to avoid doing or saying anything stupid. Unfortunately, that only lasted for two mouthfuls.

Gabriella San Vicente walked into the room wearing a long, black sundress and a floppy hat. She was arm in arm with a tall man, who sat with his back to me before I got a look at his face. What if Gabriella planned to swindle Gill out of the tea house? Was she making a deal with Cash Enterprises behind her father's back or was there something else going on? The way Keyon spoke about her, it seemed likely she'd do something underhanded.

Keyon waved a hand in front of my eyes. "Did I miss something?"

"What?" A lone scallop fell from my fork.

The host had seated the man with Gabriella behind a planter, so only the top of his head was visible.

"I thought I saw someone I know."

Keyon turned to look. "Gabriella? Who's she with?"

"Should I go see?" I stabbed the scallop, then twirled my fork in the fettuccini.

"No," he said. "We should just enjoy a nice dinner without worrying about everything that's gone on lately."

"What do you want to talk about then?" I asked, taking a mouthful of pasta.

"Why did you and your husband split up?"

My throat constricted until I was sure I'd choke. Somehow, I managed to chew and swallow before taking a long drink of water. "I thought you knew all about me."

Keyon gave my hand a squeeze. "Only that your ex wasn't Mr. Attentive."

"There's an understatement."

"What does he do?"

Pretty sure he meant besides warm the bed of every starlet in Hollywood, I placed my other hand under my thigh. I didn't want him to see how bad I was shaking when I talked about Emery. "He's an actor."

Keyon appeared impressed. "Is he any good?"

"Somewhere between the A-list and the B-list," I told him.

"He sounds like a flake. Do I know who he is?"

"Probably. He used to be a big name." I needed to stop talking before I said something I'd regret. I popped a shrimp into my mouth.

During Emery's movie about Navy Seals, he broke a leg on set, started taking painkillers, then took up with one of his costars who fawned over him the entire six months of the shoot. Echoes of arguments long unfinished reverberated through my head. Deep down, I fought the fear I'd be alone for the rest of my life. With my dog and possibly a dozen cats.

I set my fork aside as my stomach churned. "I don't feel so well. I need to go check on Sage."

"I'm sorry," Keyon said. "I just wanted to learn more about you. In case you didn't notice, I kind of like you."

I gulped more sparkling water before pushing my chair away from the table. "It's been a long day. I can't do this right now."

"Let me pay the tab, then I'll take you home."

"I'm not ready for any of this. I need to leave."

Keyon motioned for me to sit down. "You're making a scene. Just give me a minute to pay the bill, and I'll take you home. You're overtired."

I placed my napkin over my barely touched pasta. "I just need some time alone."

As he protested, I made a hasty exit past Gabriella, who met my gaze. I no longer cared what she thought or who she was having dinner with. I couldn't breathe. I needed to get out of the restaurant before I threw up.

Fresh air greeted me as I pushed opened the door and collided with Joanne and Margaret. I rushed past them as they called out. All I wanted was to be at home beneath the covers of my bed cuddled with Sammy. If I was lucky, the negative thoughts our conversation had stirred up would wash away in a day or two.

I didn't look up until I was near the tea house. Even through a blur of tears, I noticed the front door ajar and the building was dark. "Oh, no. Gill."

My stomach seemed to do a double back somersault as I ran up the sidewalk, taking the stairs in two quick leaps, despite wearing heels. As I reached for the doorknob, I thought about the police and fingerprints. Instead, I used my foot to nudge the door open farther and called out, "Gill?"

When he didn't reply, I cleared my throat and spoke louder. "Gill? It's Laken. Are you here?"

My chest tightened as there was still no answer, yet I heard water running. My imagination raced back to life with thoughts of finding his body. On the verge of tears, I listened for a sound. Any sound over the roar of blood rushing through my body.

"Gill? Are you okay?" I tried a third time.

"In the kitchen," he replied.

"Oh, thank goodness. I thought something was wrong." I sighed as I walked past the counter and opened the kitchen door.

Gill's shirt was soaked with what looked like blood and he seemed startled when I shrieked. "What was that for?"

"What happened?" I asked.

He flashed a lopsided, sheepish grin. "The ketchup bottle exploded."

I doubled over to catch my breath. "You scared the daylights out of me."

Gill shook his head and wiped excess ketchup off his neck and hands with a blue dishcloth. "You need to stay away from Keyon Blake. He's making you paranoid."

"Yeah, I know. I went out for dinner with him tonight. It was a disaster."

His cheeks paled as he rinsed the dish cloth. "Somewhere public, I hope."

"Devil's Peak."

"That dress is too fancy for anywhere in this town."

"This is one of my only dresses Sammy hasn't eaten yet." A little white lie, but not far from the truth.

"How was your date?"

"Awful." I stayed well away from the ketchup. "He started to ask about Emery, and I kind of freaked out."

"That your ex?"

"Yeah. Emery Samson." I stared at a splatter of ketchup on the floor. "I'm sure you've heard of him. Everybody has."

"I used to like his movies until Sage told me about you," he said. "Now I'd rather watch anything else. That explains why you're drawn to Keyon, though. He seems more down to earth than that louse you married."

I chuckled. "I guess. He's a paramedic and doesn't run from people when they're at their worst. How bad could he be?"

Gill met my gaze. "I'll be perfectly honest with you, young lady. You need to stay away from him. He's one of those wolves in sheep's clothing. I did some asking around. When he was a kid, he got into fights and stirred up some real trouble."

"Back in high school, he and another guy stole a rival football team's mascot and shaved it."

"What was it?" I expected him to say a goat or a bulldog.

"A bear."

My eyes grew wide. "Are you serious?"

"Oh, don't get all wound up." He laughed. "It was only a mascot costume, but it cost thousands of dollars to replace. He was suspended for a week, plus he and his friend had to pay to have it replaced and to do a couple hundred community service hours. Misdemeanor kind of stuff, but people still hold it against him."

A chill swept across my shoulders. "Does he still get into trouble?"

"Not that I've heard, or he'd lose his job."

I thought a moment. "Do you think that's why he helps Abbie with the bikes and is teaching him how to repair motorbikes?"

"A penance of sorts? I never thought of it that way."

My hands had stopped shaking. "When did Keyon come back to town?"

Gill shrugged. "A year or so ago, I think."

"What do you know about Bryan Cash?" I asked. "He's come to the tea house when you weren't here."

"He's a developer from Portland. He showed up a few months ago for a good cup of tea and fell in love with the view. Now I can't seem to get rid of the guy." He wiped ketchup off the counter while avoiding my gaze.

I snatched the cloth out of his hand then turned his face toward me. "He wants to buy the tea house to tear it down, doesn't he? How much has he offered you?"

"It's not what you think, Laken."

My turn to frown. "What is it I think?"

"That he killed Tilly to send me a message."

I caught my breath as my heart fluttered. He wasn't wrong. "You're right, I did. But why kill her if it could get hung up in probate?"

"Because she owned the place outright and refused to sell it. With her gone, the tea house is mine. Cash thinks I'll hand it over since I can't take care of it alone."

"And if anything happened to you, the tea house would go to Gabriella, wouldn't it?" I asked, closing my eyes.

Was that why Cash was hanging out with her? Chances were, if Pricilla knew Tilly had the necklace, she'd filled Bryan in on why she wanted the property so badly.

"I'm going home. My head hurts."

Gill flinched. "I'll walk you. I don't want you getting cornered by Keyon."

"Thanks," I assured him. "Lock the front door behind me. I don't want anything to happen to you either. Seeing all that ketchup scared me enough for one night."

He nodded. "I'll be it did. Could you lock up? I'm going to scrub the kitchen, then take a shower before anyone else sees me. Go home and get some rest. And stay away from Keyon."

"Sounds good." As I locked the front door, I realized there was one person in town who likely had all the answers, whether she knew it or not. I pulled out my phone and called her. "Enid, what do you know about Keyon Blake?"

I practically heard her eyes light up over the phone. "The hunky paramedic?"

"Yeah. Since he works with your son, I'm sure you've heard stories."

"Do you want the good or the bad?"

I'd probably regret asking. "I want everything you know."

There was a brief pause while she tapped what I guessed was her keyboard in the background. "I can print everything and bring it to the tea house in the morning."

"That's not a good idea."

"You're right. No one should see the two of us together. I could pop it into an envelope and drop it in Sage's mailbox during the night."

I was about to tell her that would be fine.

"I have a better idea," Enid said, lowering her voice, which made me wonder where she was. "Tomorrow at noon, take the mutt for a walk and meet me at the beach below Devil's Peak Tavern tomorrow. We can be modern day pirates and exchange treasures."

Dread filled my stomach as I asked, "What sort of treasures?"

"You want to know about Keyon, and I'm looking for information you have."

I should've known Enid's help came at a cost. "I'm not giving you any of Gill's private information."

Enid chuckled. "Silly girl. You're not as anonymous as you think. I know who you are, and I'm prepared to tell all of Glitter Bay. I want the scoop on your ex-husband, Emery Samson, in exchange for my file on Keyon."

"Oh, wow." I clutched the phone to my chest. While I knew this day would come, I never guessed it would be at the hands of a blue-haired vulture. After a couple deep breaths, I held the phone to my ear. "Fine. You can have your exclusive in exchange for information about Keyon, plus everything you know about Gill and Tilly."

"That wasn't part of the deal," she squawked.

"It is if you want an exclusive."

She grumbled. "Okay. Gill, Tilly and Keyon for an exclusive about Emery Samson. It's a deal, but you'll have to give me extra time. I'll meet you at five o'clock tomorrow on the rocks below the Devil's Peak Tavern."

"Let's say five thirty."

"Fine." Enid snorted. "Don't forget to come in disguise."

"Sure. I'll be the woman pretending to walk my dog."

After I hung up, I remembered both the tea house and Vintage Sage would be closed. I could've met her first thing in the morning.

This way I had time to check in with Cameron about the syringe and the vial, and help my sister do some serious cleaning.

Chapter Nineteen

I took Sammy to the beach for a run the next morning—him, not me. The thick, black clouds were pregnant with what promised to be a torrent of rain, so we had to get out early. Water lapped at my feet as I threw a stick in the ocean for him to chase. Keyon had sent several messages. Even as I clutched my phone, I couldn't bring myself to return his texts or calls.

"Yoohoo, Laken!" a voice called from behind me.

I turned, half-expecting to see Enid wearing some awful disguise.

Instead, Gabriella stumbled across the beach, the heels of her black stilettoes jabbing into the wet sand as she ran toward me. She wore the same flowing black evening dress she'd worn at Devil's Peak Tavern the night before. Her long hair fluttered loose in the wind. The entire ensemble made her look like an exotic bird. She and Bryan must've had a good night.

I groaned, with no desire to face her any more than Keyon. While I wanted to outrun her, Sammy paused to wait. Some help he was.

"Laken, wait up." Gabriella tugged off her shoes to close the gap between us. "I need to talk to you."

What more could she possibly have to say after the other night? Although I'd love to find out why she was hanging out with Bryan Cash.

She caught up to me and Sammy, then walked alongside us to catch her breath while Sammy strained against the leash to sniff her. "Just so you know, Pilates is no match for a run on the beach in high heels."

I chuckled. "I'll bet."

"Look, I'm sorry about how I acted the other night," she said. "I had too many drinks and was under pressure."

"Apology accepted. Pressure from who?" I asked.

"The truth is, you've been a good friend to my dad, and I was miles out of line. I haven't exactly been a model daughter."

"What?"

"Yeah, I know. Total turn around, right?" She dangled her shoes by a thin strap off one finger. "Bryan and Abbie told me you're a good person. Abbie said you gave him cash to help with his bikes, which was nice. Not everyone understands him wanting to give something back."

Rain started to fall in fat drops that splattered small craters into the sand.

I veered toward the street. "I should go. I can't afford to get sick."

"Come with me," she said, grabbing my arm. "I have a key for my dad's place. We can hang out at the tea house until the rain lightens up."

"Sammy and I need to go home."

"I'm serious, Laken. I'd really like to talk to you."

When Sammy sneezed, I shrugged. "Sure. Why not?"

Gabriella held my arm until we stopped on the wide veranda of the tea house, then reached into her bra with a wink, then pulled out a key. "Best hiding spot around."

"You're lucky. My key wouldn't have much to stop it from falling out."

"Yeah, well, these babies cost big bucks." She laughed as she let us into the tea house. "Hey, Dad, it's just me and Laken. Are you here?"

We waited several seconds but didn't get an answer. Gabriella dropped her shoes near the door and went to grab towels. I coaxed Sammy to sit on the welcome mat. Instead, he shook water everywhere and trotted across the room. At least the place was no longer in disarray. Someone had spent hours scrubbing the floors and walls.

Gabriella returned with two thick, yellow towels. "That's weird. I thought my dad would be here, but he's not."

I shrugged. "He probably went to deal with the insurance company after what happened yesterday."

"Yeah. That was awful. It took me and Abbie most of the day to clean up down here. Dad didn't want us upstairs." She dried her hair, then draped the towel around her shoulders. "Do you want tea? I'm not domesticated, but I can figure out a kettle."

Laughing, I told her, "You dry off. I'll get the tea."

"Dad told me you had cancer," she said, following me to the counter. "I should be the one to take care of you. I'm kind of useless that way."

"You could see if there are any cookies left in the back. Sammy loves the scones."

"Is that your doggy's name? He's cute. What kind of dog is he?" Gabriella disappeared into the kitchen.

"English Sheepdog, but he's not mine. I'm trying to find his owner."

She returned a minute later. "We're in luck. I found a blueberry scone and half a small cheesecake leftover from the reception."

"That'll do." I pulled out my phone to let Sage know where I was but didn't mention who I was with. She'd probably run right over to drag me home.

In no time, Gabriella had cut and plated the two halves of pecan caramel cheesecake. She set the plates on a table near the front window and chose which tea she wanted. In an odd way, it was like being home with Sage.

"Why did you come over the other day?" I poured hot water into two small teapots and placed them and the cups on a tray. "Just to tell me to stay away from your father?"

"Mostly because I was drunk," she admitted, then turned to gaze out the window. "To be honest, it was a combination of alcohol, jealousy, and grief. All I ever wanted was my parents' approval."

"Why wouldn't they approve of you?"

"Because of the company I've kept."

"Bryan Cash?"

"Yeah."

"I saw you get into his car that night and at Devil's Peak last night. How do you know each other?"

"We met months ago." Gabriella carried the tray to the table. "Bryan approached me when he saw photos of the tea house on social media and wanted to sweet-talk my parents into letting me take over, so we could turn it into a resort. Together, we'd both have more money than we knew what to do with."

I poured her a cup of tea. "But your mom wouldn't go for it."

She picked up the cup and blew off the steam. "Actually, she wanted to sell this place and move to Arizona. She hated winters here. The damp was bad for her arthritis. My dad refused to give up the place."

That didn't make sense. Why kill Tilly if she wanted to sell the tea house?

"I thought my dad was crazy to think someone murdered my mom, but it's starting to make sense."

"How?" I was more confused than ever. "If your dad held back from selling the tea house, you'd think someone would murder him instead. Is it possible...?" I paused to take a deep breath. "Is it possible your dad killed her?"

"No. Maybe." She paused to take a deep breath. "I don't know what to think. The only person besides Dad who'd benefit from Mom's death is me, and I didn't kill her."

"What about Abbie?"

Gabriella smiled. "Abbie won't even swat a fly. The kid doesn't have a mean bone in his body. Why would he kill someone who kept him afloat financially?"

"Gill gave him the money, not your mom," I told her. "I saw him sneak some out of the cash register one day, then followed him to the hardware store before he went to his garage by the marina."

"He lives in the apartment upstairs, but I didn't realize he had access to the garage."

"Why not?" I asked. "Who owns it?"

She averted her gaze. "Andy Briggs. He's a local paramedic. We grew up together, Keyon, Andy, Jonathan, and me. After graduation, we went our separate ways."

Another question burned on my tongue. I saw no harm in asking since Sage would be just as curious. "Did you date any of them?"

Her face grew pink. "All of them. Andy and I kept in touch after I left town. I was pregnant with Abbie, and an embarrassment to my family. They sent me to Portland to live with relatives."

"Is he Andy's son?"

"You really don't know, do you?" Gabriella tipped her head to one side.

I pictured Abbie, then gasped. "Keyon's?"

"Yeah."

"Does Abbie know?"

Gabriella shrugged. "If he does, it wasn't because I told him."

Keyon and Gabriella had a son. A blue-haired, teenage delinquent who was currently on probation and rebuilt bicycles for kids in need. Did Tilly know the truth about her grandson? Not unless she'd figured things out and accused the right person. Keyon had pronounced her dead, but what if she was still alive before they loaded her into the ambulance? Gill was sure he'd felt a faint pulse.

If Tilly was the only other person who knew the truth, could that be a motive for her death? Maybe it had nothing to do with the necklace and newspaper clippings at all.

My head pounded as I asked, "Did your mom know about Abbie?"

Her shoulders slumped. "She might've guessed, but I never told her."

We changed to less depressing topics and chatted for over an hour while the rain pelted the windows. Aside from Sage, I'd never had girlfriends, so it was nice to sip tea, tell stories, and giggle. Cathartic.

Sammy hung out beneath the table until the front door opened.

Water dripped onto the floor as Gill stood in the doorway. "Now there's a strange sight. What are you two up to?"

"We discovered we both like Pina coladas and getting caught in the rain," Gabriella quoted the Rupert Holmes song.

"But we do like yoga and have more than half a brain," I added.

He shook his head. "I never thought I'd see the day my little girl would smile and crack jokes again. I'm going to have a hot shower and change of clothes. Carry on with whatever you were doing."

The moment Gill's apartment door closed, Gabrielle and I burst out laughing so hard we nearly fell out of our chairs as the sun peered through the clouds.

"That's my cue to take Sammy home," I told her.

She followed me. "I haven't had this much fun in a long time."

"Me neither." I clipped Sammy's leash onto his collar. "We'll have to do this again. Maybe you could come over for dinner. If you don't mind visiting the slums, that is."

Gabriella bowed her head. "I can't believe I said that. I was just jealous. Sage has such a cute little house. I'm so sorry we got off on the wrong foot, Laken. Abbie was right. You're a sweet person, and I'm glad you've been helping my dad through all this."

"Thanks for the tea and cheesecake," I said, then paused in the doorway. "I don't suppose you'd consider helping at the tea house. Your dad could use a hand."

She shook her head. "I think you're a much better fit here than me. I'm more of a coffee house girl. High speed and high maintenance."

When tires squealed out on the street, her smile vanished. An ambulance stopped in front of the tea house. Keyon got out of the passenger side before Andy drove away. When he noticed us, he scowled.

Gabriella met my gaze and shrugged as I led Sammy toward the sidewalk. "Good luck, Laken. I'll talk to you later."

Still in uniform, Keyon stormed toward me. "What did she want?"

"We got caught in the rainstorm and had tea together. She just wanted someone to talk to since her mother died a few days ago."

"Did she pour her little pumice heart out to you?" he asked, then scowled. "Trust me, the only person Gabriella looks out for is Gabriella. Stay away from her."

I bristled and backed away as Sammy led me toward the beach once more. Considering my ex spent years telling me who to talk to, who to trust, and what to do, I wasn't about to put up with his rant.

"Laken, wait. I'm sorry." He pinched the bridge of his nose between two fingers. "I came by to see if you were okay. You haven't answered texts, so I was concerned."

"I'm fine. Last night, I freaked out. I hadn't been on a date in a long time."

"I'm sure seeing Gabby and that guy walk in didn't help," he said. "I've known her my whole life and still can't escape her."

"I'm sure that's hard to do when you have a child together." The words popped out of my mouth so fast I wasn't sure which of us was more shocked.

"She told you?" His face paled so fast I thought he'd pass out.

Warned me more like. "I don't think she meant to. She was thinking out loud."

Keyon cleared his throat. "I'll see you later. I have some things to take care of."

Sammy whimpered as Keyon walked off in the other direction.

I hoped he'd stay away from Gabriella, since I was just starting to like her. I glanced back at the tea house with half a mind to warn her. I knelt to pat Sammy's head and lowered my voice. "Ignore him. Let's go burn off that cheesecake, then pick up something for dinner. Maybe chicken and Caesar salad."

We walked up the hill toward the vet clinic. When I opened the front door, Cameron's face lit up. He steered me and Sammy straight past waiting patients, whose owners shot me dirty looks, and ushered us into an examination room.

He closed the door and stood across the examination table from me before he said, "I ran those tests, careful to not contaminate the vial or the syringe. You were right, Laken, they both contained Anectine."

Stunned, I sat on the chair in the corner to catch my breath. "Thank you."

"Now, about our date..." He hesitated. "I was going to ask if Sage would go out with me instead. I've asked her out so many times, but she always says no. I hoped you could persuade her."

I stared. "Did you ask me out to make her jealous?"

"Don't get me wrong, I like you too, but—"

"But you've had a crush on my sister since you met her."

The pink in his face darkened. "Yeah."

"I'll see what I can do. Just name a time and place."

Cameron beamed. "You're the best."

I asked him to hold onto the items a while longer, then dropped Sammy off at home while I tried to figure out how to break it to Sage that Cameron still wanted to date her. I didn't get a chance. The minute I entered the shop to help her clean, she blew past me out the door. I hoped she wasn't mad at me for going out with Keyon.

I gave up cleaning about quarter after five, picked up Sammy from home, and wandered along the beach to my rendezvous with Enid. All I needed to make the whole thing more sordid was if I'd worn dark sunglasses and a hat. I hoped Enid would be true to her word, although part of me really didn't want to know the whole truth about anything that was going on. It was getting too confusing.

I still doubted Gill would ever harm Tilly, but the more I talked to Keyon and Enid, the more questions I had. As for the information about Keyon, that was strictly personal. I didn't trust him as far as I could push him.

Sammy and I picked our way among the rocks below Devil's Peak Tavern to where Enid, wearing oversized sunglasses, a pink jacket and an orange scarf to hide her blue hair sat on a large boulder. If the gossip columnist was trying to be incognito, she'd missed the mark by a few thousand miles.

"You got the stuff?" I lowered my voice to sound gruff and play along with the whole scenario.

"I do." She lifted her jacket to reveal a large yellow envelope. "Do I have your word I get the scoop on your life with... You know."

"Yes, Enid." I smirked. Our clandestine meeting bordered on the ridiculous. "I'll tell you everything you want to know. You pick the time and place. Just leave Gill, Tilly, and the tea house out of it."

"Deal. What do you want with this stuff anyway?" She handed me the envelope.

"I need to know more about the people I'm dealing with," I told her. "Since you've known them for a long time, I figured you were the best person to ask."

"You got that right," Enid said, jumping off the rock. After all the earlier secrecy, she followed me onto the beach. "I see your friend Cash is still in town. I think that man is trouble and the sooner we can get him out of here, the better for all of us. When are we going on that shopping trip?"

"Good question. I need to help Sage clean up the store, so we can reopen first."

"Do you see that?" she asked.

Up ahead, two familiar figures argued. Gabriella had her hands on her hips, her face as red as her nails as she poked Keyon in the chest. Too bad we couldn't hear either of them over the surf.

"I'm going to walk past them," Enid announced. "I'll report back to you later."

I wanted to stop her, but Sammy pulled at the leash and barked. He wanted to walk in the other direction. I unhooked his leash before taking off my shoes. It was my fault Keyon was angry at me and Gabriella. If I hadn't blurted out anything about him being Abbie's father, I might've learned more. I doubted he'd tell me anything incriminating anyway. It wasn't the way I wanted such an interesting day to end.

I'd just finished cooking chicken breasts and Portobello mushroom steaks when Sage came home. By then, I was ready for more brainstorming. Once I placed dinner on the table, I filled her in on my chat with Gabriella. Just not the juicy parts.

"I still think she's trouble," Sage said, filling her plate with salad and Portobello.

"I saw her getting cozy with that developer from Portland."

"Let me guess. You think this Cash guy's trying to buy the tea house from Gill and using Gabriella to do it."

"Actually, his family's been trying to buy it for years." I pointed my fork in her direction. "Since Gabriella and Abbie will both inherit the tea house if Gill dies, Bryan Cash will be in a good position."

"Well, that's obvious. They're his heirs." She paused. "Do you think one of them plans to off Gill, so they can sell the tea house? That location could easily sell for a million dollars or more to the right buyer."

"Enough to keep them comfortable for a few years at least."

Sammy groaned as he curled up near my feet.

"Then why kill Tilly? She had so many health issues, she would've gladly sold the place to live somewhere warm where people could look after her all day."

"I know I would." I sighed.

"You already had that." My sister chuckled. "You still want to buy the tea house, don't you?"

Owning the tea house building, making improvements and opening both Vintage Sage and the tea garden made my imagination run wild. So many ideas, yet so little confidence I could make them work.

I shrugged. "Think about it this way. You'd get your house back, and Sammy and I could live closer to the beach."

Sage's mouth dropped open. "No way. That's not part of the deal. I'd miss you."

"True, but you'd get the house to yourself, and have more privacy when Jonathan comes to town."

She set her cutlery on the table with a sigh. "I broke up with Jonathan. I'm already tired of trying to make a long-distance relationship work. Once he takes the job in Los Angeles, we'll barely ever see each other."

"Sorry to hear that. What did he say?"

"He assured me that no Hollywood starlet would ever turn his head the way I do. I don't buy it. Look at how Emery treated you. Women threw themselves at him. All he had to do was open his arms."

"More like his zipper," I told her. "But Jonathan's not my ex. He adores you."

"That's what I thought, but he took it awfully well," Sage said, reaching for her glass.

I hesitated. "Why don't I talk to Cameron? He could take you out to dinner instead of me. After all, Grandma always said the best way to get over a broken heart was to dive right back in, right?"

Her eyes widened. "What? No. Why would you even suggest that?"

"You know he likes you." I bit into a carrot. "Promise you'll think about it."

She sighed. "Cameron's a nice guy, but he's not my kind of guy. He's boring. All he does is look after animals. That's it."

"And all you do is run a vintage shop and go to yard sales," I replied, instantly regretting my words when she took her plate and left the table.

If only Cameron Dale knew what the woman he had such a crush on really thought. He might be boring and have no social life, but he wasn't a murder suspect.

Later that night, I crawled into bed armed with Enid's clandestine information about Gill and Tilly. It was pretty much clean of anything eyebrow raising. For a gossip and troublemaker, Enid's files were pretty tame compared to most.

Gill was a former military man who met Tilly when he was twenty-two. They married six months later. Gabriella, their only child, came along after many years of marriage. Abbie was their only grandchild. Nothing I read made me think Gill wasn't a man of honor or integrity, except the ugly rumors.

Tilly, it seemed, had led a more interesting life up until she married Gill. My jaw dropped when I read the list of the beauty pageants and dance competitions that she'd competed in. After studying dance from the age of three, she became a model at fourteen, then worked a couple odd jobs until enrolling in college for fashion design and graduating with honors.

Fashion design? That fit what I knew so far.

I yawned and glanced at the cover of Keyon's file. After all the surprises in Tilly's, I wasn't sure I could absorb anything else.

Too tired to read anymore, I set it aside for morning. Then reconsidered.

I got out of bed and put all three folders in the top drawer of the dresser. Out of reach of sharp puppy teeth.

Chapter Twenty

My dreams were plagued with thieves, bullies, and my ex-husband.

Sammy wiggled closer while I glanced at the clock, then toward my dresser. I didn't have the energy to tackle Keyon's file so early in the day. I'd need a pot of tea first.

There was no way the Sweet Eden Tea House and Vintage Sage were targeted by random burglars. Someone knew full well what they were after.

The tea house was closed until further notice. I already missed sitting on the veranda watching the waves rush ashore. Missed the Hens and their chatter.

Enid had disappeared since our meeting on the beach, which hadn't stopped me from running through my list of suspects repeatedly, much to Sage's chagrin, while she moped about her breakup with Jonathan and having to find estate sales and the like so we could restock the store.

I puttered around the house that morning with far too much time to think.

That afternoon I took Sammy for a long walk on the beach then I filled a wine goblet with sparkling water and sat on the front step. Sammy lay next to my thigh while I stroked his silky fur.

"I don't understand why anyone would want to kill another person," I told him as he dozed. "Not that most of us haven't thought about it once or twice."

Sammy glanced up and yawned. He didn't seem big on having a heart-to-heart chat with his mom.

His mom.

"Oh no. I'm becoming one of those people."

Sammy tilted his head.

"You know." I scratched behind his ears. "One of those weirdos who not only talks to their pets and expects the pet to understand, but that they can communicate somehow."

He yawned again before he laid his chin on his paws.

I was doing it again.

"You're not worried if anyone thinks I'm crazy anyway, are you? I need to track down Pricilla Cash. What if Tilly stole that necklace and Pricilla knows it? Would she kill to get it back?"

Sammy groaned and probably wished I was on television, so he could turn off my voice with the remote he liked to chew on.

"Chances are Tilly had her heart attack and died before Pricilla found out what she'd done with the stones, but why does she want the tea house so badly? Tilly was the roadblock for something." I sipped my drink sure I was beyond making any sense whatsoever. "What am I missing?"

Sammy placed a paw over his face. I took that to mean he wanted me to shut up so he could sleep.

As soon as he and Keyon responded to the call, Andy gave Tilly an injection. Did he give her the Anectine, which reacted with her medication, or something else he knew she wouldn't wake up from?

Suddenly, my dog jolted out of his semi-doze and stared at the gate with his ears erect and his upper lip curled back.

Keyon unlatched the gate. "Hey, Sammy. What'cha doing?"

He leaped to his feet, ran toward Keyon, and nearly knocked him to the ground when they collided.

"I was telling him a bedtime story," I told Keyon. "He's tired of hearing my voice."

"Sounds like fun. I'd like to hear it. What are you drinking?"

"Sparkling water. Would you like a beer? There's a few in the fridge from when Jonathan was here."

"That sounds great, thanks."

I went inside to grab a beer from the fridge. By the time I returned to the porch, Keyon and Sammy roughhoused on the front lawn. Enid stood near the steps as the two of them raced around the grass before Keyon threw a ball for Sammy.

Enid clip-clopped up the stairs, wearing a pair of sparkly silver two-inch heels, a bright yellow blouse and electric blue Capri pants. With garish red lipstick and her hair and eyeshadow the color of her pants, she looked more like a rogue circus clown than how I envisioned a gossip columnist.

"It's a good thing Laken found you, boy," Enid said. "I'd hate to think what would've happened if Tilly found you first."

"How are you, Enid?" I asked, fighting back the grin that threatened to explode across my face.

"You're probably right." Keyon told Sammy to drop the ball. "Since Tilly didn't like people, there's no way she'd care for animals."

"Good point." I set Keyon's beer on the porch, then took a gulp from my wineglass. "That's odd. My water tastes strange."

Enid shrugged. "Maybe you're getting sick. You have been on the go a lot."

"I guess that's it," I agreed. "No one's ever responded to my ads or the flyers I put up around town to find Sammy's owner. Can you believe someone had the nerve to take them all down?"

Enid sat in one of the blue chairs. "I could put an ad in the paper. You've been a busy girl between working two jobs and taking care of the dog. You sure you didn't just dream you put them up?"

Sammy rolled around on the grass and took one last nip at Keyon before returning to his spot next to me.

"Pretty sure I didn't." I rubbed Sammy's head.

"Maybe his owner couldn't take care of him and doesn't want him back," Keyon said, stepping over my inert dog to sit in the other chair. He cracked open his beer and added, "Could be he was a gift for someone who was allergic, so they got rid of him."

I took another sip. The flavor seemed off, almost like wine more than water. I touched my forehead. Maybe I was coming down with something. "Tilly said she was allergic to dogs, but who'd gift her one? Gill made sure I took Sammy home without bringing him into the tea house. He even gave me a baby carrier to pack him home in."

"What's your point?" Keyon asked.

I had no idea how to answer that. Neither Gill nor Gabriella would give Tilly a puppy knowing she'd become even more irritable. Only someone who despised her and knew about her allergies would be so nasty. Abbie couldn't afford a purebred dog. The kid had to borrow money to buy spray paint.

Bryan Cash? While I couldn't rule him out, I doubted he knew Tilly had allergies.

From what I knew, Andy didn't seem like the warm, fuzzy gift type.

Something about Sammy's sudden appearance so close to Tilly's death still didn't fit. It couldn't simply be a coincidence, could it?

"Did you find more information on your suspects in Tilly's murder?" Enid asked.

"I'm not a police officer." As I took another sip, my vision blurred. Why was I so tired suddenly? I waved a hand. "Go ask the chief."

"He won't let me into the station. Something about his wife being upset about an article I wrote last summer."

Keyon snorted. "The one about him going fishing with the mayor and ending up with another woman?"

"It was a perfectly innocent misunderstanding." She flared her nostrils. "How was I supposed to know they were actually fishing, or that the chief's boat is called *My Mistress*? Men lie all the time."

"Not all men." Keyon took a swig of his beer.

Enid narrowed her eyes. "All men. Including you, Romeo."

He stared. "What did I do?"

"Don't get me started," she said. "I doubt your girlfriend wants to hear about your indiscretions. Although, a few will be featured in my new book."

"First of all, I'm not his girlfriend, and second..." As I jumped to my feet, everything grew fuzzy and grey. Only when Sammy licked my face did I realize I'd collapsed onto the wooden porch.

"Whoa. Laken, are you okay?" Keyon opened my eyes one at a time to examine my pupils.

"I guess I stood up too fast." I tried to sit up.

"Stay right there, young lady. You're flushed and burning up." Enid pinned my shoulders against the porch.

Keyon checked my pulse. The concern on his face didn't help. "Your heart's pounding like you ran a marathon and your blood pressure's probably sky high. You need to lie down. I'll get you some water, then keep you company until Sage gets home."

Once Keyon went inside, Enid released my shoulders and stood. "And I'll make my famous cabbage soup. That'll fix you right up, so we can go find us a killer."

Cabbage soup. The mere thought made me gag.

"Back off, Enid." Keyon returned with a glass of water. "No soup. No hunting. No killers. A wild goose chase is the last thing Laken needs. Here, drink up."

The water tasted off as well. Maybe I really was sick. Although, my thoughts were stuck on cabbage soup and my stomach churned. "Please don't go to all that trouble."

"It's no trouble at all. You'll love my soup," she said, then glanced at Keyon. "I have a better idea. Why don't you go pick up a couple pizzas? Any favorites?"

As I sat up and leaned against the railing, my vision swam, and my tongue refused to co-operate. "Thounds good."

"I'd rather keep an eye on Laken," Keyon told her.

Enid nodded. "Then take the doggy for a walk."

"He's fine." Keyon scowled. "And I'm not going anywhere."

"Fine. Then I'll get the food. Her blood sugar's probably low." Enid clomped down the stairs and headed toward the pizzeria. The instant she left Sammy licked my face before running to water the rosebushes. He hopped back onto the porch a half minute later and laid his head on my lap.

Keyon laughed. "He won't let you out of his sight."

I stroked Sammy's back. "I don't feel so good."

"You hit this when you fell." Keyon picked up the pieces of my wineglass and tossed them in the trash can around the corner. "If you plan to keep drinking on the porch, maybe you should invest in some plastic glasses."

"Ha. Ha." I let Keyon help me up and escort me inside. "Enid's right. I need to learn to slow down."

Keyon walked me to the couch and asked, "What was number two?"

"Huh?" I tried to look at him but couldn't focus. My eyes ached and my body weak.

"You said that first of all you aren't my girlfriend but collapsed before you said number two."

My head throbbed. "I don't remember. Everything's fuzzy and grey."

He sat me on the couch to check my pupils and pulse once more. "I should take you to the hospital."

"No more hospitals." I pressed a hand against his chest but was too weak to push him away. "I need food."

He rolled his eyes. "Works for me. At least let someone make sure you're okay."

"You just did, Mr. Paramedic. Enid's right. My blood sugar's low. If feel awful after food, I'll go to the hospital."

"Promise?" Keyon eased my head onto a pillow.

"Yup."

"It could also be you're so absorbed in finding Tilly's killer that you're not taking care of yourself. You need to stop before you make yourself worse."

I tried to touch his cheek but there were two of him. Then both faces grew fuzzy. "Aww, you like me."

He frowned. "I'm putting Sammy in his crate, then taking you to the hospital. You need a doctor."

"I'm fine." I tried to wave my hand as he left the room. My hand flopped on the couch like a limp noodle. "I'm just drunk."

"Considering you don't drink, that's not good." Keyon returned a moment later to adjust the pillows behind my head. Suddenly, he held one pillow in both hands. "You should be more careful who you trust."

"Whaddya mean?" My words slurred. What was wrong with me?

"What's going on?" Sage asked. "What are you doing to my sister?"

Keyon backed away and set the pillow down.

"Hey." My voice sounded raspy.

She lunged across the room in one motion. "Has Laken been drinking?"

"Na." I wanted to wave, but my hand refused to move as I closed my eyes. "Tired."

Sage checked my pulse. "I'm calling an ambulance."

"I'm a paramedic," Keyon reminded her.

"Fat lot of good that's doing," she said.

While I couldn't see them, I heard every word.

"I'll take her to a doctor."

"Don't touch her," Sage growled.

"Don't you trust me?"

"Get out of my house. I don't want you anywhere near my sister." Her phone beeped. Any other words were lost to the fog I slipped into.

I struggled to open my eyes, but my body refused to respond. Instead, I floated in a sort of limbo until the shriek of sirens drew closer. The next time I opened my eyes, unseen hands loaded me onto a gurney. I drifted away once more as the sirens screamed.

* * *

I awoke surrounded by people in masks. Everyone asked questions. How did I feel? What had I eaten? What did I drink? What had I done that day?

I didn't have any intelligible answers.

Everything was suspect. Any allergies? Was I on any medications?

I couldn't string two words together. The helplessness was like nothing I'd ever experienced before. Like I was underwater with no chance of drowning.

Sage took her frustrations out on Enid, who brought the pizza. I smelled peppers and cheese. My mouth watered. Keyon showed up saying I'd worn myself down trying to find Tilly's killer. Sage kicked him out again.

The doctor checked my vital signs and took more blood than I knew I had. He asked what kinds of medications I took. Thankfully, my sister had them memorized. I didn't know my own name.

"Where's Sammy?" My voice came out a harsh whisper.

Sage brushed a stray hair off my forehead and said, "In his crate at home. How are you feeling?"

"Awful. What happened?"

She walked over to close the door. We were alone in a private hospital room. I was hooked to an intravenous bag. The walls were painted in sad shades of grey blue. Not the best color for the tea house after all.

The rasp of my ragged breath frightened me. "The cancer's back, isn't it? How long do they give me?"

Sage shook her head. "It's not that."

"What's worse than another death sentence?"

"The doctor's running a toxicology screen."

"Toxiwhat?" I tried to reach for the cup on the table next to me, but my arm refused to budge. "What are you saying?"

"We think someone poisoned you."

"Poisoned me?" I recalled the odd taste of my water. "Why?"

My sister shrugged. "No idea. I gave the nurse the list of your medications in case you double-dosed, but..."

"I didn't." I frowned.

She gave my hand a squeeze. "You've been busy between Sammy, the tea house, and my shop, anything's possible. A double dose of any of them could cause side effects."

"I'm positive I didn't," I told her. "If anything, I've forgotten a dose or two."

Sage averted her gaze. "The lack of medication could cause issues as well. Either way, the doctor put a rush on your results."

I struggled to sit up but grew lightheaded. "Am I stuck here until we know for sure?"

"Considering how weak you are, that's for the best. I don't want you falling down the stairs." She hugged me. "I called Gill, and I'll keep the shop closed for a few days. I don't feel right going to work until we have answers."

Too tired to argue, I lay back. "I'd rather go home to rest. I'll be fine tomorrow."

"You're probably right." She stroked my cheek. "Get some rest. I'll let you know when the test results come back."

I took a deep breath and closed my eyes. Sage had pulled a chair next to my bed. When I opened my eyes, my sister sat bowed over her phone furiously tapping the screen.

"What'd I miss?"

She gave a snort. "Half hour of me telling Keyon and Enid to get out."

"You really don't like Keyon, do you?"

Sage shrugged. "No, but Jonathan did. He's the only reason Keyon set foot in my house. Now that Jonathan and I broke up, Keyon has no reason to come over."

I forced a smile. "Did the doctor come yet?"

"No," she said, averting her gaze so fast that I got the impression she was lying.

“What’s wrong?” I asked. “What did they find?”

Sage met my gaze. “A trace of a drug. Not enough to be concerned about.”

“Anectine?”

“No.”

I sighed. “Sage, I’m in the hospital because I passed out. Don’t tell me it was a trace of some drug but not what. What did they find?”

“Flunitrazepam.”

“Speak English.”

“Rohypnol, Laken. Someone slipped you a roofie,” she told me.

“The date rape drug? Are you serious?”

“They tested twice to be sure. Who was with you before you collapsed?”

“Just Sammy and Keyon.” I paused and thought hard. “And Enid.”

“We need to have your wineglass fingerprinted,” she said.

“We can’t. It broke when I fell. Keyon threw it in the trash beside the house.”

My sister closed her eyes, then released a long sigh. “I’ll tell the police. You need to quit snooping around before you get hurt worse.”

I wiggled my fingers to touch hers. “I know this is bad, but there’s a bright side.”

“What’s that?”

“We’re down to two suspects.”

Chapter Twenty-One

The doctor allowed me to go home after a good night's sleep and a couple more bags of fluids. My first good rest I'd found Sammy. Sage, paranoid because of the bloodwork, arranged for an armed guard. No one was to pass aside from my sister and the night duty nurse until she came to pick me up Another reason I slept so well.

No Enid. No Bryan. No Keyon. No dog eating my possessions. Just peace and quiet.

"I need to stop at Vintage Sage on the way home to pick up some paperwork," Sage said once we were in the car. "Are you okay with that?"

"Can you drop me off at the tea house?" I asked. "I have a couple questions for Gill."

She buckled me into the passenger seat like I was a toddler. Small and helpless. "Not a chance. You're not leaving my sight. Someone tried to kill you."

"What?" I gasped. "No one tried to kill me."

She ran around the rear of the car, hopped into the driver's seat and closed the door before she glared at me. "Sammy doesn't have opposable thumbs, so either Enid or Keyon slipped you the drugs."

Considering the things she'd said to Keyon at the house and the hospital, I guessed she'd already crossed Enid off her list. With a thick, black marker.

"Please." I resorted to begging. "You know I'll be safe with Gill. I'll even call ahead to make sure he's there."

Sage flared her nostrils. "I'd feel better if you were at home with Sammy. At least he'll alert the neighbors if there's a problem. Tell you what, we'll both talk to Gill once I'm done."

"Fine, then leave me with Sammy. I'll sit on the couch and drive myself crazy while you're gone." I had about a half hour window once she left the house.

After Sage helped me to the couch, she let Sammy out of his crate and into the backyard for a quick run. The moment she left for Vintage Sage, and possibly to run other errands, I locked Sammy in the crate since I didn't have the energy to walk him. The walk took twice as long as usual, but I needed to see Gill in person. I was determined to get answers. It took all my strength to climb the front steps. I managed knocked on the front door before I remembered I had a key.

Gill opened the door and gasped. "Laken, what are you doing here? Are you okay?"

"Need water."

He took my arm, and led me inside, then ran to the kitchen. By the time he returned with a full glass of water, I'd slumped onto the closest chair and had almost caught my breath. Greyish fingerprint dust covered every surface. My ex had starred in enough made-for-television mystery movies for me to recognize it.

"What are you doing here? You should be home resting."

"Looks like the police came back to search for clues." I had a feeling my sister would face the same mess at the shop.

Gill nodded, then told me, "Sage said you spoke to them in the hospital. She mentioned that someone drugged you. The police took you at your word about Tilly's death, especially after the burglaries yesterday. they didn't find anything here, but Sage sent them to talk to her vet friend. Is he a suspect?"

"They talked to Cameron. That's good. He had the evidence I gave him." I gulped down half the water, then stood to take a closer look at the counter. "I don't remember talking to anyone except Sage. Including the police."

"Laken, sit. You're still weak."

The tone of Gill's voice put me on edge. A lot of things currently had me on edge.

"I've been stuck lying in a hospital bed for I don't know how long. I needed to move." I leaned on the counter. "Sage will be furious I'm here, but I needed to talk face to face."

"You want to know about Tilly, don't you?" he asked. "You tried to ask before, but I cut you off. If you want answers, you'd better sit."

"What sort of answers?"

Gill held out a chair, then waited until I sat. Running a hand through his thinning hair, he said, "You were right about me being a womanizer. Enid and I had an affair."

"What?" That certainly wasn't in Enid's notes. "When?"

"It was a long time ago, before Gabriella was born. Tilly and I were on a tropical vacation with Enid and her boyfriend. Her boyfriend went to go explore the island and Tilly had a migraine. I didn't want to miss out on doing anything while she rested. I know that wasn't the way I should've thought, but we'd paid a lot of money to be there, and I wanted to have fun. Besides, we were all friends. It didn't seem out of line at the time."

"You and Enid hooked up on a couples' vacation?" I asked.

"We didn't plan to. We'd all gone separate directions, then she and I ran into each other at a little bar and talked. After a few more drinks, we ended up in this little cabana and things got heated. Tilly was no wild woman. She'd never do the things Enid liked."

I hoped he'd spare me the details. "Did you ever ask her to? Tilly, I mean."

"I just assumed she'd never go for it. I guess a little adventure in our lives might've helped to lighten things up." He sat across from me. "We settled into running the tea shop, then she got pregnant. Parenthood slowed us down even more until things became comfortable and dull."

"So, you and Enid, was that a one-time thing?" I'd asked Emery the same question so many times I'd lost count.

"I wish." Gill bowed his head. "We saw each other for about three months after. I stopped the affair when Tilly got pregnant with Gabriella. Enid was furious. She was convinced I'd run off with her to start a new life and knew I wouldn't leave once Tilly was pregnant. Then Tilly found out our secret. Since she and Enid were best friends, things got awkward. Banning her from the tea house was the worst we could do."

No wonder Tilly never looked happy. I could relate to her pain.

"I know about your ex-husband, Laken," Gill said. "You would've sympathized with Tilly if you knew before she died."

Sick to my stomach, I asked, "Enid never forgave you for staying with Tilly, did she?"

He rubbed the back of his neck. "Actually, Enid never forgave me for not supporting her and our son."

"Whoa. Andy's your son?"

He bowed his head. "She told everyone his father died in a car accident. I demanded a paternity test." He leaned his elbows on the table.

"Tilly found out the truth before she died, thanks to an anonymous letter she received that contained a copy of Andy's birth certificate."

"Who'd do something like that?" I closed my eyes against a serious case of vertigo.

"Someone who thought she'd sell the tea house."

"Bryan Cash or someone at his company."

Gill shrugged. "I don't know what to think. You're one of the only people I can trust, besides Abbie."

When an ambulance pulled up in front of the tea house, my first instinct was to run to the kitchen to hide. Too bad I couldn't move fast enough.

"I talked to Sage," he said. "I know you're not supposed to be here, so I called someone else I trust."

I struggled to breathe. "Me being alone with Keyon is not a good idea."

"Which is why I called Andy. He's a good man and he'll take care of you until Sage gets home." He patted my hand. "Believe it or not, some of us are looking out for you, Laken."

Andy walked into the tea house with a smile. "Did someone order a limo?"

"That's a limo?" I asked.

"A bit of a stretch," he said with a grin. "The black one's in the shop."

"Take this lovely lady home before she collapses," Gill instructed him. "I'll call Sage and let her know she needs to keep a closer eye on this one. She's too weak to be wandering the streets."

"I'm fine," I insisted.

Gill growled. "Sage told me what happened. Someone needs to always be with you. Think of it as a buddy system."

Then why send me home with someone I barely know? That made no sense. Both men walked me to the ambulance so somber I nearly burst into tears. My head hurt and my thoughts made no sense. So many secrets and lies. I didn't know who or what to believe.

Andy helped me into the passenger seat then walked around to the driver's door. He drove toward Sage's house in silence before I blurted out, "You killed Tilly, didn't you?"

"I what?" he asked?

"You were the first person to touch her besides me and Gill and I saw you give her an injection."

He frowned. "Why would I want to kill Tilly? I barely knew her."

"How could you not know her?" I asked. "You're Enid's son."

"My mother knows a lot of people. She writes gossip for the local paper. Everyone knows her. If not by face, at least by reputation."

I softened my approach to bring down his defensiveness and my blood pressure. "It can't be easy being the son of a gossip columnist. I'm surprised you haven't left town."

"Trust me, I've tried," he said. "Several times. My mom getting in trouble always brings me back. Besides, if I'm here, I know what she says about me."

I raised my eyebrows. "About you? You're her son. You're also a paramedic and save lives daily. Why would she have anything bad to say about you?"

"Because I'm her son," he told me. "And my father was some guy who died and left her stuck with a baby and little else. She's convinced I'll turn out be like him, which doesn't sound like a good thing." He stopped at an intersection, then looked for oncoming traffic. "I was born with a deep hole to climb out of, Laken, and every mistake I make is one more chance for her to say she told me so."

That was the most I'd ever heard him speak. "Does she ever talk about your father?"

"Just that he died in a car accident." Andy shook his head. "When it comes to secrets, my mother's great at digging them out of everyone else's closets, but she's lousy at giving up hers to her own son."

I wondered if Andy looked like Gill when he was younger. Maybe Gill would let me look through the photos when I was stronger.

"If you're thinking of asking her about my father, don't bother." He pulled the ambulance in front of Sage's house. "The last time I brought up the subject, she didn't talk to me for hours."

"You live with your mother?" I asked.

"Not a great selling feature when you're single, but I need to protect her. Even if it's from herself. Do you know how many kooks live around here?"

"I've met one or two."

"Then you know this town isn't safe for someone like her."

I grinned. "Do you mean a woman of her age, or someone who exposes other people's private lives for the whole town to read about?"

"All of the above."

I glanced toward Sage's house, then remembered Cameron probably gave the vial to the police, which had sparked their search of the tea house. Once Andy parked in front of Sage's, I asked, "What do you know about Anectine?"

"That it's used to numb muscles, so we can start an IV in some patients. It's also a succinylcholine and doesn't react well with some heart medications. Why?"

I met his gaze. "Which heart medications?"

"Digoxin, for one, which is what Tilly was on according to her records." Andy pulled a notepad out of his pocket. "It can also be fatal to someone who's allergic to a neuromuscular blocking agent."

"What's that?" I asked.

"In layman's terms?" He flipped through the notepad. "It's one of the drugs that can cause an allergic reaction during anesthesia."

My palms grew sweaty. "Was Tilly allergic to them?"

"Yes, she was. That's why I gave her epinephrine," he said. "I'd hoped she had a bad allergic reaction, maybe to a dog."

My eyes widened. "You didn't know her, but you knew she was allergic to dogs."

"Medical records don't lie. The shot was to combat a possible allergic reaction. Why are you asking about Anectine?"

"Sammy and I found a syringe and an empty vial labeled Anectine in the backyard of the tea house. I asked Keyon what someone would use it for, but I didn't tell Gill I'd found it."

"I suspect they did a tox screen on you at the hospital." A bead of sweat rolled down his forehead. "What did it show was in your system?"

"My usual medications. As well as something called Flunitrazepam." I played dumb. "The doctor called the police, who came to talk to me. They dusted the tea house, and probably Vintage Sage, for fingerprints, but I doubt they found much."

Andy covered his eyes with one hand, then said, "Actually, I think they found everything they needed. Did you give them the vial and the syringe?"

"Cameron Dale did, after he tested them."

"The vet?" He stared.

"I asked him to see if the drug in the syringe was the same as the drug in the vial. Why do you look like you're going to throw up?"

His expression remained as solemn as Sage's when she spoke to the doctor. It occurred to me they'd make a good pair. "Do you know what Flunitrazepam is, Laken? It's Rohypnol. Somebody slipped you the date rape drug."

"The only people at the house before I got sick were Keyon and Enid."

"Were either of them alone with your drink?" he asked. "Think hard."

I'd left my sparkling water on the step with Keyon while I grabbed his beer from the fridge. When I returned, Enid was near my drink. Not long after, I started to feel dizzy and strange. Then Keyon got me a glass of water and made me comfortable on the couch.

When Enid left to get pizza, he was holding a pillow before Sage came home...

I suddenly found it hard to breathe. "Andy, we need to go back to the tea house. I think Keyon tried to kill me."

"Are you sure?"

"He drugged me and was going to smother me with a pillow except Sage came home. He's the only other person who could've killed Tilly. I'm afraid he'll go after Gill next."

Chapter Twenty-Two

I'd never seriously suspected Keyon, especially since he put the whole notion Tilly was murdered into my head to begin with. Thinking someone was a murderer and proving it were two different things. It seemed the entire thing had been a game.

Well, if it was a game Keyon Blake wanted, he was about to get one. The only thing I could do was to confront him to find out why he'd killed Tilly and tried to get rid of me.

Andy called both Sage and Gill while I planned. He loaded Sammy into the front seat of the ambulance, then climbed behind the wheel. "Are you sure you're okay to do this?"

I nodded. "I have to be."

He drove me back to the tea house and waited while Gill took Sammy. Before I got out, Andy touched my arm. "I'd be happy to stay and help."

How sweet. My perception of him was thawing quickly. "Gill's here, and Sage is on her way. Your job is to make sure the police get here fast. Just in case."

"Will do." He leaned over to hug me. "Be careful, Laken."

"You, too."

Gill led Sammy inside, but I held back on the porch in the sunshine. Step one was in place. Step two was for me to text Keyon to meet me at the tea house. Neutral territory.

He texted back that he'd be there in twenty minutes.

My breath stuck in my throat as nausea swept over me. I needed to sit while I thought. I chose the same table where Gabriella and I had enjoyed cheesecake and tea such a short time ago. Once settled I texted Sage and Andy while Gill set up a video camera next to the glass-domed serving platter on the counter.

While Andy got the police to the tea house. Sage was in charge of tracking down Enid for front line newspaper coverage. Gill took Sammy into the kitchen for a treat.

A big part of Keyon's plan revolved around Tilly and the tea house. Was he involved with Cash Enterprises? Remembering the business card Bryan Cash gave me. I pulled it out of my pocket and dialed the number he'd written on the back, expecting him to answer, so I could ask.

Instead, I heard, "You have reached Keyon Blake-Cash, Chief Financial Officer of Cash Enterprises. Leave a message and I'll get back to you shortly."

I nearly dropped my phone. Why would the Chief Financial Officer of a multimillion-dollar development company work as a paramedic in Glitter Bay? Unless his current occupation served as a conduit for obtaining drugs and getting close to the people he needed to deal with in less than legal ways.

Suddenly, I had even more to think about than which colors to paint the walls and what type of window coverings to get. How could I confront the man who'd tried to end my life without allowing him a second attempt?

"Laken, you're early." Keyon stood in the doorway ten feet away. He wore a leather jacket and blue jeans. His sunglasses reflected the tea house.

"So are you." Easily ten minutes early. I was so absorbed in thought I hadn't even heard him open the door.

"You look much better," he said with a smile.

"Exhaustion. The doctor says I'll be fine. I'm glad you were there when I got so sick." I needed to stall him until Andy and the police arrived. "I might've died without you and Sage rushing me to hospital."

"You got lucky. Don't mention it." He stuck his hands in the pockets of his black leather jacket and seemed to fumble with something as he walked toward the table.

I took a slow, even breath to calm my racing heart. "Yeah, I did. Are you familiar with a drug called Flunitrazepam?"

"Where'd did you hear about that?"

I sat back. "I was a bit out of it yesterday, but a few things stuck in my head. They found Rohypnol in my system. The date rape drug. Apparently, when it's mixed with alcohol, it can incapacitate someone and cause amnesia. It's weird that even though I never drink alcohol, there was alcohol in my system."

"That's interesting," he said. "You still look kind of pale, you know. I have something that can help."

"It's been a long couple of days," I admitted. "I went to get you a beer that day. When I came back out, my water tasted odd. You suggested I was sick, and my taste buds were off."

Keyon flinched. "Are you accusing me of drugging you?"

"I hadn't even thought about it at first. Not until my head cleared and I could think straight. My guess is you'd already mixed the Rohypnol in some wine at home, then poured it into my drink when I went inside."

"Good guess." He smirked.

"You knew Bryan Cash all along, didn't you?" I asked. "In fact, you were working with him. I heard the two of you arguing outside the funeral home. Then I called the phone number Bryan wrote on the back of a business card. Your work number."

"I'm impressed. What else have you made up?"

"This isn't just about the tea house, is it? You're looking for a necklace you think was stolen from your family fifty years ago."

A woman, hidden by the door, huffed behind him. "I told you she was too smart for the likes of you. You were sloppy."

When a tall, blonde woman stepped around Keyon, I recognized Pricilla Cash's silvery bob and cold stare from the society pages. The first thing that struck me was her height and the fact she could've worn those gowns from the trunk fifty years later.

"I imagine you're dumb enough to carry the card around in your purse like you did the vial and the syringe," Pricilla said.

"Nope. The police have my evidence." Just not Bryan's business card. "If anything happens to me, they know exactly who to suspect."

"Just in case you and Sammy should happen to get too close to the cliffs on one of your walks?" Keyon asked.

Gill peered out from the kitchen, gave a nod, then disappeared again.

"I'm pretty sure the police will take anything that happens to me very seriously."

"Keyon thought it would be fun to send you on a wild goose chase." Pricilla nudged his arm. "Only he didn't count on someone like you being so clever."

My back stiffened. "What do you mean someone like me?"

She gave a laugh. "Oh, please, darling, did you honestly think you could remain anonymous here forever? When a former model and ex-wife of a movie star moves to a sleepy little town, it's bound to create a buzz."

So much for any delusions I'd held.

When Sammy whimpered in the kitchen, I coughed. "Tilly was clever enough to steal the necklace from your family all those years ago. Then she unset the diamonds and sewed them onto a gown."

Keyon raised his eyebrows. "What? How do you know that?"

"She's guessing, but she's partly right." Pricilla walked over to sit across from me with her back to Keyon. "Except I'm the one who stole the necklace."

My eyes grew as wide as Keyon's.

"When I met Tilly in college that fall, she showed me a couple gowns she designed," Pricilla said. "She even made me one to attend my parents' Christmas gala that got a great deal of interest. That was when I offered her a good paying job that summer. I was hooked on her talent. Hungry for it. I wanted to go into business together. She as a designer, and me as the brains behind her rise to fame."

Still no sign of the police or Andy. I needed to stall them. "What were you studying in college?"

"I was supposed to learn how to run my father's business, but all I wanted was to get my hands on the obscene amount of money my parents forked over for my wedding, so I could travel the world. I stole the necklace I was told to wear and paid Tilly to sew the diamonds onto a dress."

"Which dress?" I asked, glancing at Keyon who kept his distance.

She waved a hand. "An adorable little grey cocktail dress with crystals on the bodice that Tilly had designed for me. I asked her to add the real diamonds as a nice touch. My groom and I planned to leave on our honeymoon right after the reception. The plan was to smuggle millions of dollars in diamonds out of the country under everyone's noses."

Since there was no grey dress in Tilly's trunk, I guessed Pricilla still had it.

Keyon walked toward our table with a vial in one hand. From his other pocket, he withdrew the syringe he'd toyed with in his jacket pocket.

Tears burned my eyes. "You really want to kill me, don't you?"

Someone beyond the kitchen door gasped. Neither Pricilla nor Keyon reacted.

"Local gossip has it, Gill will reject you," he said. "Suicide is an easy option for someone whose life is already in pieces."

"Possibly, but I have friends who'll tell the police otherwise."

He lunged for my purse. "The same friends listening over your cell phone?"

I yanked my purse out of his reach. "They already know who killed Tilly and they'll know who to blame when someone finds me dead."

"Aren't you afraid to die, Laken?" Keyon asked, meeting my gaze.

A shiver ran across my entire body. Did he toy with Tilly before he killed her? For her sake, I hoped not. "Death doesn't scare me as much as it used to."

"It should," he said. "All I have to do is give you one dose of this stuff and you won't have to worry about a thing."

I swallowed my fear. "Why did you kill Tilly?"

Pricilla answered, "Because that tramp double-crossed me. She sewed the diamonds to my wedding gown instead. After the wedding, she offered to have my gown cleaned while we were gone. I didn't notice the switch until I was in Antwerp and brought my dress to my contact to remove them. We were outraged. By the time I returned to Portland, both Tilly and my wedding gown were long gone. So was the sapphire I hid for safekeeping. She was the only person who knew where it was."

The same sapphire I found in Tilly's fish tank.

When Gill peered out the kitchen door again, I cleared my throat and shook my head. "That's crazy."

"It was," Pricilla agreed.

The wedding gown from the trunk which now resided in Sage's office closet no longer had the diamonds on the bodice. Tilly must've switched them over to the blush gown after the wedding.

The beautiful gown I'd fallen in love with was one of Tilly's designs. She'd painstakingly taken the diamonds off the wedding dress and sewed them onto mine.

Pricilla didn't seem to notice my aha moment. "One day, Bryan and I stopped at this quaint little tea house and there sat Tilly. Fatter and grouchier than before, but I knew her in an instant."

"You're a liar," Gill shouted, running out of the kitchen with Sammy at his heels.

Pricilla sprang away from the table at the same time as Keyon set the vial on the table and lunged to protect her. I grabbed the vial and tucked it into my bra.

"You had no idea who she was, so you treated her like crap." Gill stood his ground.

"No, she's right. Tilly did recognize you, didn't she?" I asked, glaring at Pricilla. "She chased you out of the tea house with a butcher knife."

"She was jealous. Getting married and having a kid brought her life to a standstill," she said. "She never created another gown after I was through with her."

Gill bobbed, trying to get past Keyon at Pricilla.

A light flickered in my still addled brain. "You were afraid if she had those diamonds, she could've started a new life in New York or L.A. as a top designer."

"No, she couldn't," Pricilla said. "I broke her hand right before my honeymoon."

"You did that to her?" Gill asked.

"I had to. We argued about her designs and how to create a line of gowns. She wanted to sew wedding gowns and ball gowns for all women. I tried to pull her back to earth, so we could reach a limited market and charge ten times more money."

"You wanted to control her," he said.

She gazed out the window. "I did control her. I smashed her drawing hand with a heavy vase. There was no way she could go off on her own and become famous without me while I was out of the country."

I shook my head. "You ruined her career before it even got started."

Pricilla nodded. "Childish really, but I always get my way."

"Enough talk. Tell us where the diamonds are, so we can get out of here." Keyon reached back to the table with one hand. When he couldn't find the vial, he glanced at me. "What did you do with it?"

"You're the one who left Sammy at the tea house, aren't you? That's why no one claimed him. I'll bet you even took down all my posters."

"Give me the vial." Keyon grabbed the front of my shirt and pulled me to my feet.

When Gill tried to wrestle me away, Keyon punched him in the face knocking him to the floor.

"Gill!" Enid stumbled through the front door with Sage close behind,

"Let her go," Sage grabbed his hair, which didn't seem to bother him.

"Tilly figured out Abbie's your son, didn't she?" I asked.

Keyon slammed his hand on the table. "That's enough. Where's my vial?"

Pricilla and Sage both squawked. "You have a son?"

"Yes, he does." I didn't take my gaze off Keyon. "Gabriella told me how Keyon wouldn't support them."

Enid crouched next to Gill who batted her away. She turned her ire on at Keyon and kicked him in the shin. "What kind of louse are you?"

He spun around and narrowed his eyes, yanking me with him. "You already know everything, don't you?"

"I took pictures too," Enid said, waving her camera.

"How convenient. Give me the vial, Laken."

"Not a chance."

"You knew you were Abbie's father and yet you still tried to take everything from us?" Gill asked, getting to his feet.

Keyon backed away as Pricilla ran toward the door on her three-inch heels just as two police cars and an ambulance raced up on the street.

Sage ran around Pricilla with her arms held out at her sides. "I don't think so."

Enid joined her to block Pricilla's access to the French doors. "Oh, no, Princess. You're not leaving until the police get in here."

I yanked Keyon's hand off my shirt and ran over to help Sage and Enid. "What they said. For the record, we have proof. Right, Gill?"

He glanced toward the video camera. "Yes, we do."

Andy and the police were so close. "Keyon killed Tilly because she confronted him about Abbie. She also found out he was Pricilla's son, didn't she?"

Keyon scowled and said, "Prove it."

"You got your opportunity to kill her in the ambulance after her heart attack and tried to frame Andy who gave her epinephrine." I met his gaze. "You knew I found the syringe cap Andy dropped at the shop. Then I showed you the courtyard at the tea house. You conveniently put the syringe in the trash carefully wrapped and buried the empty vial under the roses where Sammy liked to dig."

Growling, Sammy grabbed hold of one of Keyon's pant legs and shook.

Keyon kicked him off. "I never liked you anyway, stupid dog."

Outside, sirens wailed, and tires screeched.

Once free of Sammy, Keyon lunged for my pocket. "Good for you, Laken. Now I have to kill all of you and it's all your fault."

"You have one syringe and four of us," I pointed out. "Not good odds."

"There's no time." Pricilla held a gun in both hands. "I'll bet the diamonds are at her sister's house like I told you. That's the only place you didn't search."

Keyon pinned me to the door to search me. "I was going to after I suffocated her. Shoot the rest of them. This one's mine."

"Not a chance." Enid lunged for Pricilla as the door behind us burst open.

Two officers waved their weapons with no idea who to arrest.

"Over my dead body." Gill brought one of the antique metal teapots down hard on the back of Keyon's head. He rocked forward, his forehead bouncing off the bridge of my nose before he crumpled to the floor at one officer's feet. He was cuffed within seconds.

Enid scuffled with Pricilla, then brought her to the floor with a well-timed karate chop to the throat. A shot rang out before drywall dust rained down like hail.

The entire time, Sammy barked and pranced around in a confused circle. The instant Pricilla fell to the floor, Sammy trotted over to sniff her, then sneezed and went to Sage for comfort.

Once the officers had both Pricilla and Keyon in handcuffs. They seemed confused, and wary of Gill and Enid. Rightfully so.

Andy entered the tea house. He gazed around the room then shook his head. "I don't know what to say. It looks like I missed all the fun."

"I wouldn't exactly call it fun," Sage told him.

He flashed a dimpled grin.

"Me, neither." I reached into my bra to pull out the vial Keyon had tried so hard to find. "Gabriella's right. Bras are handy hiding spots."

One of the officers blushed as he pulled out an evidence bag. No questions asked.

"Now what do we do?" Enid looked around at the layer of ceiling crumbs.

Gill set the teapot on the closest table then disappeared into the kitchen. He returned with an ice pack. "We give the cops the video and let them have their fun. Anyone want tea? I need something to calm my nerves."

Enid snorted. "I'll take a brandy."

Gill nodded. "Tea and brandy sounds good."

"I'm off duty. I'll second that." Andy helped me to a chair.

My sister sat next to me to examine my face. "Looks like Laken could use one, too."

I sat to catch my breath. "You got everything on tape, right?"

"Yup. Abbie taught me how to set that contraption up after the burglary." Gill handed one of the officers his video camera, then pressed the ice pack between my eyes.

"That's cold!" I whined, pulling it away.

Sage put it back in place.

Gill shook his head. "Abbie thought the world of Keyon. He'll be crushed to hear all this. On the upside, he and Gabriella gave me their blessing to sell you girls the tea house."

Andy chuckled. "There you go. Congratulations. Now we have something to celebrate."

"I'll drink to that." I grinned.

Chapter Twenty-Three

"You can come out now," Abbie called from the courtyard.

I set aside my knife and walked out into the tea garden. My eyes, still bruised from the full force of Keyon's head butt to the bridge of my nose, grew as wide as possible. "What have you two done?"

The spindly trees that seemed so sad by day, were covered with tiny white lights that reminded me of fireflies. Abbie and Gill had draped a table with shiny gold lamé and set it with glittering crystal and candles. The whole courtyard glowed with ethereal light, even in late afternoon.

"It's beautiful." I sighed. "Won't we need more tables for the party though?"

"Oh, we didn't do this for grandpa's retirement party," Abbie said.

I squeezed my eyebrows together and winced at the pain. "Then what's going on?"

Soft music began to play over speakers hidden beneath the eaves and Gill burst out from the kitchen wearing a tuxedo. "Is everything ready?"

"Yup," Abbie replied as he took me by the arm. "I just have to get one small detail out of the way."

"Did you just call me a small detail?"

"Yes, ma'am, I did." He pulled me into the kitchen and closed the door before peering out the window into the courtyard.

I stood next to him. "What's going on?"

"My mom has a date," he whispered.

"Gabriella?" I asked. "With who?"

Abbie clapped a hand over my mouth. "Andy asked us to have dinner ready and be long gone when she gets here."

"Wait. What?" I turned to stare. Last I'd heard, Gill was both Andy's father, and Gabriella's. "What did I miss?"

Gill placed a hand on my shoulder. "Enid and I had several shots of brandy and a very lengthy conversation after you left yesterday. She admitted to bribing the lab tech who did the DNA testing. Andy's real father was the man killed in a car accident before he was born. She needed support money, so she fudged the records a little."

I stared. "A little? Did you give her money?"

"Yes, but I don't regret it for a minute. Andy's a good man. My little girl deserves someone who treats her right and will put her in her place when she needs it."

Abbie's eyes lit up. "And he's always liked my mom, so I figured I'd send them out on a real date. Andy thought it was a great idea. Who knew?"

"You're right. Who knew?" I ruffled his blue hair. "You're a good kid, Abbie."

"Does that mean I'll still get twenty bucks a week once you take over?"

"Forty," I told him. "As long as you clean and mop the floors and take out the garbage every day after we close."

"You expect me to work?"

"If you want money to build more bikes, I do."

He huffed, then glanced at me sideways. "I suppose we might be able to come to a mutually acceptable arrangement."

"Sounds good." I stuck out my hand and we shook on it.

"Laken? Are you here?" a man called from inside the tea house.

Gill peered into the kitchen. "Sounds like your date's here."

Abbie helped me remove my apron and stuck a white rose in my hair since red, as he explained, would clash. "You ready?"

"How do I look?" I smoothed my teal dress.

"You mean aside from the two black eyes from catching a bad guy? *Bellissima.*" Abbie said, then grinned. "I think that's Italian for friggin' hot."

"I doubt it, but I'll take it. Thanks." I gave him a hug.

Gill kissed my forehead. "He's a lucky man, Laken. Go have some fun."

I took a deep breath before I walked into the tea house. A date. Not like my dinner with Keyon. This had nothing to do with murder or jewelry thefts. Just dinner.

And repayment for a favor.

My date adjusted his black bow tie. "Wow, you look even more beautiful than I imagined. Of course, I've only ever seen you attached to a dog in yoga pants." His cheeks turned red. "Not that dogs wear yoga pants. I meant that you—"

"It's okay. Thanks." I smiled.

With his hair combed and restyled, as well as wearing an elegant tuxedo, Cameron Dale didn't look half bad either. He didn't even cringe at my two black eyes when he offered me his arm. "Shall we, milady?"

"Yes, we shall, Doctor Cameron." I laid my hand on his forearm.

Feeling like a movie star and sashaying like the seasoned model I was, I strolled next to him out of the tea house and into the night. For the first time in years, life was good.

The End

Watch for more great books in the Glitter Bay Mystery series:

All That Shines (coming Summer 2025)

All That Shimmers (coming Summer 2026)

About the Author

Diane Bator began writing as a kid when she fell in love with storytelling. After ten years with various traditional publishers, she's created her own company, Escape With a Writer Publishing, to relaunch her previous work plus many new titles. She is also a member of Sisters in Crime, Crime Writers of Canada, The Writers Union of Canada, and International Thriller Writers.

A proud mom of three, Diane is also a Reiki Master, a blue belt in goju-ryu karate, and an artist who loves stopping at odd places on road trips and creating new things from old.

Her website is

Join her newsletter and Escape With a Writer!

ALSO BY DIANE BATOR

Written in Stone, A.J. Cadell Mysteries, Book 1

www.ingramcontent.com/pod-product-compliance
Lightning Source LLC
LaVergne TN
LVHW012045160826
845678LV00014B/2708

* 9 7 8 1 7 3 8 3 3 2 8 2 3 *